The Raven's Pool

A Novel

Deborah Cannon

Note for Librarians: a cataloguing record for this book that includes Dewey Decimal Classification and US Library of Congress numbers is available from the Library and Archives of Canada. The complete cataloguing record can be obtained from their online database at:
www.collectionscanada.ca/amicus/index-e.html
ISBN 1-4120-3504-X

TRAFFORD

Offices in Canada, USA, Ireland, UK and Spain
This book was published *on-demand* in cooperation with Trafford Publishing. On-demand publishing is a unique process and service of making a book available for retail sale to the public taking advantage of on-demand manufacturing and Internet marketing. On-demand publishing includes promotions, retail sales, manufacturing, order fulfilment, accounting and collecting royalties on behalf of the author.

Book sales for North America and international:
Trafford Publishing, 6E–2333 Government St.,
Victoria, BC v8t 4p4 CANADA
phone 250 383 6864 (toll-free 1 888 232 4444)
fax 250 383 6804; email to orders@trafford.com

Books sales in Europe:
Trafford Publishing (uk) Ltd., Enterprise House, Wistaston Road Business Centre, Wistaston Road, Crewe, Cheshire cw2 7rp UNITED KINGDOM
phone 01270 251 396 (local rate 0845 230 9601)
facsimile 01270 254 983; orders.uk@trafford.com

Order online at:
www.trafford.com/robots/04-1332.html

10 9 8 7 6 5 4 3 2 1

For Aubrey

The oldest site, the smallest microblade. Searching for questions. Archaeology is a quest for the things that link all of humanity

In memory of
Joanne Kellock

By and by Raven said, "I wonder what is wrong that I have such bad dreams . . . My dreams always come true. Whatever I dream surely happens."

(John R. Swanton 1909, Tlingit Myths and Texts)

PROLOGUE

The dark figure of the magician waited. Above him the crescent moon and stars shone out of the stone sky. He turned to the raven perched on his shoulder. The time had come. Once more they would look upon the drawings in the pool. Perhaps for the last time.

On the floor an enormous elliptical void, rimmed with glittering cobbles of fire, gaped into eternity. In the beginning the world lay in chaos, then *Yehlh* wrested light, water, and fire from the spirits. Above the three concentric rings of the earth, he looked to the sun, a spiral; and offered a burning stick to the men he ruled. Next were the images of *Hoon*, the North Wind; and *Kun-nook*, the guardian of fresh water.

Yehlh had known joy when first he immortalized his life in stone – but now he saw only death.

He placed the mask upon his face, and opened the Raven's beak to reveal the moon. He lifted the rattle and held it high, his robe outspread like wings.

The Eagle would not have it – the man and the frog linked in power riding the back of the large black bird, and beneath it, the hooked face of the raptor.

He moved toward the entrance. He crept through the tunnel and out to the other side behind the stone pillar. He listened.

"You should not have betrayed me."

The woman to whom the Eagle spoke did not answer.

"I would have given all to you. But now I must take what I want. Where is your lover?"

A sound came from the magician's right. He turned.

Stars burst in his head and the rattle flew. His mask tore away and his wings became arms, his beak fumbling lips. He sprawled face down on the cold floor with a warrior holding a finely honed blade to his throat.

The warrior bade him rise and he did, and nudged him toward the shadow dancing among the flickering stones of fire. He in the Eagle mask threw the warrior a length of cedar withe, and flaunted the capture of the old man's daughter.

So this was how it was to be. *Yehlh* was stripped, felled to the ground, feet lashed, hands bound behind his back. Then the chief of the Eagles lifted his hands to the woman in a false pleading gesture.

"Do as I say. For I do not wish to sever his throat before your eyes."

The woman glanced down at the doeskin covering her, then desperately at the warrior.

"Avert your sight," the chief commanded and the man obeyed.

"And the magician," she whispered. "I beg of you, do not insist I bare myself to him."

The chief raised the mask from his head, and now they could see his face. "So . . . It is true."

A knife appeared in his hand.

The warrior laughed, hurtled forward to block the woman from fleeing. The Eagle paced four feet on either side of the stone pillar. He marked two nodes with the tip of the blade. The three projections formed a triad of stone.

He went to the woman, grasped her wrists and secured them over her head. He nodded to the warrior who slid down her body to her hips. There the warrior sat, reached out, and fingered the thong fastening the doeskin to her throat.

She gasped, barely making a sound. The warrior heaved in a swift upward thrust, stripping the doeskin into the air.

"Place her here," the young chief said.

They subdued her until she knelt. Then they laced her wrists to the towering pillar. Each took a leg, forced them apart, and bound her ankles to the stones rising from the floor.

The chief crouched by the woman's head and gazed into her forest eyes.

"This was not as I intended." He placed a hand beneath her chin and kissed her on the lips. "How many times did he defile you?"

The old man's daughter was naked, lashed to the stones. The chief motioned to the warrior to join him and both hunkered by her head. The chief's eyes narrowed and he lowered an unwelcome hand.

"Again, my betrothed. How many times?"

Revulsion was naked on her face. The chief of the Eagles rose. He raised the rattle and swung it down, clipping her in the jaw.

"Whom will you have!" he raged. "The chief, the warrior, or the magician. Choose or I shall choose for you!"

She wept.

"Whom?" he shouted again.

"I will *not* violate her."

"Ah, but you will not be violating her, *Magician*. It is you she wants."

Yehlh struggled with the ropes fettering him. The woman whimpered, quivered, and he hesitated. If he did not commit the act, then the chief would order the warrior to do so.

The chief held the knife to her chin and his hand trembled. Fire leaped from the stone bowls. He drew the woman's hair away and revealed the paleness of her throat.

"Nine moons *Magician*," he taunted. "Then we shall see which one of us has won."

CHAPTER ONE

Jake shivered, though he was not cold, and released the clutch on his Bronco. Angeline, his passenger, turned to the sunny, sea swept beaches of Cedar Island outside his window.

What was the matter with him? It was only a nightmare. In the brilliant turquoise day, he could see that. But the design on her T-shirt was making the hairs lift along the backs of his arms.

"Dreams don't tell us anything," she said, measuring her words carefully. "They are manifestations of our fears and anxieties. You're anticipating seeing the rattle; it's as simple as that."

"Do you believe in inherited memories?" he asked her.

Angeline smiled, her gold-green eyes tilting at the corners like a cat's. She was part Chinese and part White, and pretty as a peach. "I don't think so, Jake."

Her black hair wrestled with the breeze from the open window. She was the kind of woman you couldn't help but stare at. She had the kind of looks that fascinated because they were so enigmatic. Her personality was a mystery, her face unreadable. They were not a couple. Jake was a professor and Angeline was a graduate student. She was from Toronto, now attending the University of Washington where he taught. She had joined his archaeology crew in the San Juan Islands for the summer.

The crew had been working almost a month, not bothering the locals much. Then, late last week, Joe Redleaf had found a Raven rattle in Connie Amos's bog. The find had attracted the attention of Clifford Radisson, a New York developer, who wanted to turn the islands into a theme park.

Jake did not want a theme park.

A windstorm last night had scattered twigs and leaves all over the road, and as he drove over a branch, it snapped and shot out the side. He swerved along the shoreline and the asphalt cleared of debris. A gnarly arbutus with thinly peeling orange bark reminded him of onion skin. The arbutus tree zipped by and a grove of hemlock took its place. Left of him, a tongue of land jutted out. Above the tumble of sandstone, a lighthouse, red and white, chrome fixtures flashing in the sunlight, stood nestled in deep yellow grass.

Jake glanced to his right, then back at the road. He slammed on the brakes.

"Dumb mutt," he grumbled, just missing a dog galloping across his path. An orange pickup truck was parked on the shoulder, and he had almost plowed into it.

He got out to see if he had done any damage to his truck. The bumper looked fine. The pickup didn't look touched either. There was no one inside it and on the driver's door an image of twin eagles fenced.

Jake clenched his fists. He recognized the logo. Did Radisson have someone scouting around here? He braced his hand on the hood of his Bronco and squinted to the east.

No one was around.

A long ramp led from a twist in the road down to a wooden dock. Beneath it, ferns, salal, and tall grass dwindled to yellow rock. The tide was out and wet sandstone textured with seaweed glistened in the sun. Further out in the shallow bay, another ramp joined the dock to floating planks where colourful boats bobbed up and down. Beyond that, the craggy peak of Lookout Island loomed sharp and green.

Angeline poked her head through the opened window. "Maybe we'd better go see if that dog is okay."

Since Connie Amos wasn't expecting them for another half hour, Jake agreed. He got back in the truck, parked properly, and followed Angeline to the beach.

Waves lapped the rocks, some birds squawked, and he could hear a helicopter somewhere.

The dog, a brown beagle, was nosing a sandwich out from a paper bag wedged between some rocks. Two ravens appeared, and one of them slipped behind, tweaked the dog's tail, while the other snapped up the food that fell from its mouth. The dog scampered away.

Jake chuckled. "The old mutt looks okay to me."

Angeline laughed too, then gestured to one of the birds with a crooked wing. "Poor thing. What do you suppose happened? Can it fly like that, do you think?"

Jake shrugged. He extended a hand and the raven hopped up and nudged his fingers with its bill. "Probably not."

He darted a look to the road above the beach. The orange pickup truck was still there.

"What's bugging you?" Angeline asked, then grinned. "You've been acting so skittish. Is the sky about to fall?"

Jake slanted his chin upward.

"Do you recognize that logo on the orange truck?" he asked. "That pickup belongs to corporate super magnate P. Clifford Radisson. He's turned more than one island paradise into a concrete haven for tourists. He's destroyed more forests and beachfronts than I have fingers or toes. The man has no regard for the natural world. I understand why he builds beach resorts and mega shopping malls, but does he have to turn my archaeology sites into a theme park?"

Angeline nodded down the beach at a lanky figure with red hair and an equally fiery beard headed their way. "We have company."

The red-haired man was dressed in jeans and a khaki vest with a surveyor's tape hanging from his hip. He glanced up as the helicopter broke through a small bank of cloud. He came closer, cracked a peanut with his teeth, and popped the contents of the shell into his mouth. The remainder of the nuts went into his pocket, and he flung the crumpled cellophane and empty shells to the ground. He lunged at the ravens and they squawked.

When he saw Angeline, a leering grin spread over his face.

"Is there something I can help you with?" Jake asked coldly as the man stopped in front of them.

"Is this Otter Cove?" he asked.

This dip of beach had no particular name and linked the lighthouse with the marina.

"Otter Cove is up past the town, north of here," Jake said. He indicated with his head the orange pickup parked on the road. "Is that your truck?"

A roar of propelling rotors descended just as the surveyor started to answer. A blast of wind slapped Jake's face. Water splashed, swirled and spun, soaking his shirt. Before he could get out of the way, another wave crested and spat in his eyes.

"What the hell is that idiot doing?" he yelled.

"Get out of the way!" the man hollered. "He's going to land!"

Jake shouted to Angeline to run as the huge shadow of the helicopter lunged. It veered, swayed, swung crazily, and came right back at him. If he didn't know better, he would swear the pilot had singled him out and was harrying him deliberately.

Angeline bolted toward the marina. Jake flew at her heels. He glanced up and the helicopter flitted and flickered, blocking the sun. Rotors spiralled overhead. They both hunched, scooting between the pylons, and under the boards of the dock.

The helicopter righted itself, hovered. It lowered, rotors whirling, slowly settling onto the ground. The surveyor waited, then went over to where the helicopter had landed and opened the cockpit door. A tall pale-haired man stepped out, and sauntered toward the marina, his expensive linen shirt fluttering in the breeze.

"I'm terribly sorry. Did I frighten you?" he asked, peering under the dock.

Jake's skin crawled. This guy was a jerk. He hunkered out from between the pylons, followed by Angeline.

"I haven't flown this machine for a very long time, a bit out of practice I'm afraid. I am truly very sorry. No one was hurt, I hope? I was looking for a place called Otter Cove. Am I anywhere near it?"

The man did a double-take and his manner suddenly changed. He extended an immaculately manicured hand.

"What a marvellous coincidence, Dr. Lalonde. Just this morning I was telling Mr. Smythe here that I must try to meet you today."

Jake stared. How did he know who he was?

He ignored the outstretched hand. The muscles in the pilot's face twitched ever so faintly. "You missed Otter Cove by miles. What did you want to know for?"

"It's renowned by the locals for its beauty. A wildlife preserve, isn't it? I wanted to see it for myself."

The man's eyes were light, almost colourless. He had a slick veneer, heightened by the stylish garb, making Jake self-conscious of his own appearance. Jake's hair was hanging in wet tangled strings, and his shirt was damp from the chest down. He glowered. He turned to look for Angeline who was standing just to the side, slightly behind him.

"I'm Angeline Lisbon," she said, offering her hand.

He took it graciously. "Yes, I know. I believe you're an archaeologist too?"

He looked at the surveyor who was teasing the injured raven with an empty peanut shell.

"Mr. Sam Smythe, this is Ms. Angeline Lisbon and Dr. Jake Lalonde. And I am Clifford Radisson."

Jake flinched. Angeline smiled as the developer turned her hand palm up and rubbed it with his thumb.

"So nice to meet you at last Mr. Radisson," she stammered. "We've heard so much about your wonderful plans to boost tourism around here."

Jake had no time for this. He gestured to Angeline to start up the beach. "We're late for an appointment."

"I'm sorry Mr. Radisson," she said as Jake grabbed her arm. "We really do have an appointment. But do you know where our lab is? Please come and visit any time. I'd be pleased to give you a personal tour– "

They started to leave and Radisson called out. "There's been talk in town about a Raven rattle, Dr. Lalonde. I understand it was found in a bog?"

He came and stood directly in Jake's face. Jake glanced from him to Sam Smythe who was tossing peanut shells onto the beach, taunting the raven with the broken wing.

"I collect Native art. I had the good fortune to purchase some very fine pieces from your museum. I think the rattle will make a lovely addition to my collection. Tell me, Dr. Lalonde, do you think Mrs. Amos will sell it?"

Jake answered, sharply. "Just what is the Cedar Island Museum doing selling off their collections?"

"Easy, Dr. Lalonde. I am just helping out. The museum is suffering from financial difficulties. Surely you don't begrudge my giving them a helping hand?"

"Which pieces?" he demanded.

"A chief's and a shaman's masks. Both Haida. One is an eagle, a lovely piece, perhaps you know it? And the other is the Raven."

Radisson's eyes moved to Angeline. Toe to hooked toe, two solid black birds, one with a violent streak of turquoise across its belly, were gripped in a death struggle, wings arced against the red of her T-shirt. Beneath their claws, a solitary salmon, outlined in black, fought to get away. The birds were solid forms, but the fish was a hollow outline, empty on the inside.

A breeze blew across Jake's neck, pricking his flesh.

He was half-Haida.

"We have to go," Jake said.

He walked to the Bronco. Over the truck's hood he saw the two men talking near the helicopter. In his stiff white shirt, Radisson moved toward the ravens. He dropped to his knees, and extended his hand to the injured bird.

CHAPTER TWO

It was him. Jake Lalonde was only a child when Connie Amos had seen him last. But some things never change. The eyes. The grey eyes and dark complexion.

She greeted the two archaeologists, but there was no recognition. Jake's look showed only curiosity, anticipation, and Connie could see herself reflected in his gaze.

Connie Amos was Native, slim, of medium height and build. She was sixty-five. Her face was smooth except for a papery quality about the light brown skin, drawn tightly over her cheek bones. Tiny lines creased the corners of her eyes and mouth. She raised a hand to the hair plaited down her back, and tucked in a silvery wisp that had loosened at the front. She was dressed in yellow. A white and canary yellow flower printed dress she had found in Wal-Mart last week.

She led them into her sunroom and asked them to wait, then brought in the rattle and placed it on the table. It was unbroken, shaped like a bird, and had a black oblong head and a straight and powerful beak. Carved in sharp relief on its back the naked figure of a man reclined head to head with the bird's. On the man's stomach a green frog sprawled. The man and the frog were linked at their mouths by a red tongue.

"A bit obscene, isn't it?" Angeline said.

Connie smiled. On one level the figures did have something to do with sex, on another they had to do with the shaman's acquisition of power. Sunlight dimmed as a cloud passed outside the window, then leaped like gunshot, landing with brilliant impact on the rattle.

"Careful!" Connie said uneasily, as Jake turned the artifact over.

The colours were faded. The principal figure depicted was a raven. Underneath, carved onto its belly, was the face of an eagle.

The archaeologist traced the avian design intently. Most of the black paint once embellishing it was gone. The almond coloured wood had darkened from natural pigments in the earth.

"I didn't know what to do since everyone wants this rattle," Connie said. "The cultural centre in Port Angeles, the museum here on Cedar Island, and Shaman Moon on Gooseberry Island thinks it should go to him." Connie paused. And then, there was Clifford Radisson.

She dipped over Jake and lifted the rattle out of his hands. She turned the artifact over, studying first the carving of the one side, then the other.

"Connie," Jake said.

"Yes? Oh, I'm sorry Jake. Did you want to examine this further?" She offered him the rattle and did not flinch when he took it.

"Are you planning to sell your property to Radisson Enterprises?"

Connie stopped in the act of pouring tea from a Corning Ware teapot.

It had sounded like an accusation, like Jake was asking her if she was going to sell her home simply because Clifford Radisson was willing to pay her a fortune for it.

Jake waited, and when she didn't answer, he asked, "Do you have any idea how big the site might be?"

She replaced the teapot on the trivet, and shook her head. "There's a property survey, but that probably won't mention anything about an archaeological site. No one knew it was there until now. Joe Redleaf should be here any minute. He'll show you where he dug up the things, and then you can judge for yourselves."

She lifted the rattle and moved her fingers with light, delicate strokes enveloping the artifact in a swatch of beige flannel. "I'll just put this away for now. I have a few other things to show you. Some basketry. I won't be a minute."

She pushed back the white wooden chair and left the table.

In her kitchen, Connie placed the rattle in the glass cabinet beneath the window and removed a small bundle rolled in an old embroidered pillow case. She stood in the doorway just out of sight of the two archaeologists and watched them.

There was something else she wanted to show Jake, but it was not in this room.

The day was waning, the sun westering across the beach when Joe Redleaf, the son of the Samish chief, finally arrived. They walked to the bog. Connie breathed heavily. An odour, damp and earthy, suffused the air. The sparsely vegetated field lay blanketed in mud. She seldom came out here now. Nothing of worth would grow on this land.

A squarish pit opened out to the sky and Jake approached it. "What made you dig here? This spot in particular?" he asked Joe.

"That basketry Connie showed you, some of it was exposed after a storm. Flooding washed a lot of the mud away. It was just lying there so I picked it up, then realized there were other things down there."

"The rattle was lying on top? On the mud?"

"No. Not the rattle. I had to dig for that. It was about halfway down I found it. Then the pit filled up with water. I guess I must have hit the water table."

"Amazing how well it preserved," Connie said.

"Isn't it?" Angeline replied. "Wood survives in waterlogged sites because its pores are saturated with water and don't permit oxygen to enter. The condition is called anaerobic and reduces the deterioration process, allowing organic materials to survive in a state of equilibrium for thousands of years."

Jake smiled. "In other words, bogs keep things from rotting."

He squinted into the sun. Connie could tell he wanted to ask something more. Maybe about herself. She was having financial problems, but that was none of his concern. She would never sell her property to Radisson Enterprises no matter how poor she got.

She glanced up at the sky, then across the field and over to her house which was banked on all four sides by a wooden veranda. The steps were rickety, painted white and peeling, and the wood siding matched neat pairs of shutters flanking windows on either side of the door. Colour undulated in the flower boxes she had placed there.

Paul had built that house for her. When he died, she had given up their only son for adoption. She was too poor and sick to take care of him by herself; and though that meant very little now, she couldn't consider moving.

"I didn't know the Samish made Raven rattles," Angeline said.

A strange look came over Jake's face. Now what could that mean?

CHAPTER THREE

It was dark. The Coleman lantern glowed. Grey daylight crept through the wide crevice to illuminate the shallow grave. Jake rose to stand in the opening of the cave and to breathe in the frosty air. A tingling began in his fingertips and toes. He took in the melting lake, the white bluffs surrounding the mirror of water. A marten poked its head up from a ridge of half frozen earth, then scurried away. Jake rubbed the numbness in his hand, the one that held his field journal. He was probably just cold.

"Can I remove the bones now?" Josie, in a dirty sweater, called to him from within the cave.

He came back inside and knelt beside her over the skeleton of the raven. A cobble had emerged from the same excavation unit, and an elliptical shadow darkened its centre giving it the appearance of a shallow bowl. The light from the lantern flickered, catching the minerals in the granite cobble. Jake stared, mesmerized by the gold flecks glittering on its grainy surface.

Josie stuck out a hand. "That is NOT an artifact. It's a rock. Now, can you PLEASE pass me a plastic bag?"

Jake ignored her, turned to a fresh page in his journal and wrote: The Marten Lake Cave Site.

Jake lifted his briefcase and placed it on the table as a stiff breeze caught at his hair. He sniffed. Rain maybe. It was damp. Hot. In the middle of this miserable field, his raingear, which was draped on a plastic chair in front of him, exuded an earthy rubbery stink. Breathing was a chore made more uncomfortable by the stench of the bog.

"Watch those hoses! You're tangled around that tree stump!" he yelled, and settled the briefcase more firmly on the table.

A crew was working halfway across the field from Connie's house twelve metres from the pit Joe had dug. It wasn't an easy job to drain water from the pits. The walls kept collapsing. Where the clay was solid, it held, but most of the ground was saturated, and no matter how long or how hard they pumped, freshwater continued to bubble up.

A shout came from the pits and Josie Davies came toward him from the crew of muddy excavators. Her matronly form was wrapped in a T-shirt, soiled across the chest, and wrinkled around the waist. She was his co-director, and was supposed to be supervising the dig at Berry Point.

Jake was here on Cedar Island to excavate a shell midden. He was interested in prehistoric shamanism and ritual, but the only way he could get funding was to run a project that would provide summer jobs for students and local residents. The Berry Point Site backed onto a beach a mile from Otter Cove. At the end of Seagirt Lane there was an abandoned house they were using for a lab, and a clearing near the forest where they had set up their camp. Close to the beach just before a rise of grass leading to the sand was the area they were digging.

When Joe Redleaf had dug up that Raven rattle everything had changed. The Heritage Advisory Board wanted Jake to excavate both the wet site and the midden. Despite Jake's protests of inadequate facilities and manpower, he was told if he didn't excavate Connie Amos's bog, someone else would do it. Josie's name had come up. The HAB had reminded Jake of the rattle. Jake had invested too much of his life obsessed with the Raven to let someone else find its origins, so he had split the crew in half, leaving some with Josie at Berry Point, taking the rest, including Angeline, to the bog.

"How goes it?" Jake asked as Josie plodded up.

"Everything's under control. What are you finding?"

Jake pointed to a piece of wood swimming in a shallow pan of dirty water.

"Don't let that dry out," Josie said to Carly who was seated at the table filling out an artifact form.

Josie scanned the ground where trays of basketry lay stacked. She picked up a spray bottle and misted the top of some spruce root splits, then tipped the tray and dampened the yellow cedar matting underneath.

"Are you going to put that fish thing in plastic?" she asked.

"Angeline says to wait until the polyethylene glycol comes," Carly replied.

"It'll desiccate if we wait for the chemicals to come. Cover it at least!"

Jake flinched at the sharpness in Josie's voice. Today was Josie's thirtieth birthday. For her, a big deal. Good thing the crew had organized a party for her tonight. Jake opened his briefcase and removed a paperclipped computer printout and passed it to her.

Nothing was going to ruin this day for him. It had taken a decade to compile this paper and now it was finished.

"What's this?" she asked.

Ravens had caught the attention of the first people even as they crossed the Bering land bridge from Siberia into North America. They were associated with the beginning of the world and the bleak region of Marten Lake supported humans in a transitional environment. The black bird was referred to as "*Yehlh*" in old anthropological journals, and Creation stories always began with the Raven in a cold empty land.

"I think the skeleton was deliberately interred," Jake said.

Josie flipped a few pages, then looked up. "Why would anyone deliberately bury a bird, Jake? It's more likely it was used for feathers or food."

"There are no butchering marks on the bones. And look at the date. A cosmology based on the Raven might have developed 10,000 years ago."

Josie shrugged. She had heard all of this before.

They went to the pub at the Innis Hotel for lunch.

Jake picked up his glass, poured beer down his throat. A waiter in a white shirt and khaki shorts unloaded a toasted shrimp sandwich in front of him.

"If Radisson gets this whole island like he wants, he's agreed to a complete assessment," Josie said, tackling her hamburger.

Jake put his sandwich down. "For Godsake, Josie. Clifford Radisson doesn't care about heritage, he just wants to rake in the bucks. This is

Archaeo-Disneyland we're talking about. RAVENSWORLD is just a sophisticated name to make the whole project sound legitimate."

"He's going to allow us to keep working here even after the park is opened to the public. There'll be interpretation programs, an education centre." Tomatoes and Kraft slices melted to a Cheese Whiz consistency squeezed out of Josie's hamburger as her fingers pressed down on the bun.

Jake knew what her problem was. She wanted a job. Not just these three month field seasons and the four months analysis. She wanted a steady pay cheque, benefits, a dental plan.

He looked down to wait for his pulse to subside, and traced the ornate edging under his fingers. The tabletops in this pub were beautiful antique wooden doors, each a different design.

The smell of grease, onions and french fries swept through from the kitchen as a door swung open. Smoke drifted by, and as Jake gazed past Josie's head to the far wall, he recognized a watercolour of the lighthouse near the marina.

Pictures with nautical and Native motifs hung everywhere. On the wall directly beside them were some black and white photographs taken in the late nineteenth century. They were familiar – the Hudson's Bay Company's side-wheel steamer, the *Beaver*; a few Curtis reproductions of Native fishers and clam diggers; several totem poles.

There was an ethnographic photo of Skidegate, a Haida village in the Queen Charlotte Islands. Skidegate was the place Jake's mother supposedly came from. Her name was Susan Tom, and other than the fact that she had given birth to him in Seattle when she was sixteen, he knew squat about her.

"Interesting photographs," he said.

"Huh," Josie answered, sullenly. She lifted a single french fry burnt slightly at the tip, drove it into a puddle of mayonnaise, and thrust it into her mouth.

Jake suddenly knocked his glass over, spilling beer onto her plate.

"Hey what the hell are you doing?" she asked.

Out of the washroom, at the far end of the bar, came Clifford

Radisson, dressed immaculately, in a white cotton shirt and tan linen trousers.

Kate had introduced Radisson to Josie last week. Kate–Katherine Leonard was the Regional Archaeologist's assistant. Like Josie, she had once shared a bed with Jake.

Josie got up. "I'm going to invite him over."

Before Jake could stop her, she brought the developer to their table.

"A pleasure to meet you again, Dr. Lalonde," Radisson said.

"Please sit," Josie said.

The developer sat down across from Jake and glanced at the spilled beer on the table.

"Waiter," he called, and a young man rushed up and immediately removed his apron, and mopped up the table and righted the glass.

"Another one for Dr. Lalonde, please young man."

Jake did not know why he couldn't speak. It was like his tongue was stuck down his throat, he wanted so badly to gag.

"Jake is not quite up to date on your plans, Mr. Radisson. I was just explaining to him how they will benefit the community," Josie said.

"*You* are the inspiration for my theme park, Dr. Lalonde."

"I can't see myself as anyone's inspiration for anything, Mr. – Radisson."

Radisson smiled. He financed the construction of shopping malls, casinos, hotels, fair grounds and zoos, internationally. He was known to personally oversee only the most important projects. If things continued his way, the theme park would soon be one.

"I am very interested in Native culture. *Your* culture," he said. "Tom Price, Charles Edensaw, Bill Reid of the Haida, and Mungo Martin of the Kwakiutl, are just some of the artists represented in my private collection."

"I would give anything to own a piece by any one of them," Josie said.

Jake cut in. "The Kwakiutl call themselves the *Kwakwaka'wakw* now."

The developer's eyes flickered over, stayed for a moment, then moved away. "Once my plans are firm, I will have jobs for all of your crew. If they want them."

"You'll need cooperation from the Native Band Council," Jake insisted.

"*You* must make archaeology accessible to the public. *I* need someone to promote and sell the place. I think if we put our heads together, this project will benefit us all."

Jake glowered and Radisson smiled, adding, "Tell me about the petroglyphs on Lookout Island."

"We haven't seen them yet," Josie said.

"They're in a cave, aren't they? That gives them a special significance."

"Until we know the implications of that particular site, you'll have to keep away," Jake replied.

There was no point in delaying the inevitable Radisson said. Funding for ten years was his offer. He wanted the park to open in five so that visitors could witness the archaeologists at work.

"Your opinion is highly regarded, Dr. Lalonde. People *will* cooperate – if you support the project."

Jake opened his mouth to retort, Josie kicked him under the table, and Clifford Radisson smiled, glanced sideways to where Angeline sat with the crew, and rose.

"I must go. Ms. Davies, Dr. Lalonde, we will talk again soon."

Jake sat silent for several minutes, glaring at Josie. Then the waiter reappeared.

"Is there anything else I can get for you?"

Jake shook his head and reached for his wallet, but the waiter nodded at the door.

"The gentleman has taken care of it."

***

Angeline stared into her bowl of clam chowder and stirred her spoon around and around. She had no appetite. Last week, her father had phoned the lab when she wasn't there. He expected her to return his call, but she hadn't.

He wanted her to come home; he thought her presence would make a difference to her mother; and maybe it would, but Angeline wanted no part of it. She was frustrated with him, tired of being told what to do.

From the first Dad had opposed her studying archaeology. Now that she was working on a MA he had become increasingly vocal. She had a place in his law firm if she wanted it, he said. But *that*, she did not want.

Angeline paused with her spoon halfway to her lips, catching Jake's eye across the crowded pub. She wished he wouldn't do that. She couldn't afford the frivolity of falling in love with him. There was nothing he could do for her except give her a summer job.

Dad had taught her very early in life that she would always be an object for men's lust. Mom had told her it was easier to marry the thing you wanted to be, than to become the thing yourself. They both wanted her to be educated, accomplished, and cultured. But instead of feeling confident, she felt inadequate, vulnerable, and weary.

At the pay phones Angeline inserted her long distance calling card. She heard the slam of a door at the other end, and a commotion in her parents house in Toronto. Teresa, her childhood friend and confidante - the housekeeper - handed her father the phone.

"Why haven't you returned my calls?" he asked.

"I did. I am." Angeline nervously twisted the telephone cord around her baby finger. "I'm sorry Dad, I meant to call earlier, but it's difficult. The lab phone is meant for project business." Her voice rose artificially light. "I'm so glad I took the job though, I'm having a wonderful time."

"Life isn't about having a wonderful time," he said bluntly.

She told him about the developer and the possibility of a theme park.

"Do you really need a PhD to work in a theme park?" her father asked. "Don't people just stand around and operate rides and sell food and blow the whistle when the kids touch the exhibits?"

"It's a project of Radisson Enterprises."

"I don't think this archaeology business is a wise idea," he said. "An undergraduate degree is one thing, Angel, but an MA, and then a PhD? What do you expect to do after that? Don't tell me you fancy yourself in love with one of those hotshot archaeologists. There's not some maverick idealist seducing you with romantic notions, I hope. Have you given your future any consideration at all?"

"Is Mom there?" she asked. But Angeline knew she wasn't.

"This is the first time you've really been on your own. There are people out there just waiting to take advantage of you. What's this fellow like whom you're working for, anyway? Where do you sleep? What do you do about washrooms and privacy?"

"I have my own tent," she said.

"I've heard how people have communal bathing and sleeping arrangements."

"I don't do anything communal," she said.

"Angel, I really don't like this."

"I know Dad, but it's what I want to do."

"Do you realize what you'll have to give up? Archaeologists are transients. They go from job to job, place to place. Your boss, how much does he make? It wouldn't hurt you to get to know people like Clifford Radisson if you really want to work in that theme park. If you aim high, you could get a position that's worthy of you. If you don't want to do law, you should consider a career in public relations. Do you know how much money P.R. people make?"

He stopped to take in a breath, then his voice changed. "You think you know how it is because I let you go west to play archaeologist for a year. I probably shouldn't have done that. I probably shouldn't have paid your way."

He paused again. "Maybe I shouldn't pay your way now."

Angeline's pulse quickened as her father's voice turned hard.

"You're too idealistic, but if that's what you want to do, then maybe you should see what it's really like out there."

CHAPTER FOUR

Clifford Radisson arrived at his branch office in Seattle late that afternoon. He sat with his feet propped up on his dark mahogany desk and watched the image of Sam Smythe on his video telephone. The thirty inch screen flickered for a moment, then the contractor's animated face cleared.

"I want him out by the end of the summer," Clifford Radisson said. He picked up a paring knife and tested its edge on his finger.

"That damned archaeologist says no way. He tells me they'll dig as much as they can this year, then close up the site until next spring."

Clifford Radisson thought about this as he whittled away at a long thin stick of wood. His fingers worked nervously, peeling layer after layer of cedar. Maybe this could be a model of a fish weir for his theme park. His thoughts roamed momentarily to the dark-haired Angeline. The knife nicked his finger and he cursed softly.

A loud squawk from the corner of the room caught his attention. Inside a golden cage the black raven with its broken wing fluttered against the wire. Clifford Radisson rose and felt the eyes of the contractor follow him from the screen.

He paused in front of the bird and held out the stick. The bird snapped at it, its bright intelligent eyes enraged to find the wood inedible. The bird could not fly, its wing had not healed properly, and it would never fly again. In this office it was safe, but he did not release it. He had no intention of releasing it. Ever.

"Mr. Radisson," Sam Smythe said. "Are you there?"

Radisson turned on his heel and returned to the phone. "What about the Samish woman?" he asked.

He was assuming a bit much by calling Connie Amos Samish, but if she didn't want anyone else to know, he wouldn't be the one to speak.

"I may have to go to see her in person," Radisson said. "She won't talk to me by phone. I think our Dr. Lalonde is having too much of an influence on her."

"She hems and haws, talks about the greater good and all that crap. I don't know what's with her. If she's flat broke, what the hell is her problem?"

Clifford Radisson settled his feet into the plush Persian carpet of his office and placed the sharpened stick next to the growing pile on his desk. The blood on the knife was already drying. He smeared it off with his fingers and glanced back at the video screen.

Her problem was him.

***

"Happy Birthday, Josie."

Jake gave his co-director a little peck on the cheek and grinned. "How's it feel?"

"Like shit."

They sat by a blazing fire in the clearing in front of the house where they had set up their field lab at Berry Point. Jake tossed in a log and smelled the piney resin rise in the smoke. Josie reached for a stick and poked at his log, straightening it, then giggled as it collapsed, snuffing out half the flame. Her eyes glowed merrily in the dark and she tilted her chin and wet her lips on a bottle of Rainier light.

"The night is young. Don't you think you should pace it a little?"

Jake kicked the log to an angle so he could shove another one under it, forming an air pocket between the coals and the wood. A puff of smoke curled into his face, making him cough.

"I think we should go have a look at those petroglyphs soon," Josie said.

The truth was, Jake *had* thought about going to Lookout Island, but not with Josie.

He looked around. Where was Angeline? He hadn't seen her in the last half hour. A log came crashing down. He shoved a thick piece of kindling into a nest of glowing coals and watched the flame leap up, then surveyed the camp.

People were drinking and smoking on the steps of the house and in front of their tents. Near the forest's edge, laughter and voices rose. His eyes returned to Josie, who was untangling a knot in her hair. He smiled, got up. The birthday present she wanted from him wasn't one he was prepared to give.

He twisted the cap off a bottle of beer and went for a stroll. At the shell midden, four shadowy figures, perched on the edge of a pit, passed around a joint. He stopped, hesitated for a minute, then told them to move for fear ash would fall into the pit or the walls would collapse.

He ambled on until he came to a grassy rise that sloped to the beach. Angeline didn't hear him as he dropped softly on the sand behind her. Her feet were bare, she wore jeans and a tank top, and her face was to the sea.

"I was wondering where you'd wandered off to," he said, startling her.

The tide slapped against the sandy beach. Jake took a slug of his beer, dribbling some down his chin, and mopped it off with his sleeve.

Angeline smiled, began to walk, and Jake walked beside her. The night was warm, the sand cool, and the moon floated above. They were quite a ways from the camp now where the fire flickered like a match flame.

"Not in a party mood?"

Angeline sighed. "I'm sorry Jake. I'm lousy company tonight. It's my father. He's decided he isn't going to help me anymore, and I don't know what I'll do for money next year."

He chuckled, making a lighthearted attempt at humour. "Don't I pay you enough?"

She looked up at him; she was a little bit drunk.

"You really don't know, do you? You don't know what it's like to feel like you can't do anything by yourself. I can't do anything by myself because everything was always done for me. Now I find out everything is so hard, and everyone puts obstacles in my way. You think because I look like *this*– " She stopped.

Just because she looked like *that,* people would always do things for her. It was true. It was one of the reasons Jake had hired her himself.

People often did things on their own. He had, Josie had, Kate had. Even Tom Jelna at the Heritage Advisory Board had gotten the position of Regional Archaeologist on his own.

"You'll be fine," he said. "You can apply for scholarships, student loans. How else do you think everyone puts themselves through school?"

Moonlight whitened the foam along the edge of the waves. The air carried the smell of seaweed. They continued walking. A cliff rose in the dark and Jake followed her around it. Twenty minutes they wandered in silence before she stopped. The silvery sand curved into a shallow bay, and they turned to look back at the bluff. They were a mile from the camp at Otter Cove.

They went up the beach to a fallen log and sat down on the sand. Crickets chirped and the tide slapped relentlessly against the shore. Jake considered what she would do if he leaned over and kissed her right now.

"Tell me about your family," Angeline said.

There are certain things you never grow out of no matter how old you get. Being shuffled around from one foster family to another was one of them. His graduating class in high-school had voted him the one most likely to end up in jail. That might have happened too, if a compassionate teacher hadn't encouraged him to join an archaeological dig the summer he turned eighteen.

It had not been easy. No scholarships at first because his high-school grades had been well below par. In those days no one wanted to give a motherless half-breed a break. In those days he didn't know what it meant to be Indian. He looked like a white guy with dark skin. He felt like a white guy with dark skin, but something had always nagged at him. Until he got into archaeology and found a reason to be, he would have been a white guy with dark skin slumming the streets.

But that was the past. Jake looked down at Angeline in the moonlight.

He drew back, smiled, as she began to talk. She was a rich girl.

Daddy was a lawyer and Mom had given up a promising career in law to marry him. Grandpa on Dad's side had been a lawyer too. But her mother's father had lived on the West Coast. As far as she knew, he had worked in a lumberyard.

"That might be why I have such an affinity for the West Coast," she explained. "Something drew me here."

"Radisson Enterprises?" Jake said facetiously.

She frowned. Jake smiled nervously.

"Were you lonely as a child?" she asked.

He looked up to where the Big Dipper twinkled in the sky. When he was a kid he used to know all the constellations. Orion, Ursa Major, Ursa Minor, Perseus, Cassiopeia, Pisces, Andromeda. *Twinkle, twinkle little star, how I wonder who you are.* But that wasn't the childhood song nagging in his memory. It was something else. A lullaby. Something about going to the creek of his forefathers to catch spring salmon. *Stay with me my mother, stay with me, O my mother, 'til the night shadows fade; 'til the fish come to welcome the dawn, stay with me until I am grown . . .*

Yes, he was lonely, but he never thought about things like that anymore.

* * *

"Where the hell have you been?" Josie squinted up at the grassy ridge where Jake and Angeline stood.

They had talked all night, returning just around dawn.

Now, on the floor of one of the pits, Clifford Radisson's contractor sprawled on his back, legs splayed, knuckles white from supporting his weight. In the early morning sun, shadows reached into the pit toward him, his biceps tensing, a tattoo in black and red twitching on his upper arm.

His tumble into the hole had partially collapsed the wall between two pits. The stratigraphy on the east wall was destroyed and the bottom of the pit contained a jumble of clam shells and the tread of work boots.

Jake descended the slope to the gridded shell midden, staring down, and waited at the edge of the pit with his hands in his pockets. His foot loosened a stone, sending earth cascading below. A beer bottle had rolled to one corner of the pit and half buried beneath it were a couple of marijuana butts from the party last night.

"What happened?" Jake demanded.

"I could've been killed," the contractor said.

"You should've been killed, doing a stupid thing like that," Josie retorted.

Jake gave Josie a look that instantly silenced her, then looked back down at the contractor, leaned over, and held out his hand.

"I don't think you could have been seriously injured Mr. Smythe. That pit is hardly deep enough."

"I could sue you people for this."

The contractor rose, ignoring Jake's outstretched hand, and hoisted himself out of the pit, damaging another section of the wall.

"It was covered overnight!" Josie insisted. "You were trespassing. He was trespassing, Jake!"

Jake gestured Sam Smythe to follow him off the work area.

They stood about five yards from Josie and Angeline while a pair of women in shorts and bikini tops headed toward the screens near the beach with buckets of dirt.

The contractor dusted off his pants and smirked. "Wouldn't mind giving either one of them a lube job. I can see why you like your work Lalonde. Being 'round that all day."

Josie made to lunge at him, but Jake stopped her with a glare. "If you wanted to see me, Mr. Smythe, you would have been better off calling before you came, so someone could be here to meet you."

The contractor growled, "Mr. Radisson will be getting in touch with you soon. He had to fly back to New York to finalize a deal. He wanted to tell you he's put in a bid to buy Lookout Island. He wants you to have a look at the rock art and tell him what you think."

The contractor sneered at Jake, glanced deprecatingly at Josie, lecherously at Angeline, and left.

"Did you hear that?" Jake asked.

Josie nodded, tipping a bucket upright with her toe. "The man is a jerk. I was over at the house making coffee this morning. He just decided he'd walk all over everything like he thought he was going to find you sleeping in the bottom of a hole somewhere."

Jake looked down into the damaged pit. "Whose beer bottle is that? And who the hell threw those joints down there?"

"I'll clean that up," Angeline said.

Inside the house, Jake snatched up the phone. When the Regional Archaeologist answered, he shouted into the receiver, "What do you think you're doing? I haven't even been over to the island to see what sort of petroglyphs they are!"

"The branch of the government dealing with Lookout Island has nothing to do with us."

"What do you mean it has nothing to do with us. It's got everything to do with us. That is an archaeological site, dammit!"

Tom Jelna refused to argue with him and said he would fly out the next day to tour the wet site and to discuss the future of Lookout Island. Jake thought it was best to take the day off and to do their Saturday chores today, so they could be on the site working tomorrow when he arrived. They went into town, stopping first at the Laundromat.

"Is Kate coming too?" Josie asked.

"No. They don't get along. Kate's had it with Tom."

"I don't blame her. She would have made a better Regional Archaeologist than him."

Tom Jelna was an idiot, controlled by government bureaucracy, but at least he did what he thought was best for the state. Kate did what was best for her. They left the Laundromat and Jake sauntered toward the museum. "Anyone else interested?"

Angeline was, and so was Josie, Carly, and her boyfriend, Steve. The rest of the crew who had come into town decided to go for lunch while they waited for their laundry.

The structure housing the collections was made of wood and stone and was more like an abandoned 19th century farmhouse than a museum. The display area consisted of a large room with no windows. It was dark inside except for track lighting along the upper walls. There were several small glass cases of the kind Victorian museums used, and one very large case that reached to the ceiling. Painted wooden carvings hung from floor to ceiling inside it. A card in front of a Haida mask gave a date of circa 1915 and described the *Sisiutl*, a two headed serpent. The *Sisiutl* ate human flesh and washing in its blood could turn a person into stone.

Carly shoved her thin wire glasses on her nose. "Dwa . . . Dro . . . Drosophila?"

"Not Drosophila," Jake said, laughing, "that's a fruit fly. *Dzunkwa*."

"Say again?"

"*Dzunkwa*. The cannibal queen."

Josie glanced over. "Cannibalism might have occurred on the Northwest Coast in the very distant past, but there is no concrete evidence to prove it."

Something was bothering Josie this morning other than Sam Smythe. Was it the way he had brushed her off last night? She had a habit of coming on to him when she was drunk.

Josie threw him a pitiful look. "Anthropologists like Franz Boas recorded cannibal dances, *not* the act of cannibalism." She stood with her hands on her hips, eyes narrowed. "Cannibal dances depend on illusion. People saw dancers mock biting members of the audience, not eating their flesh."

The round eyes, protruding ears, and pursed lips of the *Dzunkwa* hung in the display with a grisly stare.

"What do you know about her?" Angeline asked Jake.

"You can read, can't you?" Josie said.

The *Dzunkwa* was similar to the old lady in the Hansel and Gretel story. She was an uncivilized, savage woman, who lived in the forest. She suffered from some sort of sleeping or drug induced disorder (just like Josie), and her eyes were slitted and her movements trance-like. She prowled the edges of villages sating her appetite for children's flesh.

They moved further along the case. There was no air conditioning in the museum, but Jake's hands suddenly went cold. In front of him was the short hooked beak and raptor eyes of an eagle.

The label said: "Displayed with the generous permission of Mr. P. Clifford Radisson, New York, NY."

Beneath it hung the Raven.

CHAPTER FIVE

"Clifford Radisson will make a huge difference to the economy here," Angeline said.

The developer's handsome face, full of false pleasantness, was always on the verge of a slight – a *very* slight, arrogant sneer. No one else seemed to notice, but when those pale eyes smiled their blind emotionless smile, Jake felt something inside his gut recoil. Gag.

They had left the museum and he and Angeline had decided to walk back to Berry Point while Josie and the others drove his Bronco back with the laundry. As they rounded a bank of trees, stepping out of the shade, the air grew warm and the sun shone hot on the golden sand. Children frolicked in the water, and a little girl in a red and white polka dotted swim suit climbed up the beach dripping wet with a plastic bucket.

"Imagine this– " Jake stopped, and waved a hand to take in the beach. "RAVENSWORLD opens to a marching band of costumed Indians and archaeologists. The main attractions light up in giant flashing signs. Raiders of the Lost Petroglyphs. Indiana Jones and the Temple of the Coast Salish. Indiana Jones and the Last Shell Midden. Get your tickets here for the wildest ride of your life. A park to rival Disney World . . . I can see it now, Harrison Ford swinging through the trees, a giant stone ball rolling over his head and landing smack on top of ours. It's sacrilege, Angeline."

"But– "

"No buts about it. Do you know what Radisson's plans for marketing are? A giftshop pavilion along the beach, a boardwalk selling everything from fedoras and bullwhips to arrowheads, miniature petroglyphs and basketry reproductions. I wouldn't put it past him to try and sell the real things. Who's gonna store all that stuff once we get it out? Do you know how much stuff can be excavated in ten years? Every little projectile point, retouched flake, bone fragment has to go somewhere. Why not sell them and just keep the good stuff for display?

It all makes sense to me."

"You're being facetious," she said.

"It's all authentic and it's all from here. No justification necessary. People will buy it." Jake waved his hands fitfully in the air. "We'll never have to worry about storage space again."

"That's illegal. There's legislation to protect cultural property from being sold for profit."

"Who's going to enforce it? Do you want to know who's gonna be providing food services? McDonald's. I'm not kidding, it's all propaganda. A tourism boon, boosting the economy to make up for fishing and forestry shortfalls."

Jake didn't say it, but he was damned if he was going to sit back and watch Radisson hit on her either.

They walked silently down the beach, and as they approached Otter Cove, the sand curved in a deep sickle toward Berry Point. Jake's face relaxed, and he looked down at Angeline. He had feelings for her that he didn't dare show because he didn't know if she had any for him.

She had no idea what he was thinking, and wandered down to the shore, and he followed. The tide quietened into a gentle slapping. The water was oddly clear and sheltered from open swells. Their faces reflected back, and below the rippling green, olivey sea lettuce wallowed in the gentle suck and surge. Shells and pebbles tumbled, and a fish darted into the shade.

"Look there's a sculpin." Angeline pointed a running shoe into the pool, took off her shoes and socks, and sliced her foot into the water. Jake started to speak, changed his mind, and rolled his jeans up to his shins, and splashed up beside her.

"I can't believe how beautiful it is," she said lightly, then pirouetted until she faced the shore. The sandstone bluff, capped with firs, towered over the beach. At its base, where Indian paintbrush flushed its orange foliage, a small black head bobbed up and down.

"An otter?" she suggested. They grabbed their shoes and followed it into the forest.

In a shadowy glade maidenhair fern, salal, and lady-slippers, crowded the forest floor. Runoff babbled noisily, and Oregon grape, wild peas, purple liverworts and mosses grappled a stony bank. A twisted oak had fallen, and along its upthrust roots, bracket fungus, creamy and brown, ate into the bark in uniform rows. Something dark flashed overhead, and Jake lifted his head to red arbutuses, maples, alders, and dark green conifers.

Angeline pointed to a large black bird in a tree. "So what's this theory Carly's been telling me about?"

"Theory?" he echoed.

"She says you've been researching the origin of the Raven myths, and she's been helping you. She says you think you might know where they came from."

Jake had an idea, and yes, a theory, placing the origin of the Raven myths in prehistory.

"Don't you find it odd that a Raven rattle should turn up this far south?" he asked.

"Now that you mention it, the thought had occurred to me. The motif on Connie's rattle is Haida or Tlingit, isn't it? I once wrote an undergraduate essay on Raven rattles for an art history class, and that one reminded me of some examples from the far north. Now, what is an Alaskan shaman's rattle doing in Washington State?"

Angeline fell silent, and Jake told her his theory.

"You think the Raven myths were inspired by a real person?" Her voice rose in pitch. "You could never prove that."

"Then why do the stories say that the Raven was a magician or a shaman?"

"Because, Jake, they're myths. Myths are fictitious, imaginary. Fantasy. They aren't real. Just because he was greedy, a practical joker, and a notorious womanizer, doesn't mean he was ever a living person. That kind of personality makes for good stories. Especially the womanizing part. Everyone likes a spicy adventure with plenty of sex and violence."

Angeline shrugged as though there was nothing left to say, and searched for the sleek black animal that might have been an otter. Jake decided not to pursue the subject. There was plenty of time to convince her, especially if the site they were excavating revealed any artifacts belonging to a shaman. She led the way back out into the sunshine, and he followed. If his paper on the Marten Lake raven burial was published, maybe she'd believe him.

Jake drank in the green sea, forested hills and golden beach. Otter Cove was one of the most beautiful, pristine spots anywhere on the islands. If he failed to thwart the development, it was destined to become a tourist haunt.

***

"About the photograph . . ."

Connie Amos left the sunroom and went into the bathroom. She had hung it in here because it was the one place in her home where Clifford Radisson would never see it. She lifted the picture of the totem pole from its hook on the wall over the toilet tank and brought it back with her. She placed it on the table where the developer sat waiting, and forced herself to relax.

"This pole was raised at a potlatch at Salmon River in 1832," Radisson said. "The white man," he pointed under the wings of the Thunderbird, "was made into a Native crest figure whose yearly arrival was panto mimed with braid-trimmed frock coats and striped trousers."

Connie stared.

"How do you think a white man ever ended up as a Haida crest figure?"

"He came to the coast as the young master of a fur trading brig in 1825. He was so successful that the Hudson's Bay Company hired him and put him in command of the *Grand Corbeau*. He married a high-born Haida girl," Connie said.

Radisson smiled. "Yes. He had a daughter."

"Who gave birth to Martin Moon's grandfather."

"Perhaps."

Connie held the plastic laminated photograph and placed a finger on the figure of the white sailor. Before she could speak, Radisson did.

"Whenever the captain appeared on the deck of his ship people would shout out his name. To the white sailors, the cry sounded like, *Go to Hell!*"

How apt, Connie thought. Is that how you feel about the world? Is that why you've come to my house to ask me to give it to you?

"I think Dr. Lalonde might be interested in this photograph," Connie said, and looked thoughtfully at the developer's face . . .

Mine, the little boy had said to her.

Yes, she had replied, but she would keep it for him until he was well.

A month had passed and when the boy returned to his foster home they had both forgotten all about it.

CHAPTER SIX

Josie showed Tom Jelna around the wet site the next day. Angeline, ankle deep in mud, hosed off a medium sized basket, flattened like a road kill. It was woven of spruce root splints and shaped like a truncated cone.

She wondered if she could get a job in Radisson's theme park. When she finish her MA, maybe did a PhD, and had a job waiting for her at the end of it all, maybe then her father would see that archaeology wasn't a waste of time.

"A house! I've found a house! Come quick! Am I right?" Carly shouted.

Josie and Tom came running from another trench. Angeline trudged through the muddy bank to where Carly crouched with a hose in her hand. The edge of a wet cedar plank stuck up from soft yellow clay. Toppled by a mudslide, it had lain untouched by sunlight for thousands of years.

Angeline climbed out of the trench, picked up one of the nearby hoses, and immediately rinsed herself off.

Josie's voice rose over the gurgle of running water. "I knew it! Shouldn't we shut down the midden and concentrate our efforts here?"

"Well, that's definitely a house plank," Tom said. "Someone better go tell Jake."

Lately, Jake had been spending a lot of time with Connie Amos, trying to head off the momentum of Radisson Enterprises. The developer had agreed to give free shares to each resident who sold him property. He had also promised jobs. He wanted authenticity. And Indians, whose heritage this represented, were as authentic as he could get.

Native people could run rides, displays, food services, tours, and simulated archaeological digs. Even an IMAX theatre was planned to show the history of the excavations and to dramatize ancient whale hunting exploits, tribal rituals, and warrior prowess. Radisson had gone so far as to discuss "Living History" concepts – Native people playing prehistoric roles for visitors.

A stiff breeze rose as Angeline walked to Connie's house. She hesitated on the porch, peering through a half open window. Jake stood at the far end of the room, his back to her.

The room was sparsely furnished, and the only things of possible value were some small Native prints hanging on the walls. Connie came into the room, laden with her Corning Ware tea service, and through the window, their eyes met.

Connie smiled, set the tea things down on the coffee table. "I think someone wants to see you, Jake," she said.

Jake stepped onto the veranda. "What's up?"

Angeline smiled. "I've got great news. We found the first house."

Jake moved to the rail of the veranda where he began to pick at projecting slivers of white painted wood, and perused an ant that had somehow managed to crawl up onto the railing.

"A house, huh? You sure?"

"Yes. Carly found a cedar plank. Isn't that wonderful?" When Jake didn't answer Angeline said, "You knew this was a village."

"I guess somewhere in the back of my mind I was hoping I was wrong. I guess I was hoping it was only a refuse dump. A garbage heap that Radisson wouldn't be interested in."

Jake's hand rose in the air and landed with a smack on the ant.

"If you didn't want to excavate why on earth did you ever agree to?" she asked.

"I didn't. The HAB was going to give the site to Josie. I didn't have a choice. It is officially now a salvage operation. Shit, you know, they aren't even going to let me excavate it properly. I won't be able to stop Radisson from putting the pressure on Tom to haul everything out as quickly as possible. Dammit Angeline, I refuse to be an exhibit in Radisson's theme park." Jake scowled at the site where the Regional Archaeologist poked about in the mud.

Angeline shrugged. "It's only a theme park. There are lots of theme parks all over the place. And what about the Raven rattle? Excavating the bog might shed more light on that."

"Exactly. And do you realize what this means? This is what Radisson was waiting for. Tom and Kate will ratify the proposal. Everyone will have to move. Do you really think Radisson is going to allow that little community to stay here? For Christ's sake, since when do archaeologists work in theme parks?"

In the distance, Josie stood up. She was directing the crew to find the rest of the house's walls.

"There's another side to this," Angeline said. "We could get jobs. Important jobs. It's all right for you, you have a job, but I don't want to be a dig bum all my life."

Connie's face appeared behind the screen door. Jake didn't notice. His eyes were dark and his tone ugly. "Are you blind? You're nothing but a pretty ornament to him."

***

Angeline left. Jake felt the words sour in his mouth. He shrugged at Connie's questioning glance, thanked her for the tea he hadn't drunk and the conversation they hadn't had, and begged a raincheck. He was wanted at the site.

When he arrived, Tom Jelna waved a bone harpoon point enthusiastically in his face.

"Isn't this exquisite?" he asked. "Bilaterally barbed."

The Regional Archaeologist passed the artifact to Carly who slipped in the mud, letting out a squeal as she saved it from destruction.

"Bag that Carly, before it gets broken," Jake said.

The site looked like a giant mud puddle. He turned and stooped by the edge of the trench where the first cedar plank had been left.

"It's a village," Tom said. "No doubt about it."

"Maybe not. Maybe it's an isolated find."

"I think not." Tom faced the trench where Steve, Erika, and several other students gently dislodged another cedar plank, then he pointed to Joe Redleaf. "This place is crawling with them. Your man there has located another board ten metres over."

Jake had no choice but to acknowledge the facts. It was a village all right.

"I want you to start giving the feasibility of a theme park some serious thought."

"The theme park has nothing to do with me," Jake said. "And just what is going on with Lookout Island?"

"Go and have a look at it. The island is government property. It's slated for development."

"What about the petroglyphs?"

"There is no safer place for them than inside a theme park."

"It's not like we're gonna have dinosaurs on the loose eating people," Josie insisted, rising from where she hovered over the trench.

Carly crawled out from behind her, and laid the artifact on the table where Angeline had gone back to work.

"Do you really want Connie and Joe to be part of a freak show?" Jake asked.

"That's really their business, isn't it?" Josie replied.

"If it's done right, we'll give the public a sense of pride, responsibility and respect," Tom said.

"They'll think it's nothing but fun and games, and treasure hunting."

"That's why we want you in charge of it. By overseeing the development, you'll have curatorial as well as marketing control."

"So now you're not even waiting for an assessment?"

"If you have any serious objections. I'll listen." Tom placed a hand on Jake's shoulder and Jake flung it off. "Give me one valid reason why I shouldn't consider Radisson's proposal for a theme park."

Jake threw up his hands, and stormed back to the trench. Behind him Tom's voice continued to mutter. Jake shaded his eyes against the sun and watched Steve run tepid water along a cedar board.

The foundation of the house was surfacing. Broken bits of wood from support posts and rafters. Erika had found a hearth complex – a series of fire-cracked stone circles. There were benches and sleeping mats, a baby's cradle. Another pit fed into this one and on the floor, fish bones, broken stone axes, deer bones and shell wallowed out of the earth.

Tom followed. "I'm shutting down the shell midden and moving everyone over here."

Jake glanced at Angeline, but she looked away. It was a nasty thing he had called her – an ornament. But that was what Radisson thought of her, and she should know it.

"Josie can take up the slack at the east end of the trench, maybe open up another one. That'll get things moving faster," Tom said.

The damage was already done. Even as he stood here, bacteria, enzymes and sunlight were breaking down the fibres of the wood objects in the bog. Jake mumbled an excuse to Tom and headed toward the road.

"Where are you going?"

Jake said nothing, got into his truck, and gunned it through the forest.

In front of him the ferry terminal rose. He was tempted to drive straight onto the dock, off the ramp, and right onto the boat heading for Port Angeles, but instead, he turned down Beach Road. There was the marina. The town. He dropped to the speed limit and ambled between two rows of painted cottages. A string of colourful buildings rolled by – the Innis Hotel and the pub below it, the Laundromat, the museum, and the general store. The library.

He drove on through Main Street, then swiftly out of town. He passed the Surf Lodge, more beach and forest, then Otter Cove. He stopped by the side of the road and watched the clouds swell and cleave over the sea. He opened the door and walked around the truck, then leaned against the side of the hood and stared at the splash of colour at the base of the cliff. Something struck him. That wasn't Indian paintbrush fluttering in the breeze. There was a row of orange flagging tape on the beach below.

CHAPTER SEVEN

The shell midden was a likely place for discarded ritual paraphernalia and one of the prime reasons Jake had chosen this site. The alkaline nature of the shell helped preserve artifacts made of bone. Shamans often carved bone into smooth shiny pendants and talismans. Almost anything could be found in a midden from food refuse to broken tools and art objects, but so far, no shaman's implements had surfaced.

Jake was frustrated. The entire crew had moved to the wet site, and he sat brooding in the lab filling out requisition forms. The shell midden, regardless of whether it ever revealed the evidence he was looking for, represented months of preparation, and now the Heritage Advisory Board wanted to shaft his project and dig up the bog.

Radisson wanted to reconstruct the village, to have visitors zipping down the corridors of time through life sized vignettes of Indians demonstrating daily tasks. Radisson's people would be real people, Natives dressed up in ancient garb, splitting logs with antler wedges, cooking soup with boiling stones and knapping arrowheads with hammer stones. The whole thing would be in its natural setting, the structures chemically treated to protect them – come rain or shine. If Joe Redleaf and the Samish people didn't mind, why did he?

Rain slapped suddenly against the dirty window, thrumming steadily. Jake ran outside and spread a plastic sheet over the midden, jogged through the camp zipping down tents, then went to his Bronco.

Silvery rays slashed his headlights, and when he reached the wet site, most of the crew scurried about searching for dry spots to stash their things. Carly raced up, arms laden with wooden objects on trays, and he unlocked the rear hatch of his truck for her. At the trenches, Angeline knelt on all fours bagging some artifacts. The front of her T-shirt was soaked where her jacket blew open, and rain ran in rivulets down her cheeks and off her chin.

She glanced up, sealing the last bag, and rose. He had one thought–

how her skin glowed and her lashes formed twin starry arcs over her eyes. She stood there as though she were waiting for something, and if ever a woman gave a sign to a man, this was it.

The sky was dark, the wind blew, and behind her, the shutters of Connie's house rattled back and forth. The sea beyond was an angry grey, foaming white and boiling. He turned from her, bellowed at Josie who was jamming the poles holding up the shelter.

"Take down that plastic! It's not going to hold!" He wiped rain from his face and Angeline left with a stack of bagged artifacts. "Steve! Over here, we have to take the pumps back!"

Jake gestured to the tall, skinny boy who slogged over. They grunted and groaned with the heavy equipment; something tore in his shoulder. He ground his teeth. The thing weighed a ton.

Every vehicle was loaded down with heavy equipment and the day's finds, and there was barely enough room for passengers. Angeline was one of the last coming back with hoses and screens.

"In here!" he yelled, but she ignored him.

She ran to Josie's Land Rover, only to find it full, then went to Steve's van, but it too was full. Frustrated and in pain, Jake strode over.

"Unless you want to walk back, you're coming with me!"

Some of the tents tumbled head over heels when the truck pulled up in the driveway, and along the road near the house, the blue plastic doors of the portable toilets slammed back and forth. He braked and the crew got out.

"Grab rocks!" Josie hollered. "Anything to weigh the tents down!"

"Take them apart! They're not going to stand up to this!" Jake was amazed at the destruction. He had only left here an hour ago. Most of the crew had modern, arced, polyurethane coated nylon tents with fibreglass poles. All their gear inside should have weighed them down, but personal things were scattered everywhere. Jake had always refused to buy one of those plastic domes and now he was glad. While everyone else's went spinning like carousels out of control, his conventional canvas tent remained anchored firmly to the ground.

"Has anyone seen mine!" Angeline's white and turquoise nylon tent was gone. Wind whipped at her jacket, skewing her hood. They hadn't seen it on the road, so it must have blown over the knoll. Jake ran past the plastic shelter which had fallen into the pits and now writhed like a downed balloon. Over the rise, he pushed back his hood to see through torrential rain. A drop landed in his eye and something moved. A mangled dome, blue and white, half rolled, half sailed toward the pounding sea.

***

On the other side of the grass, just before the cedars rose, a bulging hedge, purple and green, grew in a riotous tangle. It was laced with thick clusters of blackberries. The sun was at just the right angle, slanting between the trees, striking the morning dew on the fruit, leaving them sparkling. They were ripe, bubbly and dark, drooping heavy on thorny branches. Angeline pulled her sweatshirt over her T-shirt and lay it on the grass. When she had gathered enough of the berries, she took them down to the beach, sat down in front of a dead log, and ate.

Jake had rescued her tent, but they couldn't fix the damage in the howling wind. She had spent the night in Carly's tent and risen early before anyone else had awakened. She stared at the sea, and the tumbling twigs that had snapped off in the storm. The air smelled fresh this morning, clean after the violent weather.

He had called her an ornament.

Angeline rose, peered over the rise at the camp. Most of the crew was up – it was eight-thirty – and the majority of them had decided to go into town. Better hitch a ride with somebody before everyone left without her. She went back to Carly's tent but she was gone, and only the Land Rover and the Bronco were left in the drive. She could not ask Jake for a ride, could not quite forgive him for thinking so little of her.

Josie's tent was the dark blue one and Angeline knew she was there because one wall bulged from someone pressing against it. She peeked in, saw Josie, saw immediately that Josie was not alone.

Jake sat on his haunches, half clothed, sitting on Josie's sleeping bag. Josie, thighs exposed, clad in an oversized T-shirt, knelt beside him, hands busy. He moved his head slightly and now Angeline could see Josie massaging his left shoulder. Eyes sleepy. Brows unruly. Mouth soft. His head was tousled and on his chest, dark hairs curled shallowly stretching from nipple to nipple and down his tanned belly.

Angeline turned, ran, and slammed into Sam Smythe.

"What's the hurry, sweetheart?" The tall red-bearded man towered over her, fingers digging into her armpits, a flash of gold showing in his teeth.

"Well, hello Angeline." Clifford Radisson's face appeared behind Sam Smythe. "Where are you off to in such a flurry?"

"I was trying to catch a ride into town. I guess I missed my ride."

Radisson's eyes creased gently at the corners. "I'm going that way myself. If you can wait ten minutes, I'd be pleased to give you a lift."

A white Lexus leisure vehicle was parked behind the contractor's orange pickup truck, which was parked behind Jake's Bronco. She tugged at a lock of hair, and followed his gaze up and beyond her head.

"Ah, there you are, Dr. Lalonde. How are you this morning?"

Angeline flushed, and Jake gave her a bemused glance, then turned his eyes on the developer. "Did you want something?" he asked.

Dressed in stylish khaki, Clifford Radisson stepped around her. "I hope the storm didn't cause too much damage? I see you've had a few casualties with the tents, but the site is intact?"

Jake straightened his shirt impatiently. "I don't know. I haven't been out there yet."

Josie had put on a pair of jeans before leaving her tent, and smiled at the developer. "Is there something we can help you with?"

"I can see I came at a bad time. I wanted to leave these blueprints with you." Josie accepted the roll of paper Radisson handed to her. "I hope you'll have a look at these. I'd appreciate some input. I'm looking for a central focus for my theme park. I was hoping you archaeologists could help."

Josie smiled amiably, and didn't hesitate. "Well, it *is* called RAVENSWORLD. Why not centre the displays on the myths of the

Raven?"

Jake's face turned slightly off-purple. "The site is not for sale yet."

"Be reasonable Dr. Lalonde," Clifford Radisson replied. "It's only a matter of time before we will all be working together. Well, and now I must go. I've promised this young lady a lift into town. I'll be out to tour the site next week with the Heritage Advisory Board. I'll see you both then."

CHAPTER EIGHT

"Jake!" Josie's voice rose irritably. She clutched the architectural plans, waving the roll in his face.

"Get those blueprints out of my sight," Jake said.

Clifford Radisson stood at the passenger side of the white Lexus waiting for Angeline to get comfortable before closing the door. The car roared to life and backed down the driveway. As it disappeared through the trees, Josie's face contorted into a slight smirk.

"They're going into town," she said. "I told the crew they could rent a room at the Innis Hotel and have showers."

"Whose paying for it?"

"We are. It's coming out of the budget. Living or miscellaneous expenses, as you like, but you can't expect them to work in mud and never have a shower."

"Hotel accommodations were only budgeted for once a week, on weekends."

Josie shook her head at him like he was being unreasonable. "Is that shoulder still bothering you?"

Jake rotated it and winced. "When's everybody coming back?"

"Noon. I'm going into town. Are you coming?"

"No, I think I'll go out to the site."

While Josie went to the lab to put away Radisson's theme park plans, Jake went to his truck. He took the long route, passed Otter Cove, and drove deliberately into town. The white Lexus was parked on the side of the road, but there was no sign of Angeline or the developer.

He started the ignition and headed back to Beach Road. A few minutes later, he rolled up to the marina, pulled onto the shoulder and parked. Over the glittering sea, several dark specks winged their way to Lookout Island.

Ravens. Jake followed the specks until they disappeared.

Below, on the bustling wharf, people were renting dinghies to go fishing. Down by one of the rowboats someone in an orange hard hat and vest was having an animated conversation with a man holding a clipboard. Jake frowned, and suddenly had an impulse to take a boat and go to Lookout Island. Instead, he threw the truck into gear and drove.

Connie waved from a wicker chair on her veranda as he rolled up.

"Any damage to the house?" he called, slamming the front door of the Bronco. He climbed the stairs. Connie straightened up in her seat and returned his smile. He stood opposite her, looking over the house for signs of the storm, and when he leaned into the rail it creaked from his weight.

"Careful! That was quite a storm yesterday, wasn't it? My house took quite a beating." Behind her a couple of wooden shutters had partially detached from their hinges. "How did you people make out?"

Jake jiggled the handrail gently. "Our tents got tossed around, but no serious damage. I can fix this railing for you, if you've got any tools."

Connie looked toward the deserted bog. The plastic shelter over the excavation had collapsed, and the entire site was flooded just as it had been before the crew had pumped it out.

"That's kind of you," she said, and stood. "Lovely day, isn't it? Seems to be the way after a storm. The forecast is for more rain though."

"Seriously?" He followed her down the steps. "Maybe there's no point in our setting up again."

She shrugged. "The forecast has been known to be wrong. Here we are."

They left the wooden shed where Jake had found a hammer and some nails, and returned to the house. He studied the wooden slats joining the handrail to the veranda. Nails had come loose in several spots and were working their way out. He raised the hammer and slammed it against a nail, moved down, steadied the next slat, and pounded in a few more. The veranda was soft in places, and he was careful not to stick anything into where the wood crumbled.

"You're going to need this replaced soon," he said.

Connie climbed the steps and stood on the veranda behind the rail. She was dressed in a floral print cotton shift, and her long silvery braid drooped down.

"There won't be much point if this house ends up being bulldozed." Her braid hung even lower and their eyes met. "I think you should have a look at those petroglyphs on Lookout Island."

***

Connie wondered if she should show Jake the photograph today. Bacon sizzled on the stove and she reached for the kettle.

"Tea? Or I can make you coffee."

"Don't go to any trouble," Jake said. "I'm fine with whatever you're having."

Connie filled the kettle with water, placed it on the back burner and noticed Jake staring at the old wooden cabinet under the yellow curtained window. There were photographs and little green nephrite carvings on top of it. He seemed to be looking for something. The rattle? It wasn't here. She had moved it to the coffee table in the living room.

"Your husband?" Jake indicated a large framed photograph among the others on the cabinet.

She left the frying pan with two golden yolked eggs bubbling in it, and lifted the picture. The man in the picture was White, a fisherman, and beside him, a young woman with long dark hair and a bright demeanor leaned against his cheek. At twenty-two, she wore long dangling earrings and pale pink lipstick. Connie felt colour reddening her cheeks. Jake must be wondering about the earrings and the lipstick.

"Oh dear, the toast!" Connie dropped the picture to the cabinet and quickly retrieved the toast before it burned. "This toaster has a mind of its own," she said, drawing a plate toward her. "I've been meaning to replace it."

She let Jake butter his own toast, and set a knife and fork and the plate of bacon and eggs in front of him.

"I really think you should go and see the petroglyphs," Connie said. "Is the Band Council aware of them?"

She nodded and refilled their cups with tea. Like the photograph of the totem pole, the petroglyphs interested Clifford Radisson more than they should.

Jake finished his breakfast and dog-eared a paper napkin in his hands. "Connie. Would you mind if I looked at that Raven rattle again?"

Connie picked up his cutlery, his empty plate, and their cups and stacked them by the sink, then went to the living room, and brought the rattle back with her.

Yes, it seemed right for him to hold it. It seemed to take on life in his hands.

She felt a sudden powerful urge to give Jake the photograph hanging in her bathroom.

"I hope you're keeping this rattle in a safe place?" he asked.

She nodded.

"Then I'd better go. It must be almost noon."

Jake handed the Raven rattle back to her as a white Lexus pulled up beside the house.

***

Jake paused on the steps as the developer approached, and behind him, Connie stopped too.

"We can't seem to stop running into each other today," Clifford Radisson said.

"That's not surprising since you keep materializing at my sites," Jake replied.

The developer smiled. "I didn't actually come to see you."

Jake started down the rest of the stairs. "Fine. I don't have time to talk to you anyway. I have a site to visit."

"The petroglyphs?"

This time Jake couldn't control his face and spun around. On the stairs, Connie said nothing.

"A wise idea. The sooner they are evaluated. The better for all of us."

Jake crushed his anger. The sooner he saw the petroglyphs and verified their authenticity, the sooner he would find a reason to protect them from being developed into an exhibit.

"You and Mrs. Amos appear to have become quite good friends," Clifford Radisson said.

So?

It suddenly dawned on Jake that the man was troubled by this idea. Connie was the only resident of Cedar Island who had not voiced approval for the theme park and the developer blamed *him*.

He smiled as she responded, coldly. "My name is Connie."

"I would like to see the Raven rattle, Mrs. Amos."

For some reason Clifford Radisson found it difficult to call Connie by her first name and Jake didn't understand why she would want him to be that familiar with her anyway.

"It isn't here," she lied. "I've sent it to the museum to be conserved."

Clifford Radisson remained at the bottom of the stairs looking up at the Native woman's hard face. Surprisingly, there was almost a kind of pleading in the colourless eyes.

"Excuse me," Jake said, and brushed past the developer toward the site.

The crew was busy positioning pumps and screwing on hoses as Jake neared. Erika was setting up a work table and Joe was already in one of the pits describing, to a local resident, what they were doing. Angeline went to help Erika, then picked up a shovel and walked over to the trenches. She had changed into a clean pair of jeans and a Levi's shirt with the sleeves rolled to her elbows. She stepped back as Josie walked over to her, lifted the shovel, and snagged it clumsily on the leg of her jeans. Without so much as a glance up, she swore softly, untangled herself, and turned to leave.

"What's with her?" Josie asked as Jake approached.

He had an idea but didn't voice it. He surveyed the site with a wide sweeping gaze. A mud pool lay where two pits used to be and Josie pointed this out to him.

"The rain really did a number over there. Looks like we've got a big job for the pumps."

"You better get started then," he said.

The mess in front of him, brought on by the violent weather, made him wonder once more why they were doing this. When he thought about it he was surprised the Band had even granted a permit to excavate this site. Usually they gave archaeologists a hard time just to make sure they were not being exploited. For some unfathomable reason this time was different. With full government support, and for whatever reasons, this was Native history and suddenly the Natives had a very strong interest in it.

Jake called out to Angeline and filled her in on his plans for the afternoon. She told him he didn't need her to look at the petroglyphs. He convinced her he might require a second opinion.

What he really wanted was to get her alone. She came reluctantly and Jake opened the passenger door of his Bronco. He affected to be every bit as suave as Clifford Radisson.

They started down Beach Road, south, to the marina. He accelerated, and the wind from the opened window caught Angeline's hair and blew it about. He leaned over to adjust the window for her.

"The automatic mechanism sticks," he explained. "Is it too windy? I don't know what's the matter with this thing. Damn truck's falling apart. I should've had it fixed before we left Seattle."

"It's all right. Leave it," Angeline said.

Jake glanced sidelong at her profile. But before he could break the tension, she did it for him.

"We have a professional relationship," she said. "I don't care what you think of me, or what you think Clifford Radisson thinks of me, or what Josie thinks of me."

He glanced at her, but she glanced away and he turned back to the road. Sometimes he wished he would think before he opened his mouth. And now he was completely stumped for words.

They hit a wide curve and passed the ferry terminal. The marina was not much further.

He parked. Few people were about, a lot of boats had been rented, and Angeline wandered down to inspect what remained. Across the channel Lookout Island appeared small and volcano-like, and around the craggy summit a bird circled. A man gestured at him from a small blue kiosk in the centre of the dock. Jake went over to rent a boat.

Jake rowed, his back toward Lookout Island. The sky was clear except for a few clouds. The sea was peaceful, his reflection on the water oily. He perspired and paused to rest his shoulder. It ached.

Angeline removed her orange life jacket. Underneath it she wore a white T-shirt, and over top of the T-shirt was a denim Levi's shirt. She removed the denim shirt and tied it around her waist. He raised the oars and dipped them into the water.

"Shit."

She glanced over. "What's the matter?"

"Nothing," he said.

He pulled in the oars and rubbed the pain in his shoulder until it dulled. A seagull screamed overhead and then two more. A whole flock descended on the marina. Something must have died or someone had brought in a good catch today. He picked up the oars. It was incredibly calm, and only his splashing disturbed the channel. He dipped, pulled back, and dipped again. Angeline turned at the waist, her left hand crossing over to rest on the gunwale while the wind flapped the sleeveless T-shirt under her arm.

"See anywhere we can land?" he asked.

Angeline indicated a flat strip of rock washing out of the dark sea. Jake rowed to the sandstone ledge, dragged the oars into the boat, and snagged the rock with his hands. She leaned over and anchored them while he got out and tied the mooring to a nearby shrub.

"I think we better pull it up further," she said.

Under normal circumstances, this boat would not have been heavy, but as it was, it took everything Jake had to keep from wrenching his shoulder again. The ointment Josie had rubbed on it this morning was wearing off.

He wrapped the mooring around the shrub several more times then tugged to make sure it was secure.

They climbed up through cedars and firs and spruces. A thick grove of ferns tangled their feet, then it was mostly hard packed soil, rock and moss. Just below him, Angeline clung to the side of the hill. She had a build for lounging at beach resorts in colourful bits of printed cloth. She was not meant for mountain climbing or ditch digging. Seeing her like this with her teeth clenched and her eyes hard, made him wonder what drove her to do archaeology.

CHAPTER NINE

Jake groped in the dark.

Nothing met his pawing fingers but his foot hit something hard. He stopped, and a beam of light came around him to point the way, then Angeline slipped past and shone the light to the back of the cave.

They could stand upright where the rocky walls potbellied up and out. Now he could see that both the ceiling and floor were covered with nodes of stone created by the swirling action of water.

It was humid, which wouldn't do much for preserving paintings. Fortunately, most of the images were carvings. Angeline was warm from their hike up the mountainside and untied the Levi's shirt from around her waist, leaving it on a lump of stone.

Jake took the flashlight from her, strode deeper into the cave, and lit the blackness further down. To his left, a long grainy pillar rose from the floor, not quite touching the ceiling.

He went back to where Angeline sat on a projection of sandstone.

"If there's something you want to say to me," he began.

She took the flashlight from him before anything else left his lips, wove her way around the stone formations, and left him stumbling in her wake. On the wall, from ceiling to floor, pictures were scratched into the stone.

A prickle crept up his spine. It was like they were being watched. As if the cave had eyes and lungs. It breathed as though it were alive. And whispered and blew and dripped. He was hot. Cold. Clammy. He felt disoriented as he focussed on the engraved images above his head.

Those amorphous shapes and watching eyes were spirits looking down. Below them, people and animals scratched into the rock with a sharp implement stood testimony to another time. Some were coloured a brownish red with the greasy clay pigment ochre. The humans had large round heads and stick bodies and enormous circular eyes. They were chiefs, shamans, dressed in full ceremonial regalia, shields of some sort on their chests and spiky headdresses atop their scalps.

"Is that a lip ornament?" Angeline whispered.

Jake stood behind her, silent, and studied the grotesque face with the unusual T-shape just above its chin.

"People around here didn't hunt whales, did they?"

Jake turned to a scene where several men, some seated, some standing in a boat, chased a large oblong creature.

The beam of light danced. Every available space, except the ceiling and the floor (which were too bumpy), and the smooth, flat, west wall (where the stone pillar grew), was etched with images or painted with red ochre. On the very back wall a drawing was prominently enhanced by the same greasy paint. There were contorted twisted figures and shapes, ovals, lines and something else, a large winged creature with a sinister eye and a sharp heavy beak.

Jake sucked in a breath. "If that's what I think it is, it's a *Nuxalk* story– a Bella Coola myth."

"But that tribe is way north of here. On the central coast of British Columbia. What is it doing here?"

The winged devil was the Raven. He perched inside a canoe lined with small circles. In front of him was a smaller figure, delicately rendered, and distinctly feminine. Below and slightly behind them were a series of oval drawings, reminiscent of the fish carving the crew had retrieved from the bog. Inside each, a human face peered out.

Native mythology told of people who lived in villages at the bottom of the sea. Every year, the docile, benevolent, Salmon People transformed into fish and offered themselves as food to the men of the land. Should the men at any time fail to show honour, respect, and gratitude, the salmon did not return the next year.

Angeline traced the drawings with the flashlight. Shadows flittered and flickered, and Jake felt a wave of vertigo almost topple him.

The Raven wanted a wife, and the only way he knew how to get one was by trickery. He pecked holes in the canoes of the Salmon People, so they wouldn't be able to follow him when he abducted the daughter of the Salmon Chief for his bride. After a feast at the chief's home, the ungrateful Raven asked for help to load food into his canoe. When the

Salmon Princess offered, the Raven seized her and paddled away. Her people immediately transformed into fish and followed.

"Each tribe has a different story don't they?"

When Jake didn't reply, Angeline said, "I wonder if Clifford Radisson has seen these petroglyphs. Why else would he put in a bid to buy Lookout Island? Can he do that? I mean, who does this island belong to anyway?"

The developer knew about the cave; he had said so.

Angeline stepped backwards, turned, and lit her way over the rough sandstone to the opening where a dull grey light left a silver oblong on the ground.

"I've seen enough. I can hear it raining outside. I think we'd better go before it gets worse."

Jake stared, hypnotized by the etching on the wall.

"Jake! Are you coming?"

He swivelled to the mouth of the cave, hesitated. Angeline vanished through the opening, and he turned his attention to the petroglyphs once more.

Suddenly, he heard a scream. He ran outside.

***

The sinkhole Angeline had fallen into was less than two metres across, but almost twice that deep. She lay on her back and tried to move her left foot, and winced.

"What happened?" Jake shouted down.

"Something pushed me."

Jake looked around, but all he could see was dark forest and bare rock blurred by a curtain of rain.

"Don't worry, I'll get you out of there."

He skittered the rest of the way down the hill, rain sluicing along his back. The trees at the base of the mountain grew straight to the sea. He stood at the bank in the streaming downpour and searched the channel. The marina, the whole of Cedar Island, vanished in mist. He tried to get his bearings. The bank curved, rocky and steep, to a point where a cluster of trees jutted into the water. He climbed some protruding rocks, made his way around the bend, and finally sighted the ledge of sandstone where their rowboat sloshed back and forth.

On his knees he tried to undo the mooring, but it was fused into a nylon lump. He leaned into the hull, rummaged through an aluminum kit until he found a knife, then scrambled back to the bow and sawed at the rope. He hacked at the thing and sawed back and forth, and jerked at it until it finally twanged free; then he coiled the line up and charged up the cliff.

Oh shit, the boat!

Jake spun around and stumbled back to the beach to make sure it was still there. It was tottering on the ledge on the verge of making good its escape. He gripped the edge of the hull, yanked, and dragged the boat up past the shrub to solid ground.

He barged up the hill, stumbling blind, and leaned into the downpour. Where was she? Everything looked the same in the rain.

Their footprints had been washed away. Jake searched for the top of the mountain and retraced their descent. He had gone too far. Angeline had almost made it down before falling. He whirled about and started downhill again. Rain pattered on the leaves above him.

Angeline had managed to sit up, rain matting her hair to her head. Next to her foot, at the bottom of the hole, half buried in mud and rotting leaves, the silver handle of the flashlight stuck out.

He tied the rope to the trunk of a tree, brought it to the pit, and dropped it in. The hole wasn't more than three metres deep, the walls were slightly sloped, and the odd rock protruded for footholds. That should make climbing easy.

She tried to get to her feet, but mud sucked her back. He swung the rope, and she grabbed it and dragged herself up on her good foot. The mud was so sticky she couldn't hop and her back was covered with leaves. He instructed her to tie it under her arms. She fumbled with the slippery nylon but it wouldn't hold.

"I'm going to try to climb!" she said.

She heaved, slipped, dropped back, and tried again. She leaped at the rope, caught it, and pulled. One foot found a rock, slipped, and sent her crashing to the mud.

"Tie it around you!" Jake yelled.

This time, Angeline managed a fairly stable loop. Jake wound the slack around a large rock, dropped to his stomach and pulled. His shoulder seized up, one hand let go. Angeline dangled, two feet off the ground, and that was all. He lowered her and she slipped out of the noose.

He winched the rope back up and measured it in lengths, looped knots at one foot intervals, and when the entire thing was done, brought it back to the sinkhole and fed it in. Clinging for dear life, he eased himself down, landing with a splat next to her. He retrieved the flashlight, and shoved it into his back pocket.

"That okay?" Jake touched Angeline's left ankle gently and she flinched. "I can't see anything in this mess. We'll have to wait till we get up top. You ready?"

Hands locked around her hips, Jake heaved until Angeline was perched on his good shoulder and hanging onto the knotted nylon.

When she was about four knots up, Jake reached around her knees until he found the mooring and hauled himself up. At the top of the hole he saw a flash of orange.

"Climb!" he yelled.

The rope hung still.

"Everything all right up there?"

He scaled up, shielding his face, pulling hand over hand till his head pressed into her back. They were smack against the side of the sinkhole, her head right at the top.

The rope vibrated.

"Jake, I don't think it's going to hold!"

Suddenly they fell in a tumble and she was sitting on top of him.

Angeline was almost in tears. Jake picked up the rope and stared at it. He was getting her out of here even if it killed him. He fixed a knot around his waist, clawed his way up using the jutting stones, and dragged himself through sheer will up and over the muddy edge of the sinkhole. Then he tied the rope to another tree, dropped it down and ordered her to climb up.

***

That rope should not have broken. Jake collected several loose rocks and formed a circle near the mouth of the cave. He placed a flat piece of stone on the floor, found an appropriate stick, and pared it down to a point with the knife.

He twirled it, as he had seen the Samish do, rolling back and forth on the kindling, waiting for it to catch a stray spark. For a whole minute he did it, then two, then three. Nothing happened.

The brittle clink of stone on stone came from the back of the cave. The flashlight flickered behind him and the chipping continued. What was she doing back there? She wasn't damaging those petroglyphs was she?

Silence. Then the chipping of stone. Jake settled down to drill again. They don't make fire this way, do they? He drilled and drilled and considered striking two stones together, but knew, in reality, such things only worked in cartoons.

The flashlight wavered above him. Squatting, Angeline flicked some of the kindling aside and made a bare patch on the stone where he had been drilling. Then she sprinkled something glittery on it.

"Let me try something." She reached for the cedar drill, but he held it fast, and resumed drilling. A burning smell, but no smoke.

Silence again. No doubt she thought this was another example of his stubbornness. If they intended to spend another minute together he had to say something now.

"Angeline."

He did not stop drilling. Water dripped from her hair onto the stone just missing the kindling as she glanced up. "The other day . . . What I said at Connie's house when you came to tell me about the cedar planks . . ." Jake paused, drilled harder. "I didn't mean it."

Angeline picked up a loose piece of sandstone, and pushed his hands away from the hearth, then she wiped the stone across the iron pyrite, generating a spark, smoking the brittle leaves.

"Unlike some people," she said, a smile breaking from her eyes to her lips. "I know how to start a fire."

Jake grinned, blew on the smouldering kindling till a flame burst up. "Where'd you learn to do that?" Angeline went back to the far end of the cave, and he twisted around. "Where did you find the pyrite?"

"There's lots of strange stuff back here, wood too, and granite cobbles." Her voice echoed. "Maybe they're artifacts, I didn't look too closely."

Flames gobbled the branches greedily, flaring up and smoking. The wind was in their favour and sucked most of the smoke outside. The occasional raindrop found its way in, spitting as it hit the blaze. Jake went to the rear of the cave where the flashlight stood on the floor, and Angeline picked it up and showed him where some split logs were piled against the wall. He knelt down, retrieved a piece, and inspected it.

"Do you think it's archaeological?" she asked.

He rotated it in his hand. "Right now, I don't care if it is."

Three pieces went into the flames. Jake stirred the coals beneath the wood and propped a splinter of cedar between the larger logs to allow for the passage of air. Since Angeline had not followed him back, Jake returned to where she crouched, examining the granite cobbles.

He lifted one and turned it over in his hand. The fool's gold glittered in the beam of the flashlight. The rock had a smooth flat depression in its centre, reminding him of the cobble at Marten Lake. He placed it carefully on the floor and rolled another one toward him. All of them were approximately the same shape and size.

He rose, went to where Angeline sat rubbing her hands together over the open flames. He waited several minutes not talking, just letting the warmth penetrate his fingertips and face. He fetched more wood and fed the blaze until it soared toward the ceiling.

"That's better," she sighed, and thrust out her injured foot.

Jake crouched in front of her and held out his hand. "I better have a look at that."

Her foot was so swollen he could barely get her running shoe off. Her jeans were sodden and tight around the ankle and he couldn't remove her sock. She would have to take off her pants.

Her denim shirt lay over a node of stone, and he went to fetch it. "Get out of your muddy things and put this on."

Jake turned his back to her, waited for her to change into the dry shirt. Angeline had taken everything off including her underwear and they lay on the stones adjacent to the fire. He stooped, pretended to ignore the fact that she was naked under that shirt, and shone the flashlight onto her foot.

Her ankle was swollen and purplish, and he ran a thumb along the side, on top of the many small tarsal bones. She didn't flinch.

"I don't think anything's broken," he said.

Angeline leaned over to look at her ankle, then up at him. "I swear, Jake, something pushed me."

"Maybe it was a spooked deer," he suggested.

"Maybe." But he could see in her troubled look that she didn't think so.

They sat. Now he had her alone, he couldn't think of what to say. He wanted to avoid staring down at her bare legs or up at the opening to her collar and her throat.

The fire surged, tossing shadows to the ceiling. Jake glanced up and over Angeline's shoulder, got to his feet, walked to the rear of the cave, and gazed at the image on the wall. The Salmon Chief's daughter leaped, danced in the flickering light. A cold draft rose from the floor.

Angeline slipped up beside him and placed a hand briefly on his arm. Jake turned, looked down, and she moved in closer. He stepped behind her, and slid his arms down hers to her waist and locked them. He brushed his cheek against her temple. In front of them, graven eyes, ovoid and sinister, stared toward the spike of stone.

Jake breathed into Angeline's ear. He stepped around to face her, his hands touching her elbows. A whispering came from deep inside the cave. A distant drip, drip, dripping, and a gusting like laughter. He reached up, touched her cheek, slid his fingers into her hair and drew it back from her face.

Shadows leaped. Light danced. The pictures on the walls swam and swirled. Then he engulfed her, his arms so tight, her breath was almost gone.

CHAPTER TEN

"If you want some privacy, use the phone in the bedroom," Radisson said.

As the short, slight man returned indoors, Clifford Radisson cracked a peanut and offered it to the caged raven. It poked its beak between the wire, ruffling its neck, and snapped at his fingers. He drew back, threw the peanut onto the beach and reclined in his lawn chair. In front of him the golden cage sat on a plastic table holding two glasses of Perrier with a translucent slice of lemon floating on the top of each drink.

The bird was unusually agitated today. Rain pattered rhythmically on the wooden roof sheltering the four feet square of flagstones outside Radisson's ground floor cabin at the Surf Lodge, keeping him dry. He scanned the misty sea where there should have been a clear view of Lookout Island. The raven fidgeted, demanding its freedom, and the ice cubes settled with a snap and a clink.

He reviewed his day as was his habit. He had a very analytical mind. That was how he had come to his fortune. He studied every situation he encountered and every person with whom he interacted. Only by knowing how things worked could one control one's destiny.

Connie Amos was going to be a problem, but he wasn't too worried. In time she would relent. Once everyone else saw his point of view, she would find she had no choice. He suspected she didn't really believe the theme park was a bad idea. After all, he was doing it for people like her. He was doing it *for* her. Native people needed a place to keep their heritage alive and he had the means to do it best.

She was stubborn. He could see that. She had scruples and didn't like him. That was wrong. That was *very* wrong. To dislike him was very wrong. Didn't she realize when she had shown him the photograph of the Moon family's totem pole that he had known what it was?

He was entitled. He had the knowledge and the expertise and the finances to make things right for this community.

He stretched his legs under the table. How nice it would be to have a family. He had lived most of his forty-three years alone. In that respect, he and the archaeologist had something in common. Jake Lalonde had no family. Radisson knew this because he never ventured into a business proposition without knowing about the people with whom he dealt.

He watched the rain lighten to drizzle.

He would try to convince Connie Amos again that the Raven rattle belonged with him. He would treasure it, take care of it, protect it. Better than Jake Lalonde could ever do.

Lalonde only wanted Connie's friendship for his own selfish agenda. He was an academic, and academics did not care about anything real. They wanted to put the treasures away into boxes and make up stories about them. They wanted to write about them and keep the information all to themselves. What was noble about that? Clifford Radisson could make up better stories and he would share them with the public.

The tide was out and in the mist he could see several sticks poking out of the shallows. He rose and walked toward the sea, oblivious of the mizzling rain. Yes. Many sticks jutted out of the waves, the remains of a fish trap. He wondered if it was archaeological and if the archaeologists knew of its presence here on this beach. When the tide was up it would be completely submerged. He would have to study it more carefully on a sunny day. He would like to include an example of a salmon weir in his theme park.

The screen door creaked open, caught on its springs, and Clifford Radisson turned to see Tom Jelna step out onto the flagstones.

"Did you make your phone call all right?" he inquired as he rejoined his guest on the patio.

The raven fluttered its flightless wings inside the cage. Tom Jelna pulled up a chair and sat down.

"Yes thanks," he said. "I had to check in with my office. You know how it is when you're away. Things turn to chaos."

"Dissension among the ranks?"

"Something like that. I have a woman who works for me. Nothing but trouble. Always tries to make decisions on her own. Doesn't realize that institutions can't be run on the whim of one individual. Sometimes I think she should have remained a field archaeologist. I have a good mind to send her out here for the duration of the project. She used to work with Jake Lalonde."

"Oh?" Clifford Radisson's interest was piqued. He cracked another peanut.

"Yeah. Didn't work out too well. Business and romance, you know, doesn't work out so well." Tom Jelna smiled mischievously. "Jake's a good archaeologist, but too sanctimonious. It'll be his downfall. He thinks archaeology only belongs in universities. But if we don't set up interpretive facilities, archaeology will lose its appeal to the public." He shook his head. "Just because he's so self-righteous, he thinks everyone else should hold his views. That's what happened between him and Kate, the woman I was telling you about. They don't exactly see things eye to eye."

"From what I've seen, he seems to have his little world under control," Radisson said. He taunted the bird with another peanut.

Jelna laughed. "Far from it. I've never known anyone who has fewer friends than Jake, except the women of course, though I have to admit, he loses his appeal pretty quickly once they get to know him. I didn't know ravens ate peanuts," Jelna added.

Clifford Radisson glanced sidelong at the gold cage, and took a sip of his Perrier. When you have money, when you know how to make money, you can have anything. Especially women. Dr. Lalonde apparently did not have enough money, nor did he know how to hold on to women. This Kate - Katherine Leonard - was intriguing.

Radisson's thoughts drifted to the pretty dark-haired Angeline. She was unusual. Exotic. Everything about her was incongruous with what he knew about her ancestry. She had light skin where it should have been olive, green eyes where they should have been brown. But then, he was hardly one to judge. Genes manifested themselves in the most unexpected ways. The archaeologist for example, whom he knew carried the blood of the Haida in his veins, certainly did not resemble the flat-faced, stocky Indians he had seen on the Queen Charlotte Islands.

He had taken Angeline into town, driven her to the hotel where she had showered and changed. Then he had driven her back to the site. It was progress just getting her into his car. He was a gentleman. She had liked that. He wondered how old she was. He wondered how much she mattered to the half-breed archaeologist.

"Mr. Radisson?" Sam Smythe came around the side of the cabin, ducking the drizzle. On his head was an orange hard hat and he held a large carton in both arms. He was out of breath. "Sorry I'm late. That other errand you wanted me to do took a bit longer than I expected."

Job done? Radisson asked with a glance. Smythe shrugged. Radisson tossed him a look, telling him he must go back to confirm the job. He threw the peanut onto the beach as the raven eyed it ravenously, and indicated a dry empty spot on the table.

"The museum wrapped it up for me," the contractor said. "It can't get wet. Don't worry."

"What is it?" Jelna asked.

Radisson reached out and lifted a bundle rolled in tissue and bubble wrapping out of the box, carefully removed the paper and plastic, and hoisted the eagle mask into the air.

The raven squawked, sending feathers flying. Tom Jelna gasped. It was almost three feet long, painted red and green with white eyes outlined in black. It was a functional piece, despite the decorative paint job, and had an opening in its underside large enough to fit someone's head.

Lovely, Radisson thought. Graeme Redleaf, the chief of the Samish Band, wanted to borrow this mask for his son's betrothal potlatch next month. The museum had not objected. He, himself, had agreed on one condition. That they use it for the Thunderbird dance.

CHAPTER ELEVEN

Angeline awoke with a start. She heard something. A scrabbling of rock.

She started to get up, but Jake had his arm around her. A stone projection hit her hand as she moved to feel her way out of his hold. She heard the sound again, like gravel grating on metal, and turned to see a light shower of rubble at the mouth of the cave.

"Jake, wake up!"

It was quite dark. The fire was low, the embers glowing eerily under a single burnt log. She got to her feet, hugged the shirt she wore around her chest, and step-hobbled to the entrance.

The rain had stopped, and the air smelled earthy and wet. The stone under her bare feet was cold. Jake slipped up behind her and touched her arm. He was groggy, had pulled on his pants, and was holding them up with one hand.

"What's the matter?" he asked.

Angeline waited but heard nothing more. The sky was clear and dusk was settling in. If something had knocked her into the sinkhole earlier, then it was probably the same creature sniffing around the outside of the cave.

"Nothing, I guess," she said.

Jake bent down, picked something up.

"What's that?" she asked.

"Flagging tape. I wish Radisson's men would stay away from this island."

"There's no law against them being here," she replied, though she agreed with him. Sam Smythe gave her the creeps. She quickly buttoned down her shirt and went back in.

Jake threw a log on the fire, and watched her get dressed. She sat down to pull on her running shoes, but the swollen ankle made it difficult to lace the left one up.

"Maybe you should leave that one off," he suggested. "I can carry you down the hill."

"It's okay," Angeline said. "It really doesn't hurt that much."

Jake put the stick aside that he was using for a poker. He leaned over, cupped her chin in one hand and kissed her on the lips. Contented, he rocked back against a hump of sandstone and relaxed.

It was strange how it had happened. This morning she would not have imagined herself doing what she had done with him. It was like he was swept away, like they were both swept away by some uncontrollable force. It was the kind of feeling you got when you had drunk too much.

She finished tying her shoe and looked around at the cave drawings. They flickered and leaped as the flame licked up, reminding her of their task. She asked Jake what he thought of the petroglyphs. His eyes had a funny faraway look in them.

She squinted to where he was looking.

The Raven danced in the wavering light, luring the Salmon Chief's daughter away. Beside the carved images the tall column of stone shot straight for the ceiling.

A gust of wind blew into the cave and with it came the sharp pungency of the sea. Jake smiled. She felt strangely elated. Maybe this would work after all. Maybe she could get a job with Radisson and still have Jake.

Jake leaned on the palm of one hand to avoid a shower of sparks as the burning log settled. He cursed softly as something pricked his hand.

He groped behind him, and held up something for her to see. A peanut shell.

"Maybe it's a good thing Radisson Enterprises wants this cave," she said. "I know it's a bit unusual to do archaeology under corporate sponsorship. But when you think about it, what's really so bad? Funding is funding isn't it? And the company will be able to protect the cave which is more than the government can do."

Jake shook his head. "This isn't about money. If they gave us the money and left us alone, that would be fine. But they won't leave us alone. They aren't even content with just one site. Radisson wants all of the sites. He'll build a plastic jungle. A huge commercial enterprise with causeways and airways and boatways all tangled up with each other. I had no idea you were so mercenary."

Angeline scowled. Just because she could picture herself working for Radisson's theme park did not mean she was mercenary.

He reached a hand out for her, but she ignored it.

"Do you even know what I'm doing for my Masters thesis?" she asked.

He lifted a brow because he had no idea what that had to do with the theme park.

"Something to do with subsistence? When marine resources first became important?"

This was not what he wanted to talk about, but so what?

She had listened to his ideas on the Raven eagerly. She could tell him exactly what his theory was, and why it was flawed. What could he tell her about hers?

The heavy reliance on sea foods on the Northwest Coast was older than even his theory of the Raven. And though most archaeologists thought Native North Americans crossed the Bering land bridge from Siberia chasing bison and mammoth, she believed they came to the New World following the salmon runs.

"You don't even know, do you?" she accused.

"I am not your supervisor," he replied. "Thank God for that, given–"

Something caught his eye at the mouth of the cave. She rose and followed him outside. There was a rustling as though something were heading downhill fast, then a grating sound and a splash at the bottom of the mountain.

The stars were out and night had fallen. Jake walked to where the trees thinned near the beginning of the slope, and stared out at the channel. The sea was empty, black. But a few minutes later they saw movement. A single light glided silently, bound for Cedar Island.

***

Connie watched the man labour until the perspiration beaded on his

brow. Clifford Radisson had sent his contractor over with a tool box
and brand new shutters. A shutter grated as Smythe removed it from its
hinges and placed it on the floor, then he picked up one of the new ones
and measured it against the window.

Below the sill, white and orange begonias clustered, and red
impatiens overflowed the brim of the wooden flower box. The
contractor shifted the shutter, knocking the head of a begonia to the
floor, scattering petals. Connie frowned. The man was wantonly
damaging her flowers. And his employer – his employer was the most
presumptuous man she had ever met.

This morning she had awakened early to the sounds of hammering
outside her bedroom window. "This is not necessary," Connie said.
"Please stop the work, and leave."

"Sorry ma'am. Mr. Radisson has already paid for the work to be
done."

"I did not contract this work to be done!"

"That's between you and him. I do what I'm paid to do."

Shrugging, Sam Smythe turned back to his chore and pounded in a
bolt to hold the shutter in place.

"You've put the wrong shutter on that window, it's too small,"
Connie accused.

"So it is. You'd best not be distracting me ma'am. You'd best go on
inside and let me do my job."

Connie was incensed.

"Well, we'll just see about that." She shut the door to her house, and
marched down the steps to the road.

***

As soon as the Bronco rolled to a stop, Angeline got out and headed
to Connie's house. Jake told her he would join her after he had checked
on the site to see if any more damage had occurred since yesterday's
rain. She walked over the grass to the porch and almost tripped in her
tracks. She had seen a man working on Connie's windows as they
drove up the road, but she hadn't paid much attention and so hadn't

noticed who it was.

Sam Smythe grinned at her, a cigarette sticking to his lower lip, as she walked up the steps. "Mrs. Amos ain't home. Anything *I* can do for you?"

"I just came to borrow her shower," Angeline said.

An ugly gleam came into Smythe's eyes and he put the hammer down. He released a plume of smoke without removing the cigarette, and leered at her. Connie had offered the use of her shower anytime she wanted to use it. After falling in the mud hole yesterday and spending the entire afternoon in the cave, Angeline desperately wanted to wash and couldn't wait until Saturday.

"Well, I don't know when Mrs. Amos will be back," the contractor said. "She didn't say where she was going."

He looked through the windows toward the sea and spilled ash onto the sill. "You can always go skinny dipping. In fact, I'm pretty much finished here, maybe I'll join you."

A black and red tattoo flexed on Smythe's upper arm as he removed the cigarette from his mouth. He puffed out a perfect grey circle, and grinned. Then he looked over Angeline's head.

"Got a problem, Lalonde?"

Jake, who had returned from checking on the site, waved smoke from his face. Angeline told him that Connie wasn't home so they might as well go. Sam Smythe puffed deep rings into the air, watching them; then he hunched down, dripping ash to the porch, and settled his tools in his kit.

A bundle wrapped in beige flannel poked up from the hammers and wrenches, and it struck her as something odd to keep in a tool box. When Smythe noticed her noticing it, he shoved the bundle down with one hand, and quickly shut the case and rose.

"If you change your mind sweetheart, I'll meet you at the beach."

Jake glanced from her to Smythe, and every muscle in his body tensed.

"What was that?"

"Nothing."

Smythe hid his smile and popped the cigarette that was dangling from his lower lip into his mouth.

A last gust of smoke bloomed in Jake's face and Smythe dropped the cigarette onto the porch floor and stamped it out with his boot.

Jake almost leaped onto the contractor's back as he hopped down the steps; but a taxi pulled up, and he decided to let him go. A smiling Connie got out of the vehicle and joined them.

"Did you hire Sam Smythe to fix your shutters?" he demanded.

"No," Connie replied. "Clifford Radisson decided to do me the favour. I just came back from seeing him and I must say, that man simply astounds me."

She gestured them both through the door and into her kitchen.

Angeline did not think it odd that Clifford Radisson cared about Connie's shutters. He was a generous man, and did many unasked for things to help the community. He knew Connie didn't have much money so he had done for her what he had done for everyone else. It was the same reason he had paid thirty thousand apiece for the masks at the museum. Now the museum could buy a hygrometer.

At the old wooden cabinet under the window in her kitchen, Connie hunched over and said, "I want you to have the rattle, Jake. I want you to take it for safe-keeping."

She opened the glass doors and looked inside, then abruptly rose, grappling the counter beside the sink to steady herself as though she couldn't believe her eyes.

She stooped and removed some books, some coloured drinking glasses, and a pair of pewter candlesticks. As a polished carving of a bear with a fish in its mouth crashed to the floor, Angeline rushed over.

"Don't worry about that," Connie said. "It's not valuable."

But the rattle was. Connie got to her feet and strode out of the kitchen into the living room where she scanned the coffee table, then walked down the hall, pushed open the bathroom door, and touched a photograph of a totem pole hanging above the tank.

"I remember replacing that on the wall, then– oh dear, then what did I do?"

She unhooked the photograph from its place, glanced at Jake, then hung it back. She returned to the kitchen, and collected the books, glasses, and candlesticks, and replaced them on the shelves.

"Can't you remember where you put it?" Jake asked.

"I thought it was here. The last time you came to see it, I put it here in the cabinet."

"We better report the theft. I'll take you to Port Angeles," he said. There was no local police on Cedar Island.

"I don't know if it was stolen. Nothing else was touched."

"You didn't lend it to anyone? The museum? Or Shaman Moon?"

"No. *No*," Connie said, adamantly. "I didn't."

***

Jake went back to the site and Connie put on the kettle. She turned to see Angeline sitting at her kitchen table gazing at the picture of Paul. Paul used to leave her for months on end and she wouldn't know when he was coming back. Sometimes she thought for sure, he would never come back.

"Jake's upset isn't he?" Connie said. "He's just too polite to say so. I should have known better than to keep the rattle at home."

Angeline shrugged and held out her cup as Connie brought the teapot over.

"It was more than just an artifact to him," she said. "I knew that, but I thought it would be safest with me."

The discomfort in Angeline's eyes told Connie not to persist, but she couldn't help but wonder what had happened between them. All the other times she had seen them together, they had seemed so fixed on each other. Like she had been with Paul. *Ma Poule*, he used to say. *Je reviendrai toujours*. I will always come home.

Connie gazed solemnly at the picture of her husband. Despite what he had promised, in the end, he had not come home.

Angeline stayed ambivalent on the topic of Jake, and Connie suddenly realized she had no right to ask. She had lost her husband forty years ago and had reclaimed her maiden name. The French fisherman was gone, and it was time to let go. She wondered if Angeline liked dangly earrings and pastel coloured skirts.

They finished their tea, then Connie said, "While you're having your shower, I'll toss your clothes in the wash."

As she brought Angeline to the bathroom, she glanced at the black and white photograph hanging over the toilet. Every time she saw the totem pole she felt compelled to explain why it was there. It made her uneasy. She must not wait much longer to show it to Jake. She would have done it today had she not been so disturbed by the loss of the rattle.

Angeline studied the picture herself – the white man clad in a buttoned tunic and seaman's trousers decorated with piping near the top of the pole, just under the Thunderbird.

Connie slipped out of the bathroom and called softly. "Hand me your things through the door, dear, when you're ready."

After a few minutes, Angeline did.

"There's a white terry bathrobe on the back of the door you can use." Then Connie left to put the clothes into the washer.

So many things on her mind. The totem figure, the Raven rattle, Clifford Radisson, the theme park- and Jake. Connie entered the kitchen and stared at the antique cabinet, then returned to the living room and sat down. Two people had a stake in owning the rattle. But it belonged to only one of them. She observed her collection of artifacts on the coffee table in front of her. Some were genuine, others, not. There was a mask made from a piece of whalebone carved into a human face with grinning teeth and copper eyes; and a club of green jade, perforated at the rounded handle.

Like the Raven rattle, they were both shaman's objects.

"Has your family always lived on the San Juan Islands?"

Angeline stood in the doorway in the white terry robe, pointing to an aerial shot of Cedar Island.

The islands were part of Washington State, and Connie was only here by marriage.

"I haven't seen any members of my family for a very long time, and of course my parents are dead." She nervously rearranged the artifacts as she said this. "What about you, Angeline? Jake tells me you're from Toronto . . ."

Connie had never been to Toronto. She was not much of a city person. Victoria was as close to a big city as she had ever seen, and she had never even visited Seattle.

"I imagine your parents must miss you very much, you being so far from home," she finished.

She gestured for Angeline to come in and sit down, and reached for the stone club. It was difficult to talk about family. She cradled the club gently, then suddenly realized how strange that must seem.

"That photograph in the bathroom," Angeline said. "Was it a real totem pole?"

CHAPTER TWELVE

Jake lifted a finely polished circle of bone, and bent his head to the sheet of paper under his hand. Whale or sea lion bone? He dropped the pen in favour of a pencil and tentatively wrote *Orca*. He turned the object over. It was pretty, face up, incised with the pattern of a star. It was about the circumference of his palm, and now that he thought about it, more the size of a sea lion's epiphysis than a killer whale's.

He looked out the window of the lab. Angeline would have known what type of bone this was, but she wasn't here. A groan came from beside him as Carly tried to label a bone needle.

"Can you read that?" Carly asked. She blotted the technical pen on a scrap of paper. "I've got three needles, an antler pendent and an awl. God, this shouldn't be taking so long."

She flexed a hand and shoved something along the table toward him.

Bird motifs were common among Northwest Coast artifacts and the handle to the comb Carly passed to him was definitely a raven. He lifted it and angled it sideways, noting the sharp beak and the oval slit of an eye.

"How's the library research going?" he asked.

Carly spun the awl until the wide end faced up and shook the pen.

"Want me to fetch my notes?" She drew a couple of zigzag lines on a scrap of paper, then set it down, straightened her glasses which had sloped to the tip of her nose, and swung a leg over the bench.

Through the window he watched Carly dip between her own and Angeline's striped tent. The blue and white dome fluttered slightly in the breeze. The tent was brand new, brightly coloured; and he had fixed it for her following the storm.

After that incident in the cave Jake felt wary. All the time they were there, it had felt like a dream.

Carly returned. "I'll show you what I've got so far."

She set the binder down, thumbed through some pages, and tucked her legs under the bench. She smoothed a sheet of paper flat where it puckered from a water stain.

"A woman was weeping because her brother kept killing her newborn sons. Heron told her to go to the beach, find a smooth round stone, and heat it in a fire. When it was red hot, she swallowed it and gave birth to the Raven."

Carly paused. "I wonder if that's a universal theme. Like how *our* folklore says that babies are brought by the stork. Interesting isn't it? All these similarities even in Euro-North American cultures . . . Here's a bunch of other adventures he had. A tree collapsed and squashed him, a canoe slammed shut on his body, he tripped into a burning pit and was boiled in a copper kettle."

She giggled. "Hey, the Raven was just like the Coyote in the *Roadrunner*. Human ideas really haven't changed in hundreds of years, have they?"

Her finger wandered down the page. As the Raven came into adolescence, his appetite became so rapacious he ate the black spots off his feet, then he wandered in search of more edibles and other amusing situations. On the horizon he sighted a fire, stole a burning branch, and inadvertently set himself aflame, frying off some of his beak.

Jake listened, but none of these stories were new. He had hoped Carly would have come across something he hadn't.

The Raven was a thief and stole salmon eggs, his sister's berries, and numerous shiny things. In some of the stories, when humans caught onto his tricks, he was physically mutilated and carved up into little bits, but he always managed to regenerate himself.

Jake nibbled a hangnail on his thumb. The image was sharp in his mind. The Raven beaten to a pulp, coiled and trussed, and dropped to the bottom of the sea. That wasn't the only myth recounting the Raven's demise. The ability to return from the dead was one of his greatest powers. But what if, in one of them, he didn't return? The idea plagued Jake, and now he was almost certain he was right.

On an overturned artifact form he began to sketch. Lines and swirls emerged, transforming into several stylized figures. "Tell me what you know about the Raven," he said.

Carly gazed at him. "The Raven brought light to the world and put fish in the sea. He was killed and resurrected. He taught people how to use fire and freed the first men. He also took a lot of wives. He had very human traits, but he was a spirit."

Jake bowed over the paper, squelching the growing sense of unease. They were all gods in a sense. Sea bear, *Wasgo*, Thunderbird. They could all take on human form.

"He was immortal."

Memories were immortal.

Carly smiled, eyes darting uncertainly at his sketch. "So what am I looking for in all of these stories?"

Jake lifted his finished drawing and held it up to the light.

The figures were arranged in a ring. A large fisherman sat with a line in his hand, forming one side of the circle, while his wife, her neck and back arched, comprised the other. In the centre was a halibut with a hook over its open mouth, and below them was the Raven. He lay prone, his head and beak seductively shaped to the curve in the woman's spine.

Tires grated on dirt outside the lab. A Honda Civic pulled into Seagirt Lane and stopped within view of the windows. The rear passenger door opened and Angeline stepped out. She was dressed in a two-piece thing, sort of a pastel peach coloured skirt and a matching top cropped at the waist so that her midriff showed when she lifted her arms to wave good-bye to Connie and Joe who sat inside the car.

Jake held his breath as Angeline came toward the house.

"There you are," she said to Carly, as she walked through the door. Her hair blew back, and clutched in one hand was a bulky white plastic bag.

Carly waved an artifact in the air. "We need you."

"Later." Angeline looked casually around the room, directed her next sentence right at Jake. "Right now, I want to have lunch. Will you drive us into town?"

"Where did you get the duds?" Carly asked.

"From Connie." Angeline paused, twirled. "Back in style, don't you think? I've got some for you, then let's go into town."

***

A movement by the totem pole caught Clifford Radisson's attention. He sat angled toward the restaurant's entrance with Katherine Leonard, the woman from the Heritage Advisory Board, facing him. Seated slightly to his right was Josie Davies, the chubby woman archaeologist, and Tom Jelna sat to his left.

How curious. The two people from the government were seated as far apart from each other as was physically possible around the circular table. Radisson raised his eyes to see Jake Lalonde enter through the glass doors.

The hostess of the Surf Lodge stood just inside the dining room smiling. She asked Lalonde something and he shook his head, indicating Radisson's table. He walked over, swaggering a little, and placed his hands on the back of Katherine Leonard's chair. He looked around at their drinks, then met Clifford Radisson's gaze.

Radisson rose, extending his hand.

"I'm glad you could join us, Dr. Lalonde. I hope I didn't take you away from anything important?"

Jake grunted, and grudgingly obliged him with a handshake. He pulled out a chair from a neighbouring table and inched it in between the two women.

On the patio, Radisson glimpsed the pretty dark-haired Angeline and her bespectacled friend under a red, white, and blue umbrella. So the game of musical chairs continued. He returned his attention to the table and filled Josie's glass with a clear grapey Sancerre. It had taken nothing to switch her from drinking beer to wine. He righted the bottle without spilling a drop and tilted it at Jake, who shook his head and ordered a Heinekin.

"Have you thought my proposal over?" Radisson asked.

"What's the hurry?" Jake replied. "With a wet site to excavate, we won't be finished here for months. We are conducting an archaeological assessment. It is not finished yet. When it's done, you will get the report."

Katherine Leonard cast her former lover a disapproving look to which Jake scowled. Radisson smiled. How he must hate being manipulated by women. If any woman dared look at Clifford Radisson that way, he would soon put her in her place.

So now he had all three of the most important women in Jake Lalonde's life here in the same place at the same time. Since Jelna had wanted to get Katherine out of the office, he had suggested she be directly involved in the project as well.

"Have you been out to see the petroglyphs?" he asked mildly.

Josie Davies reached for a bagel crisp from a basket in the centre of the table, and smeared it liberally with butter.

"Jake has," she said. "I haven't been out there, myself, yet."

Katherine rattled some clunky metallic rings on her fingers, propping an elbow on the table. "Rock art is very fragile which is why we try to keep the public away from the site."

Radisson nodded. "Petroglyphs are one of my pet interests. I'm intrigued by symbolic ambiguities, and rock art is nothing if not symbolic and ambiguous."

Katherine smiled, agreed, and added that she owned several books on the subject herself.

"I haven't had much time to keep up with the literature, but I am always looking for sources. More wine Ms. Leonard?"

Kate's long fingers looked even longer and skinnier with all the cheap jewelry as she held out her glass. Radisson felt a slight twinge of contempt.

The Regional Archaeologist was not to be outdone by his assistant. "All of these ovoids and formlines, inner ovoids, S forms, U forms, and split U forms characteristic of the classic Northwest Coast style require an understanding of basic style and motifs," he said imperiously.

Katherine interrupted. "It's especially hard to tell the difference between all the various beaked birds." She had several contemporary Native prints at home, and if it wasn't for the fact that the artists titled the pieces with the names of the animals, she could never tell the difference.

Radisson's eyes crinkled. He was beginning to define some patterns. Katherine Leonard was highly competitive, which was why she had left Jake Lalonde, and why she despised her boss, Tom Jelna.

"Maybe I can help there," Radisson offered.

"The Raven and the Eagle?" Tom suggested.

"The Eagle's beak is short and ends in a strong downward curve while the Raven's is quite straight. The Eagle has ear tufts, and the Raven usually has a tongue."

"*Mocking* one might say?"

He had forgotten about Dr. Lalonde.

"One might say so. At best, the Raven is a joker." Radisson raised the bottle of Sancerre to the Regional Archaeologist and topped his glass. Tom swirled the wine, and asked for his thoughts on the meaning of the work – especially if the artist was no longer alive to explain it.

"The more highly abstracted a design is, the more difficult it is to interpret the symbolism accurately," Radisson explained. "Rock art– primitive art, originated when man first tried to give substance to his subconscious."

"I'd be careful what you call primitive, Mr. Radisson," Jake said. "What's primitive to you and me, is not primitive to the people who created the art. And while we're at it, who says a man created the first works of art? Maybe it was a woman."

Radisson almost laughed. He glanced briefly at the patio where Angeline and her friend huddled over a bottle of wine. "I beg your pardon, Dr. Lalonde, you're absolutely right. In any case I would be very much interested in hearing your assessment of the petroglyphs on Lookout Island."

"The cave is not for sale. I have not had time to make a proper assessment yet. In case you've forgotten, we are excavating a wet site. That takes precedence over anything else."

The Regional Archaeologist threw Jake a contemptuous look. "The sale of Lookout Island has nothing to do with you."

"For Christ's sake Jelna, that cave is an archaeological site! I've seen it!"

Katherine glowered, reminding Jake the luncheon was not to discuss the sale of Lookout Island. She turned back and smiled brightly.

"Did you know rock art, in North America, dates from 4500 BC to AD 1800?"

Jelna answered, "Rock art is hard to date. We can't do C14 dates in the absence of carbon. And no one has really established a reliable method of dating petroglyphs– at least not that I know of."

Interesting. Radisson fiddled with the silverware by his glass. They wouldn't be able to detect a fraud then, would they?

"I don't suppose you own any petroglyphs?" Jake demanded.

Katherine did something under the table, causing Jake to wince. Radisson suppressed a smile. When RAVENSWORLD became a reality–

No, even before that, he intended to own the petroglyphs on Lookout Island.

He sipped his wine. Katherine Leonard and Tom Jelna obviously did not get along, and watching their bickering was like watching an old married couple whose lust had turned to revulsion. But when it came to RAVENSWORLD they were of one mind. The fat archaeologist he could count on too; she was not going to cause trouble. Lalonde on the other hand was a problem. He was belligerent, contentious, outspoken, rude. Tenacious. And a man of good will. An interesting set of attributes, but out of date. Dr. Lalonde would have done well fifty or sixty years ago, but the modern world had no place for him.

"Now that we're one big happy family," he said, "I think I'll go invite those two young ladies outside to join us for lunch."

CHAPTER THIRTEEN

Carly squinted behind her wire framed glasses. "See that? Jake is sandwiched between his two ex's."

Angeline looked, face contorting slightly, and her eyes darkened.

"Yup. He's had an on again, off again, relationship with Josie for years. And Katherine Leonard just pops in every now and then, though I think she was more recent. Well, actually, I'm not even sure it's completely over between them. Either of them. I saw him come out of Josie's tent in the wee hours of the morning after that thunderstorm. And why the hell does he hang out at the HAB's offices so much except to see Kate? He and Tom Jelna aren't exactly bosom buddies now are they?"

"I thought there used to be something between him and Josie, but I didn't know about Katherine Leonard," Angeline said.

Carly grinned. "You should pay more attention to the gossip."

Angeline was not amused; instead she seemed particularly disturbed by this bit of information, and Clifford Radisson decided it was time to make his presence known.

He ducked under the striped umbrella, smiled and said, "How are you ladies? It's been awhile since I've had the pleasure, I thought I would come over and say hello."

The two young women raised their faces to his.

"Lovely afternoon isn't it? I was going to ask you to join us inside, but I can see that would be a mistake. Why would you want to come inside and talk shop when you can sit out here and enjoy all of this? May I ask what you are drinking?"

"Chardonnay," Angeline replied, composing herself with an affable smile, and lifting the bottle out of the clear acrylic cooler.

Radisson took the wine bottle from her and studied the label. "I think you ladies should be drinking champagne."

Carly squirmed in her seat. "We can't afford it."

"You don't have to."

Clifford Radisson signalled a passing waiter and ordered a vintage bottle of Moet & Chandon. Then he remarked on the beautiful weather which had expedited progress at the site. He noted the younger woman's brazenness and compared her to Angeline.

Was Angeline aware of the effect she had on men? He was certain her nearsighted crew mate knew, but that did not affect their friendship.

The sun was hot and the short top that Angeline wore rode up as she leaned forward to hear him better. He tipped the umbrella backwards to shade her.

"Thank-you," she said.

"You're welcome."

The waiter set the champagne down in a new acrylic cooler, laid out champagne flutes, and took the Chardonnay away.

Radisson glanced toward the beach. The day was fine, the sun shining over a sea as calm as lake water. An unusual shade of blue for the North Pacific, he thought. Like molten jade melting into indigo. A soft wind blew in from the beach carrying the sea and a breath of roses.

From across the table, he could feel Angeline's lovely greenish eyes studying him. He was glad he had not barged in on them without waiting. Hearing what he had heard, knowing what he knew, and seeing Angeline's reaction, confirmed everything he suspected. He couldn't imagine a more appropriate time to ask.

"Would you care to have dinner with me tonight, Angeline?"

Her eyes lifted, stopped, and registered a troubling mix of emotion. He looked behind him, expecting exactly what he saw. Jake Lalonde stood in the doorway, the sleeves to his cream cotton shirt rolled up to his biceps and his jeans faded and frayed at the pockets.

"Are they joining us or not?" Jake asked gruffly. "The waiter wants to take our order."

His hair was too long and unkempt; his shirt, opened at the collar, exposed a tuft of brown hair.

He looked like . . . (Radisson secretly chuckled) like an archaeologist. Radisson adjusted his crisp white collar, and deliberately stroked his smooth, freshly shaven chin. He turned back to Angeline and repeated his question.

"Dinner would be wonderful," she said.

Jake's mouth dropped open.

"What time?" she asked.

"Seven o'clock? That will give me time to tour the site and inspect your facilities. I'm really looking forward to seeing what you people have found. Then, I'll take you to the mainland. We'll dine in Seattle. Would you like that?"

***

Clifford Radisson was enjoying himself. After a tour of the site, Katherine Leonard had remained behind while her superior, Tom Jelna, returned to Seattle. Josie Davies was showing him around the lab, and any minute the beautiful Angeline would come bouncing in after changing out of her work clothes to join him for dinner. He wondered which of the three women he could count on. Probably not Angeline. She had complex feelings for Jake. He could change that though. Maybe.

He noticed his roll of blueprints on one of the tables and reached for it. "Have you had a chance to look at this?" he asked.

"I think your plans are very innovative," Josie said, nodding vigorously.

Radisson placed the roll back on the table. "Tell you what. Let's not wait until things are formalized. Are you interested in working for me?"

The fat woman's eyes grew eager, wide. Of course she was.

"And Ms. Leonard?" he asked. "Can I count on you as well? I am going to need a very large staff."

Katherine's lips parted, then shut, as someone entered the house.

"Dr. Lalonde," Radisson said.

"What the fu . . ." Jake sputtered clumsily in an effort to keep his composure, and turned his wrath on the women. "What the hell is going on here? What are you two doing? We have work to do!"

"It's Sunday Jake."

He frowned at Josie.

"I'm sure you have many things to do," Radisson said, as Angeline slipped in through the door. "So I will just get out of your way. Thank-you for the tour of the site. It was very enlightening."

He turned to Angeline who had put the pretty peach dress back on, had combed her hair and, he looked a little closer, yes, even applied a little lipstick.

He offered a hand and she took it. Jake's face turned three shades of purple. Radisson smiled. The man should learn to control his temper. Women were put off by blustering fools. He looked back, once, as they stepped onto the porch, but didn't linger to hear what else was about to go on in there.

***

They were over the sapphire waters of the Juan de Fuca Strait. The sea shivered. Here and there islands floated, dark green. North, was the elongated mass of Vancouver Island, and south were the San Juan Islands where Angeline had boarded Radisson's private plane. They cruised the Strait of Georgia over another cluster of islands - Salt Spring, Pender, Galiano, Gabriola. The legends came alive. *Dzunkwa*, cannibal spirit, *Sah Sin*, hummingbird, *Sxwaixwe*, two-headed serpent, *Yehlh*, bird creator, and then there was the Thunderbird, the most powerful eagle of them all.

Angeline felt Radisson's eyes on her hair. Two weeks he had been courting her. He hadn't kissed her yet, except on the cheek. She knew he wanted to sleep with her.

Radisson touched her hand.

"We've seen the petroglyphs," she said in answer to his question.

"They're authentic?" he asked. "Significant?"

No one was talking about them because the only people who had seen them were her and Jake. Jake had no intention of sharing his opinions with the developer, and Angeline did not want to think about them at all.

Those images had come alive. They had seduced her. *Jake* had seduced her. If he hadn't been intrigued by the petroglyphs they would never have gone to the cave. She would never have slept with him. And she wouldn't be here with Clifford Radisson trying to decide her future.

A raven sat on the floor, caged, in front of her feet. It was obviously injured, the right wing bent at a most uncomfortable looking angle. It tripped something in her memory.

The wings of the plane dipped. She turned, sighted the bustling harbour of Victoria, the capitol of British Columbia.

"Picture this," Radisson said, leaning over her shoulder. "Cedar Island, Gooseberry Island, Lookout Island. A prehistoric world linked by land bridges and boats to take visitors from one time period to the next." A laugh came from deep within his throat. "My contribution to the economy, Angeline. Exciting, interesting jobs. Just think of me as a kind of Walt Disney, but without the cartoons."

She rearranged the seatbelt over her hips, and smiled. "Walt Disney didn't have a lot of money to start. Just a dream."

"You haven't told me yours."

The silver at Radisson's temples was so perfectly symmetrical that on anyone else it might have been placed there on purpose. He had an aquiline nose and impersonal eyes. He exuded power and strength. He was mostly absorbed in his own affairs, but was not above granting dreams. Would he grant her hers?

"Dreams are what make people fly when they have no wings," he said. "Climb mountains when they know they'll very possibly get frostbite, lose a nose, an arm, a leg, or even their life. What are you willing to risk for your dreams, Angeline?"

She wasn't sure. She had dated those men her father had paraded in front of her. Each and every one of them wanting a maid, a hostess, a whore. They had credentials and suits and money and nothing else. They never talked to her. They never questioned her aspirations, sought her opinions, or encouraged her ideas.

They were like her father. Like Jake, except that Jake didn't have their money. Evaluating her dress, her hair, her body. And giving her a place in their social spheres. She could have a job if she liked, but if she married any one of them, it would have to take a backseat to theirs.

Not anymore. No one was ever going to cage her, treat her like an ornament again.

The raven banged its head against the wires of its prison. Its beak pecked savagely at the metal. It was thin and sickly, but its hunger to be free was fearsome. She felt pity, but also wondered how a flightless bird would fare in the wild. Wasn't that why Clifford Radisson had caged it? To protect it? To allow it to live?

His hand moved toward her, his shirt rustling slightly. She glanced up. Now she remembered. Two men, one in jeans and khaki vest, the other in crisp linen. He had rescued the injured raven on the beach.

"Poor devil," Radisson said. "No matter what I do, it doesn't seem to want to feed."

"They like salmon," Angeline said. "And almost any kind of human food."

"Not this one. Perhaps he would prefer his freedom to his life."

She suddenly did not want to discuss the raven anymore.

"How did you become interested in Northwest Coast Native culture?" she asked. "The idea to build a theme park around it is quite unusual."

"Do I look Native to you?" he asked.

She shook her head.

"Somewhere in my ancestry there is Native blood. But my interest in aboriginal arts comes from my mother." A wry smile came to his lips. "If you don't want to, you don't ever have to work again. When I've bought this place, I'll give it to you as a gift."

Angeline looked at him, heartbeats quickening. Then she dropped her eyes to the caged bird, pecking relentlessly against the metal rods.

*   *   *

A cloud of smoke billowed as Jake flopped a couple of raw beef patties on the grill. He adjusted the heat, looked up at the house, then across the camp to Angeline's tent. Over the past couple of weeks, Angeline had been seeing more and more of Clifford Radisson.

"What time's dinner?" Josie asked from the doorway of the lab. She pushed up the sleeves to her purple fleece jacket and plodded down the stairs.

"Ten, fifteen minutes. You like your meat rare?"

"Well done. I don't want to get hamburger disease."

Angeline left her tent holding a plastic bottle of water. Carly placed a gargantuan bowl of mixed greens on the table where Angeline went to sit. Jake watched Carly layer some napkins on a stack of paper plates and tear open a bag of white plastic cutlery; then she dumped them out on the table and sorted them into spoons, knives, and forks. Neither woman spoke. Then Carly came over, and Jake jerked his eyes toward the picnic table.

"What's with you two?" he asked.

"Maybe I don't like the company she keeps." Carly took the spatula and poked at the meat, reached over to the sideboard to the right of the grill and flipped up the plastic cap of a bottle. A generous blob of barbecue sauce landed on three of the burgers, and fat dripped, sending smoke into the air.

"Get me that plate," Jake said, taking the spatula from her. When she brought the stainless steel platter, he piled on the cooked burgers, and laid a few more raw ones on the grill.

Smoke irritated his eyes, making them water. He picked up a paper plate from the sideboard and lifted a meat patty, then Angeline came over and stood beside him as he passed the plate to Carly.

"I need to talk to you, Jake."

He needed to talk to her. Everyone was standing around munching on burgers and salad, so he laid down the spatula and gestured Angeline into the house.

She went to the table and sat down. On the surface, cluttered with papers, books, and uncatalogued artifacts, was his sketch of the Raven and the Fisherman. Angeline studied the picture. She did not see what he saw when he looked at this– the Raven beaten to a pulp, coiled and trussed, and dropped to the bottom of the sea.

The phone rang. Jake reached across the table and answered it. The

voice was a man's. Asking for Angeline. He handed her the phone.
"The Royal Ontario Museum?" she said softly into the receiver. "It
must be about the volunteer job. I guess I forgot to tell them I was
going to be out west this summer. Don't bother to call them back, I'll
do it myself." She paused, her brows squeezing together, voice low.
"That isn't why you called, is it, Dad?"

Jake returned from where he had gone to stand just outside the door.
Angeline replaced the receiver.

"I'm needed at home," she said. "Clifford Radisson is going to fly
me to Toronto tomorrow."

Jake fought to keep his voice even. "If that was your father just now,
obviously, you made plans to leave before he called. Why? Not
because of me, I hope."

"Of course not!"

"When are you coming back?"

"I don't know. It's . . . it's a personal matter. You don't have to
worry about a replacement for me, I've asked Joe's girlfriend, Marina,
to take my place. I won't know if I'm coming back until the Fall. I'm
not sure I want to do archaeology anymore."

Of course you want to do archaeology, Jake wanted to shriek at her.
Isn't that what this is all about? Clifford Radisson can give you a
future. I can't.

"What about the First Salmon Ceremony?" he demanded. "I thought
you wanted to attend that. It's coming up in a few days."

"I'm afraid I'll have to miss it."

CHAPTER FOURTEEN

Angeline shivered as she stood in her underwear trying to shimmy the black crepe dress up from her feet to her shoulders. The air conditioning was working over-time.

The skirt was narrow and curved smoothly over her hips. The neckline accentuated her long creamy neck, scooping from shoulder to shoulder, sleeveless. The waist sloped, the cut of the fabric and the style of the dress making her narrow waist look even smaller than it was. She turned from side to side, peering critically at the three-way mirror in Toronto's Holt Renfrew on Bloor Street.

Of course she hadn't left because of *him*. She had merely made up her mind.

Would Radisson like this?

She turned and twisted, adjusting the skirt. Her legs were bare right now, but tonight, she would wear a pair of sheer black stockings. Black was always elegant. And she would carry a black beaded handbag. Did she have gold earrings? Not these studs; they were too small. Something bigger that would glitter against her dark hair after it was cut. It was too long. Starting to look messy. Or sexy. It depended on how you chose to look at it. *He*, she decided, would like her hair shorter, stylish. Classy.

She glanced down at her watch. She'd better hurry. Her appointment was in half an hour. She was expected home by six. Dad was ecstatic. A billionaire was nothing to scoff at. For the first time in recent memory, he wasn't working late. But Mom . . . Oh dear. Shoes. It had been so long since she had dressed like this. She needed a pair of high heels, black, to match.

"Are you all right in there?" the saleswoman called through the door.

"Fine," Angeline said.

"Can I get you anything else?"

"No thanks."

Angeline quickly slipped out of the black cocktail dress and pulled her jeans back on. Saleswomen had an annoying habit of wanting to come in when you were naked.

***

Jake grabbed the bow of the boat as Josie climbed over the gunwale. They hauled the small power boat onto the beach. They were just in time for the First Salmon Ceremony on Gooseberry Island. Carly, along with the rest of the crew, had already joined the spectators.

Shaman Moon holding his rattle stood ankle deep in water. He trailed a red goat's wool robe decorated with square mother-of-pearl buttons. A group of men waited on the beach dressed in soft buckskin shirts, laced at the seams with ribbons of matching leather. On their backs and chests sea creatures were beaded into stylized designs with dentalia, abalone, and tusk shells.

The fisherman had just delivered a catch of Sockeye salmon.

Jake looked around and saw Connie among the women. He left Josie and went to stand beside her. Connie smiled. She pressed a finger to her lips and turned her attention back to the ceremony.

A cluster of children knelt before the shaman. The men in the beaded shirts formed a human avenue. From the water's edge up to the cooking fires at the top of the beach, they stood shoulder to shoulder. The children rose one at a time, red ochre on their faces and white eagle down in their hair. Each child took a fish from Shaman Moon and carried it up the beach, dorsal fin in their teeth.

At the top of the beach, Pauline, the shaman's wife waited. Behind her, alderwood fires blazed in shallow pits. The child at the head of the procession handed Pauline her salmon and she placed it on a newly woven cedar mat.

Guiding her husband's hand with a knife, she slit the belly of the first salmon.

Shaman Moon rose, leaving the women to their task.

The cooking fires died, ashes were swept away. Hot rocks glowed at the bottom of the pits. Pauline and the other women placed alder chips over the stones followed by the salmon. The fish were covered with seaweed, branches, and leaves, then shovelfuls of sand.

"Hi Connie," Jake said when the formal part of the celebration was over.

"I'm so glad you could make it," Connie said, gesturing him to accompany her for a walk.

"Any word about the Raven rattle?" he asked.

She shook her head.

He had a feeling it wouldn't be found by the police or by anyone actively searching for it.

"I'm sorry, Jake. I should have been more careful. I should have given it to you or to the museum as soon as it was discovered."

He located a low boulder for her to sit on, and hunkered on the ground by her feet.

"Is there evidence of a shaman's hut in the bog?" she asked.

"Not so far."

"Perhaps it's just as well. There's someone I'd like you to speak to after the festivities. Someone who might be able to clarify things a little for you. I know you've been obsessed with the Raven for a very long time. He was a curious mythological figure. I can understand your fascination with him."

Offshore, a blue heron stood on one leg in shallow water motionless as a stick. It moved, lunged. The long grey throat stretched skyward, and a small silver fish slid down its gullet. The wind lightly ruffled its feathers.

Jake got to his feet, looking at the activity surrounding the cooking pits in the distance.

"Shall we go back?" he asked. "It looks like they're about ready to serve."

The baked fish were laid out on traditional planks of split cedar, their heads turned to face inland, upstream, the direction the run was to go. The feast would have been traditional except that folding tables and chairs were available for people to sit on, and paper plates and cups were handed around.

Jake was starving. The side dishes included bean, potato, and leafy salads, wild peas, bread and rice, eulachon grease, and a bowl of steamed Blue Camus bulbs. He helped himself to a scoop of everything.

"Slow down," Josie said. "There's still the salmon."

Chief Graeme Redleaf's wife led a line of women bearing the planks of fish to the tables, ceremonially praising them in song as they came.

***

"How about if we take about three inches off here?" Symone asked.

Angeline glanced up at her stylist. "Not too short?"

"No. I think it will make you look very sophisticated."

That was exactly what she wanted. He started to snip away and little wisps of hair fluttered down, sliding on the smock that covered her and landed on the floor in a puddle of black.

"Hot date?" he asked.

She had to think about this. She was going to *La Rose*, one of the most exclusive restaurants in Toronto. It was the first formal date she had had in over a year. Going out with archaeologists didn't count. They never paid for you anyway. And they never asked you out. With them, things just happened. You ended up having dinner with them at some cheap bistro or at a movie or in a sleezy bar. Or sometimes you ended up in bed with them because you had drunk too much.

She flushed and hoped Symone didn't notice.

"I thought you were going to be gone all summer," Symone said. "Hair started to drive you crazy?"

Angeline let a smile break through her melancholy. As a matter of fact it *was* driving her crazy. It was impossible to keep clean when you were camping.

"I watched a documentary last night," Symone said. "Scientists think there was some interbreeding between Neanderthals and modern humans."

"Oh?" Angeline said. "I thought they'd stopped all that speculating."

Symone shrugged. "They can take DNA samples and compare them to modern humans."

"To prove what?"

He shrugged again. "Not exactly sure. Archaeology isn't exactly my thing. I just watched a bit of it as I was flipping through the channels. It made me think of you. What are you people digging up on the San Juan Islands anyway?"

"Rocks, bones, broken pieces of wood." She didn't feel much like elaborating. She didn't want to think about Jake. She thought about Clifford Radisson instead. Most people thought he was heartless and cold. A ruthless businessman. She knew better. Underneath that facade was true humanity. Otherwise, why would he care so much about Connie?

"There was a Raven rattle," she said.

"Sounds exciting."

Angeline glanced into the mirror to see if Symone was being sarcastic. His face was perfectly blank.

"Do you ever find burials?"

"Sometimes, but not while I was there." She grinned. "No Neanderthals of course."

He came around to her face, stooped, and brought the scissors just under her chin.

"So, when are you going back?"

***

Pauline, the shaman's wife, came around with a plank of leftover fish.

"I am so stuffed," said Carly. Josie took another serving but the others declined. Carly noticed that most of the guests were collecting their paper plates to make room on their tables for dessert. She asked Pauline if she could help clean up.

Paper plates, cups, napkins, all went into plastic garbage bags, but not before the bones and leftover skin and flesh were scraped off and gathered together on a cedar mat. Pauline handed the remains of the salmon feast to Graeme Redleaf's wife who took it down to the beach and dumped it, mat, fish bones and all, into the sea.

The custom reminded Jake of the petroglyph in the cave on Lookout Island. Which reminded him of Radisson. Which reminded him of Angeline.

The sun fell below the horizon and the sky flamed orange. Fires were built up to illuminate the night. Jake picked up a can of Pepsi but it was too sweet. He wanted a beer, but none was served.

"Try this," Josie said. A paper cup of whipped soapberries slid over the table toward him. The confection, called Indian Ice Cream, was frothy and pink, its flavour sour-bitter despite the obvious sweetening with sugar.

"I like the real thing better," Carly said. She burped behind her hand. "I don't know about you, but I think it's repeating on me."

Jake smiled and so did Connie when she realized what was going on. Indian Ice Cream was an acquired taste.

On the beach, some people gathered in costumes in front of the fires. Joe Redleaf appeared in a spirit mask.

"Sit down Jake," Josie said.

"That mask– "

"It was borrowed from the Cedar Island Museum," Connie said. "And yes, that's the Raven mask Clifford Radisson bought."

***

Angeline swayed her hips to the music coming from her stereo. She moved in a black lace bra and matching panties. She waltzed over to the bed and lifted the black crepe dress. It felt crisp and new and smelled faintly of scented tissue paper. She twirled with it as though it were him. She had never danced with him.

The music stopped. She started to go over to change the CD, but changed her mind. She didn't have that much time.

The dress slid over her head, and she twisted around to view the back and to reach the zipper. She gripped it between her red polished forefinger and thumb. Careful. These nails had taken an hour to do after Symone had cut her hair.

She ran her fingertips gently up her calves to her thighs. The silk hose glistened slightly in the rosy light of her bedroom. Then she slipped on the black high heels.

At her dresser, brush poised, she studied the mirror again. Symone had created magic. She was beautiful. Her hair curved smoothly behind her left ear and fell softly forward over the right, curling slightly around her jaw to her cheek. Her eyes tilted upward, exotic, lashes long and sweeping. Lips perfectly sculptured red.

A soft click, and a tap, then her door slowly widened. At first she feared it was Dad, who came home early these days now that Angeline had returned. Mom, on the other hand, left whenever Dad was home.

Teresa smiled from the doorway. At Angeline's beckoning, the housekeeper entered the room, and perched on the edge of the bed.

"It seems like only yesterday– "

"Don't do that," Angeline said affectionately, turning up her nose and twirling for full effect. "You like?"

Teresa nodded. "You look very sophisticated. I hardly recognize you anymore."

Good.

"I've read about Clifford Radisson in the papers," she said. "I know the man's a billionaire, but he's twice your age."

"Dad likes him," Angeline said.

Teresa sighed. "Why have you come home? Your dream was to become an archaeologist. What's wrong, Angeline?"

The doorbell chimed. Angeline did a last minute touch-up to her hair, blotted her lips, and ran, then stopped, drew in a breath and tread lightly down the stairs, leaving the housekeeper staring after her.

Her father opened the door.

"Come in," Jason Lisbon said, grasping the man's hand.

Clifford Radisson was dressed in a dark, expensively-tailored Armani suit, white collar contrasting sharply with his royal blue necktie. Just as dapper in his formal lawyer attire, her father beamed from the foyer, and she almost couldn't tell them apart.

Jake had called her mercenary and an ornament. What could be wrong?

***

At the far end of the room in front of an ancient wooden buffet, against grass-mat wallpaper, a statue sat, carved from yellow cedar. It was a clam shell filled with little people attempting to escape and rising from the top of the shell was the imposing figure of the Raven.

Connie had brought Jake to the shaman's home. She watched as Jake touched the fine wood, recognizing the story the sculpture represented. The shaman was not here. His wife was.

"Connie tells me you study the past," Pauline said. "Why do you want to know about the Raven?"

The past linked the present and the future. The past offered continuity. Connie knew Jake was looking for his roots.

"The Raven was my mother's crest," Jake said.

"The Raven is a human invention, created as the embodiment of good and evil in the world," Pauline said. "As an archaeologist, you must know mythology is a way for people to make sense of the world."

Jake nodded. "But the Raven– the character of the Raven, was different from any of the others. Haven't you ever noticed that? He wasn't like the Bear, the Wolf or the Beaver. None of those mythical creatures possessed such sublime human qualities. *He* . . . The Raven was based on something real."

Connie arced her brows, studying Jake's face. "What makes you think that?"

"I just know."

That didn't sound very scientific.

"The Raven was a man, a shaman, who conjured up sights and sounds and made people believe the magic was real," he said.

Pauline suppressed a smile. There was no such magician, she said. They used mythology today, and always had, to maintain cohesiveness among their people. They maintained the traditions by recreating the images in art, myth, and dance. The Raven was nothing more, nothing less, than an invention of some old men sitting around a campfire.

Jake stroked the cedar carving. It was quite beautiful. He traced the bird's beak from its head to the tip of its clawed toes.

"I am not talking about hundreds of years ago," he said. "I am talking about thousands. The Raven might have been one of the first people to come to the New World."

Connie indicated the time, apologized to Pauline, and ushered Jake out of the shaman's home before his wife could respond.

"Why did you do that?" Jake asked. "I wanted to know what she thought."

"Look around you, at these houses, at this beach, at this reserve," Connie said as she nudged him toward the sea. "Proving the Raven was a man won't solve anything, but it might encourage more publicity. It might give Clifford Radisson more reason to purchase our islands."

They strolled past lighted windows and shallow peaked roofs. Dusk had melted into solid night, and behind the houses a bluff rose dark and menacing.

A porch light flashed on and some boys exited through a front door, jumped down the stairs, and ran past.

"At first, I thought development might be best," she said. "But in the end, selling your culture is always a short term solution."

Connie hung back, digging a pebble out of her shoe. Jake had not noticed and was still walking. Connie listened to the sound of the waves. Houses were built right down to the beach, but further ahead the skeleton branches of conifers spiked the sky from the tall cliff. Jake walked to where the houses ended and a wall of rock hovered bare and high. He stopped, turned around to search for her.

"Your past isn't here," Connie said softly as she approached. "The Samish did not have totem crests. If– Jake watch out!"

A boulder came tumbling off the bluff, just missing him.

"Dear God, are you all right?"

On top of the wall of rock, something moved.

"Jesus, that was close," he said, then frowned.

"What is it?" she asked.

Jake glanced over at Connie, then up at the bluff again.

"That cliff has been eroding for years. They should have a sign up here. Children could get hurt. Are you sure you're all right?"

***

A silver spoon clattered to the floor and Angeline leaned over. Clifford Radisson gripped her wrist. "Someone will get that."

Of course, someone did. A waiter came rushing over to replace it. Radisson smiled, releasing her gently. He reached across the table and poured out another glass of champagne.

The view below the restaurant was breathtaking. The city fanned out in a million glittering lights. Where the lake swallowed the land it was velvet black. A few lights blinked where the Toronto Islands floated offshore. The air-conditioning was gently maintaining a comfortable interior temperature and the stifling heat was trapped beyond the windows.

Angeline perused the crisscrossing streets marked by yellow street lamps and the blazing headlights from cars.

"What would you like to try?" he asked. "The food here is exquisite."

Angeline surveyed the menu. *She* was exquisite.

"Tell you what," Radisson said, taking the menu from her. "I'll surprise you. How's that?" He ordered for both of them and then pushed back his chair. "Come over here, I want to show you something."

She got up and went with him over to the other side of the empty restaurant.

She gazed up into the sky and then down below to the lake. If you were to reverse your position, he thought, the sky would be the land and the land the sky.

"Have you ever thought about the fact that we may be living in only one of several universes?" he asked. There were countless planets out there, countless stars. They floated in countless solar systems in countless galaxies. "Do you feel insignificant, Angeline? In the greater scheme of things?"

She smiled at him like she didn't know what he was talking about. "Do you ever think about dying? What you would see? I imagine it to be something like this– To be up somewhere high, looking down, from a black universe watching the bustling going on below. No one knowing, no one caring that you're gone. I don't ever want to be gone without anyone caring."

"That will never happen," Angeline said. "You've done so many good things. You've brought prosperity to so many places and people."

"Still, it makes you think. Life is so fragile. It could be snuffed out just like that. A single person doesn't count for much in the greater scheme of things."

She was not sure what he was driving at.

Maybe it was better that she didn't.

Clifford Radisson held Angeline's hand, drew it to his lips, and waited. She looked up at him and he kissed it, and brought her very close to him until her hand rested on his chest. He left it there and brushed his lips to her hair.

"Come to New York with me," he said.

He traced a line from her chin to her throat. Her neck was bare. The skin was pale, glowed in the dim light of the restaurant and the reflected starlight outside. Its luminous quality reminded him of pearls.

What did she bath in? She smelled so fresh, so clean. The rose scent was fine, subtle, hardly detectable except now that he had her as close as he dared.

"I have something for you," he said, and led her back to the table and sat her down. He knelt on the floor at her feet, careful not to crush his Armani trousers. He took out a velvet box.

"Oh!"

Clifford Radisson jerked up at the exclamation which had not come from Angeline, but from someone hovering above them.

"I'm terribly sorry sir. I didn't see you in the dark. Should I come back later?"

The waiter stood behind him with a trolley laden with plates of food, apologizing profusely. He looked like he wished he could die.

CHAPTER FIFTEEN

Jake sat alone in the house at Berry Point surrounded by books and journals. He paused from paraphrasing a myth he had found in the collections of the anthropologist, Franz Boas. A draft from the open door of the lab fluttered the papers on the table, and he slapped a hand on his notes.

"So that's where you've been hiding. Help me with this." Josie stood at the doorway, laden with a tray of artifacts. Jake rose, took the tray from her and set it down beside his books.

"Have you finished the preliminary assessment?" she asked. "Have you even started it yet?"

"None of you care what I think. What do you need a report for?" He turned away, reread what he had written and added a postscript.

She rearranged the artifacts that had slipped to the lower end of the tray during their transfer from her car to the lab. She flicked the cover of a book. "This has got nothing to do with our site or even the region. What do you think you're going to find in these?"

When he didn't answer, she shook her head. "You aren't thinking about that raven skeleton at Marten Lake again? Jake, your paper won't get published. Even if you could prove that Raven worship came from somewhere in the north, you can't prove that any one person was the inspiration for the myths. Think about what you're saying. That someone, a shaman, born in Alaska was the source of all these stories. Raven tales are not restricted to the Northwest Coast. Are you implying they spread to other parts of the world from here? That's stretching it. The myths were oral, passed on by word of mouth from generation to generation."

She set a plastic bag of cedar matting on the table and picked up a felt marker, wrote the date on the bag, and recapped the pen. "Come outside and help me get the rest of the things."

Jake rested a hand on the roof of Josie's Land Rover as she unlocked and raised the hatch. She slid a tray to him, and he took it out of the car and set it on the ground. A mat woven from cedar bark enveloped the skeleton of a large fish, and was partly buried in a shallow block of soft clay.

"Maybe Angeline is right," he said. "She doesn't know if archaeology is what she wants to do, well maybe I don't either. It's not about learning anymore, it's about making a buck. I was never good at that."

"Which is probably why she likes Clifford Radisson," Josie said.

He frowned but didn't comment. The bones in the cedar bark were stained a sepia colour, and Jake lifted a twig from the gravel to gently prod the skull below the fish's right orbit. It was a whole articulated salmon, head bones overlapping each other, the way they had in life, before the flesh had been eaten away by decay.

"Great isn't it? Like someone was preparing it for storage or a picnic." She slammed the hatch and stood towering over him.

He pulled himself up by the bumper, placed his elbows against the hood of the car, and tugged at a greasy lock of hair. His T-shirt was dirty, his hair unkempt, and his chin unshaven.

Josie said, "You know, Radisson hasn't been on the island since Angeline left?"

"I don't know if I like that."

Dusting her hands off, she shrugged. "I want to photograph this before we take it inside." She snapped a few shots, then looped the camera around her neck. "Did you ever look at Radisson's blueprints?"

The drawing Josie unrolled when they were back inside the house showed a scheme of Radisson's target islands in the Juan de Fuca Strait with causeways and tunnels joining the three islands. Jake thought about Gooseberry Island, the fact that a rock had almost fallen on his head while they were there.

"What's on Gooseberry Island other than people's homes?" he asked.

"I don't know. Gooseberries? That's not our problem."

"If it's got sites on it, it is. Who's doing the archaeological assessment?"

Josie was silent.

"Well?"

"A lot of the property there has been sold. There was nothing important on it. It was surveyed years ago and a couple of small sites were excavated by the University of Victoria. There was never a village there, just temporary fishing encampments."

Radisson was set on building joy rides, high-rise hotels, beach resorts, and shopping malls, and the government was playing into his hands. Jake picked up a black film canister and squeezed it, flipped off the lid, and watched it spin around on the diagram of Gooseberry Island. If only he could get a World Heritage Site designation from UNESCO. *That* would change things.

Josie released the blueprint and it sprang into the shape of a tube. She dumped the lid of the film canister out of it and exposed another plan underneath.

This was Otter Cove under development. Jake remembered the orange flagging tape he had seen there a few weeks ago. Below the cliff where the forest was now, a large pavilion was schematized. A boardwalk stretched along the shore from this main building to several others. It was designed to hold gift shops, theatres and food outlets. Jake flattened his palms on the blueprint, leaning forward. "There was never any settlement at Otter Cove. I thought Radisson was going to stick to an authentic layout of the village."

"You know he can't do that. The park is too big. There has to be room for tourist facilities: washrooms, food services, and retail." She rolled the rest of the blueprints together and looked up. "Now phone Kate. Tom wants your report."

The United Nations organization for education, science and culture was not interested in wet sites, but what if Cedar Island was the burial place of the Raven– a ten thousand year old prehistoric shaman? UNESCO's primary mandate was to protect, preserve, and conserve. A theme park would be exploitation and Jake couldn't think of one example of a World Heritage Site that was exploited in that way. The Egyptian pyramids were safe and could only be viewed as they stood.

There were no roller coaster rides on the pyramids.

CHAPTER SIXTEEN

Clifford Radisson lifted the fine gold chain out of the brown velvet box and held it for Angeline to see. Timing was everything, and that stupid waiter at *La Rose* last week had bungled things badly. What kind of job would they find for him at the unemployment office? McDonald's or Burger King?

She continued to sit, mesmerized, as the light spun and hit the gold sending sparks into the subtle darkness of the *Jazz Bar*. The musicians were taking a break. Angeline liked jazz. She liked the saxophone.

"Does it please you?" he asked.

"Oh, yes."

"Let me put it on you."

Radisson rose from his chair at the small round table and went behind her. Angeline lifted her hair while he fastened the clasp. He let his knuckles linger at the base of her neck where velvet hairs stroked her nape. The chain fell across her chest just above her breasts in a fine sparkling wave against the electric blue silk of her blouse. He went back to his seat.

"You are breathtaking, Angeline."

She smiled and touched the chain.

In the jewelry store it had seemed rather small, insignificant, but Radisson knew diamonds, at this point, would only frighten her. Now that he had it against her skin, its delicate beauty came into its own. It was a very classic piece of jewelry. Angeline had a way of making the most simple of things elegant and refined.

He looked into her lovely eyes. Pleasure certainly, he hadn't expected less, but something else. Did she still have *him* on her mind?

"It's exactly you," Radisson said.

Angeline's lips parted very slightly. She had such a sweet mouth. He could smell her hair, her scent.

"Thank-you," she said.

Her face was twelve inches from his own. He leaned very slightly forward bracing his hands on the table on either side of her. He was very tempted to move his fingers a little bit closer, just that much closer, until he . . .

He sat back. The musicians were returning to the floor.

***

It was Friday night and the library stayed open until nine o'clock. Jake stared at the book in front of him. The odd person was reading, and every now and then someone broke the silence with a tapping at the computer. He had come to the library to look for the myth of the Raven and the Fisherman. Something had preyed on his mind, impelled him to find it, to read it once more. The story told how the lecherous bird had taken on human form and seduced another man's wife.

The fisherman's wife had given a pot of boiled seawater to her husband who drank it. He then vomited into a massive cedar box, tossed a fishing line into it, and landed an enormous halibut. She cooked it, he ate it, and when he left the house, the Raven decided to take her for his own.

Jake got up, slammed the volume shut and placed it on the Return cart as he walked out the door. He got into his Bronco and drove.

It was almost dusk. He headed out of town. He had a strong urge to go back to the cave. But soon it would be dark and he had nothing to see by, not even a flashlight. He thought about what Connie had said at the First Salmon Ceremony. If his interest in the Raven had to do with his search for his own heritage, then he would not find it here. He needed to talk to Elders, people who had known his mother. He needed to go to *Haida Gwaii*, the Queen Charlotte Islands. But that was not the driving force behind his obsession with the Raven. No matter what anyone said about his need to know his parentage, he knew that the Raven, the man who inspired the myths, was real.

His head started to bob. He yawned, snapped himself awake, and eased his foot off the clutch. He had no idea where he was going; he only knew he didn't want to go back to camp.

No one on the road except him. Through this stretch of forest everything was in shadow. He drove for perhaps ten minutes before two points of light appeared out of the murk. Headlights. A long way off. He blinked, trying to clear the fuzziness from his eyes. Dark shapes flickered across the windshield and he stepped on the gas.

Jake widened his eyes, heart pounding. He gripped the wheel, breath tight. A fast moving object was racing toward him.

***

An hour passed or maybe it was only a few minutes. His entire body ached. Jake wasn't sure if he was dead or alive. He lay sprawled out, flat on his back in a ditch. Gingerly, he stretched an arm up. Withdrew it. A shadow stood over him, the moon hovering above. He gasped, coughed, almost choked, and let his head loll back. He wasn't seriously hurt, only battered and bruised. But his head was damp, his palms wet and his feet cold. He coughed, sputtered some more, and the cool night air entered his lungs.

"Are you okay?" a voice asked.

The only response Jake managed was a grunt.

"What on earth did you think you were doing? You could have killed us both." A familiar face looked down at him as Jake wiped his mouth on his sleeve. "Why the hell didn't you have your headlights on?"

Jake squinted. It was still light when he had left the library, but he could have sworn he had turned them on shortly after he drove off. He looked askance at his Bronco and it sat in the dark like a steadfast lump of rock. He turned back, peered into the gloom and waited for Tom Jelna's face to come into focus.

"What are you doing here?" Jake demanded.

"I had a meeting with Josie. I was on my way to the ferry when you came bombing out of the dark."

Jake tested his arms, his legs, his head, and rose. Tom Jelna thrust out a hand and helped him to his feet. "I can't believe you're still alive. You got nine lives or something, Jake? You're always doing crazy things. Things that would kill anybody else."

"What do you mean?"

"I mean, I heard how you and that grad student – the pretty one, fell into a sinkhole at Radisson's cave."

"That is not Radisson's cave."

"Well it may as well be. When he sets his mind on something, it's his."

Jake did not like the tone of Tom Jelna's voice. He was not just referring to the cave.

"Did you damage my truck?" Jake asked.

"Of course not. We barely touched. You braked so hard, you sent the door flying and yourself with it. You should wear your seatbelt if you're going to drive like that. And you should get the door on that rattletrap fixed."

"You'd better get going," Jake said. "The last ferry's at eleven o'clock. You wouldn't want to miss it."

Tom looked down at his watch then out towards the water. Why had the Regional Archaeologist requested a private meeting with Josie? He never came into the field unless he was coddling some government bigwig or some equally self-serving business tycoon. As far as Jake knew neither were on the island at the moment.

CHAPTER SEVENTEEN

From the balcony of the Four Seasons penthouse, downtown Toronto spread out in a bustling metropolis. The air was thick and cloying, filled with smoke and summer humidity. Traffic was relentless, clogged in a bottle-neck caused by an accident further down the street. Horns honked and voices shouted obscenities. It was too late to be trapped in the city.

Clifford Radisson inhaled a shallow breath. The air was thick like New York in the summertime, but not as foul. He placed a hand around Angeline's waist, slid a hand to her hip, and moved around to stand at her left.

"Come, let's get out of the traffic fumes," he suggested, and guided her back indoors.

The raven squawked from its golden cage inside the bedroom.

"Maybe he's hungry," Angeline said.

"No, I'm quite certain he's not."

From the lacquered buffet against the wall, Radisson lifted a fluted glass, noting its elegant shape and the fine, slim stem. This, he thought, was Angeline, exquisite like expensive crystal. He poured a glass of champagne for her from a silver ice bucket, and nestled the bottle back in the ice. He watched her take a sip with her lovely sculptured mouth. She wore lipstick for him. He had never seen her wear lipstick for anyone else. In the reflection of his own glass, he could see her silhouetted, like a fashion model, a socialite, a debutante. The image pleased him. It made him want her. More than he had ever wanted any other woman.

He set his glass down on the buffet and removed his Armani jacket. He had waited long enough. Tonight she would sleep with him.

"Come over here and sit down," he said, gently.

She raised her arms, fending him off with a smile. "That was a lovely dinner, but I really should be going. I have to work tomorrow."

Radisson reached for her hand, took the glass from her, and kissed her fingers. "Don't I treat you well, Angeline?"

"Yes . . . yes, you do."

"Then stay."

She shook her head. Her look pleaded for understanding. He had none. He had heard it all before and was tired of her excuses.

He drew her close to him and smelled her hair. His hand went to her face and he tilted her chin up. She had beautiful, sexy eyes. They were feline, rich in colour, seductive. His finger traced the line of her jaw to her ear, then down her neck. He fingered, possessively, what hung there. It was the gold chain he had given to her.

He caressed her smooth ivory shoulder. He wanted her.

Now.

She inhaled tremulously and closed her eyes. He took that as an invitation and bent decisively over her mouth, kissing her deftly, leaving her irresolute. He nudged the strap of her dress, drawing her breast gently up, and lowered his head. She was soft, yielding to his caress. His lips traced the curve of her breast, then upward, past the gold chain to her throat, her chin, her lips. His thumb moved over the raw silk, found the nipple, felt it harden.

The raven squawked raucously from the bedroom. Angeline jerked her head away, lashes fluttering open. She backed away, pulling her strap up, covering herself. One of her arms was still in his hand. He had very large hands, and her arm didn't amount to even a handful.

"I'm sorry, it's getting late. I really have to go."

Her smile was insulting. Inappropriate. But he stemmed the rising ire. He softened his eyes, made them meek and apologetic, and slackened his hold, remembering this coyness was exactly what attracted him to her.

"I'm sorry, Angeline. Maybe I was mistaken. Last week when I gave you this– " Radisson touched the gold chain. "I thought it meant something. Obviously we weren't thinking the same thing. There were rumours around Cedar Island that you were attracted to me, you know. Since I am extremely attracted to you myself I acted on the assumption."

"People were talking about us?"

"They could hardly help but notice how I feel about you."

She hesitated. "Well . . . they weren't wrong. It's just that– "

Radisson nodded, and let his face fall with just the right amount of pathos.

He went to the leather sofa and sat down. Angeline remained where she was by the buffet. Her hair fluffed out in a shortish cloud around her lovely face. The white raw silk dress she wore was cut well above the knees, sleeveless with straps that crossed alluringly over her shoulder blades. Her legs were well toned, the calves shapely with delicate ankles.

He crossed his legs. He was aroused. More than aroused. And annoyed. How much longer was she going to make him wait? How long had it taken Jake Lalonde to get her into bed?

The raven squawked again from the bedroom. Angeline glanced over at the door, then came and sat down beside him. She waited, and he almost reached out and grabbed her again.

"Before you came to Cedar Island, before we started seeing each other . . ." she began.

Yes, yes, yes, he wanted to say. You dumped the archaeologist. Jake Lalonde didn't know how to handle you, how to pleasure you.

She was close and he could smell her. Not perfume, something else, her hair, and whatever lotion it was she used on her skin. Women like her had a scent, a special scent, that needed no perfume.

"The man is not worthy of you," Radisson said. "He will never be able to give you what you deserve."

Her eyes glistened. He felt like slapping her. He felt like taking her here on the sofa or on the floor just for thinking about Jake Lalonde. What did it take to get him out of her mind? Her naked flesh was accentuated by the whiteness of the dress. He wondered what kind of underwear she wore. No bra, he had already ascertained that. This dress did not allow for any type of bra.

She rose. Her breasts bobbed slightly under the white raw silk.

"Angeline, if you go now, I have no choice but to assume you aren't interested in seeing me any more."

"But I thought . . . Are you giving me some kind of ultimatum?"

He thought about this. About how she would respond to an ultimatum. "No. I'm just saying I have certain expectations after four weeks."

She studied him, then walked slowly toward an end table at the other side of the sofa. She stooped over the phone. It rang, startling her. She stood and stared at it as it continued to ring. He leaned over, and lifted the receiver.

"Hello," he said. He glanced over at Angeline, cupped the receiver and apologized, then carried the telephone into the bedroom.

"I'm sorry, I hope I wasn't disturbing you," the voice at the other end said. "I know you often work late."

Jake was going out of town tomorrow, she told him. Jake would be out of their hair for a little while. They were working overtime to have things ready for his next meeting with the investors. Tuesday, wasn't it? Josie thought he might want to know that. Someone from the Heritage Advisory Board would fly in for the meeting by the way. She just wasn't sure who, yet.

Josie continued to babble on about the progress at the site as he kept one eye on Angeline through the bedroom door.

"I must go," he interrupted. "I'll see you soon."

He slammed the phone down, and started toward the door. Out of the shadows, the raven flapped, lunged at the cage, and he glared at it.

Clifford Radisson lowered his brow, scowled. He turned aside, walked to the bird, and opened the hatch. It recoiled, lunged, nipping him smartly on the hand. He reached in and it screeched. He clenched his jaws, grabbed the bird, and snapped its neck.

Angeline stood in the doorway, mouth open.

"I have to go," she said and hurried to where her purse lay on the buffet.

"Angeline, wait. You weren't going to go without saying good-bye?"

Her back stiffened as his touch slid over the X of fabric crossing her shoulder blades. He pressed, sliding his tongue between her lips.

As he grew more aggressive, tracing the sensuous curve of her spine, she shrank back. He hadn't intended to do that, but now it was too late. Now he had to go all the way. He went to the nape of her neck, pushed hard, and forced her lips back to his. Then his other hand found the hem of her skirt and groped up.

Angeline·flinched, trying to breathe against his powerful grip. He wound the chain around his fingers, twisting it. A thrill rippled from the base of his spine to his neck. A button from his shirt ground into her cheek and she cried out.

He slackened his hold, withdrew his arms, and allowed her to push him away.

She rubbed her throat, then her fingers slid down, and snagged on the gold chain.

"I don't know what came over me," he said quietly.

She did not speak.

"Angeline?"

He watched her, calculating. His eyes went blank, cold.

"No, don't call a taxi. Let me drive you home."

CHAPTER EIGHTEEN

"I'm glad you could come, Jake."

Kate stood beside her tiny desk in her tiny Seattle office, fiddling with the blinds on her tiny window, rattling the cheap silver rings on her fingers. Outside, Jake could see the intersection of First Avenue and Union Street and between the buildings the road sloped down to Elliott Bay.

It was not really an office; it was a cubicle, partitioned off by wheeled walls of burgundy-painted particle board. Only Jelna had a real office, constructed with real walls, and an actual swinging door on hinges that shut. Jelna wasn't here today. He was out doing whatever it was the Regional Archaeologist did when he wasn't in his office pushing paper around or creating more pieces of paper for people like Kate to push around. Kate came back and sat down opposite him and picked up one of those pieces of paper.

"I wasn't sure you would take the time off, but these requisition forms have to be signed. I hope you brought that preliminary assessment with you?"

Jake grunted, and didn't answer. Of course he hadn't brought it with him. He hadn't even written it yet. He took the pen she passed to him and scribbled his signature. "I almost didn't come, but I needed to get away from the site for a few hours. Josie's driving me crazy."

"Well don't go back right away, we can have dinner. I know a wonderful little place, you'll love it . . ." Kate's voice trailed off and Jake recognized the look in her eye. She hadn't met anyone better than him in all this time. He shook his head, stifled a smile.

"For old time's sake?"

"No. I gotta go back. I just wanted to know that you'll hold off on anything until I've made a proper assessment of those petroglyphs."

"Why? You've already seen them. What difference will it make?"

"There's something wrong. Some of the images depict stories from the north."

"So?"

"So, it makes all the difference in the world if those petroglyphs are fakes."

***

Angeline paused as she stood in the lobby of the Royal Ontario Museum, briefly waylaid by a visitor. Something moved in her peripheral vision. On the marble landing at the top of the steps, Clifford Radisson stood by a white stone column, tapping his foot on the floor, straining his eyes, searching. She did a double-take, then directed her sight deliberately at the person speaking to her.

"I'm glad you enjoyed the tour," she said, as the man departed.

Clifford Radisson took two steps forward. Their eyes met, and it was too late to disappear. Her group had deserted her and she stood exposed in the middle of the museum's rotunda, in a short navy skirt, white blouse, and matching jacket.

Someone asked her directions to the dinosaur exhibit, a fat ruddy-faced man. She hoped, to discourage the developer, he would monopolize her attention for awhile. He left, and she looked up, and saw that Radisson was gone. She walked briskly toward the steps.

"May I speak to you, Angeline?"

Out of nowhere, Clifford Radisson had reappeared.

"I have another group in ten minutes," she said, nervously.

"I think we should talk."

Angeline took a deep breath. "I'm not sure we have anything to talk about."

"They don't pay you to do this, do they?" he asked.

She looked down at her feet which were clad in navy and white sandals. He was right. She was a volunteer.

"I think we have things to talk about," he said.

When she didn't reply, he added, "Toronto will suffocate you. You belong on the West Coast. That is the culture you want to interpret for the public, not this."

Radisson had hit on the truth, and knew it; and despite the shock he had given her last night, she still needed a job.

"We're putting on a special show of Northwest Coast Art," she said. "It's going to be downstairs in the Special Exhibits gallery next to the archaeology display."

She avoided his eyes, searched the rotunda, an enormous circular lobby with a high domed ceiling, then turned back to face him. "Unless you plan to stay for the tour, my group is assembling."

A slender grey-haired woman approached them, stuttered in broken English, and gave up. "*Rencontron-nous ici pour le tour guidé?*" she asked Radisson.

Angeline replied for him. "*Oui Madame. Il commençera dans dix minutes.*"

"*En français?*"

She nodded. Radisson smiled. "I had no idea you were versed in the Romance languages."

"I speak French," she said.

"Well, I suppose there isn't any point in my staying for the French version since I don't." He looked her solidly in the eye and asked, "What time do you get off?"

***

Radisson elbowed his way through the clusters of sweating bodies outside the museum and stood on the street in front of his rental sports car.

No, he thought. He felt like a walk. He needed to clear his mind, to compose himself before he came back for Angeline.

He went for a walk up Bloor Street. Toronto was the largest city in Canada, and its multi-cultural mix showed on the bustling streets. There were turbans and saris, blue jeans and business suits, dark skins and light, long eyes, round eyes, almond eyes. A mix of foreign tongues came from passers by– Middle Eastern dialects, Asian, and French. There were some he couldn't recognize. Slavic languages, perhaps; and now and then he caught a word of English.

During the summer, Toronto was a sauna. Traffic stood bumper to bumper all day, and for those who were unlucky enough to be stuck on the subway during an electrical malfunction, they could expect to suffocate in the dark, airless cars. He almost tripped over a homeless man, holding a baseball cap in his lap. The man was Jake Lalonde's age, greasy and olive-skinned. On the ground in front of him was a sign that read: *Plese help! My wife is kidnapped* . . . Radisson didn't bother to read the rest. It was doubtful the man even had a wife.

He arrived at a Native arts gallery. Most of the artwork in the window was Ojibway. He recognized the flat bright colour, outlined in black, characteristic of the Woodland artist, Norval Morrisseau. A silk-screened print sat angled on the floor of the display case, but it was not Ojibway.

A cool rush of recycled air met him as he opened the glass door. The shop owner, a middle-aged man, dressed as though for a funeral, rose from a desk at the far end of the gallery.

"Where is that print from?" Radisson asked, indicating the only non-Ojibway picture in the display.

The man came around, lifted the picture out of the window and placed it in his hands. "It's a beautiful piece, isn't it? It was done by a young Native artist in the Queen Charlotte Islands."

A thrill of recognition coursed down Radisson's spine. He knew the story. The villagers had found the woman with the Raven, and her father had flown into a rage. If the Raven could not marry the old man's daughter, he would have the fisherman's wife. The fisherman had returned, beat up the Raven, and thrown him into a latrine. A pale moon hovered over him. He had only begun to sate himself, had only just penetrated her, when she screamed. This time the fisherman beat him till he couldn't move. He tied him up with twine, bundled him in a boat, rowed as far out to sea as he could – and cast him into the deep.

"This young artist has a promising future ahead of him."

Radisson glanced down at his watch, noticed it was almost five o'clock, and handed the picture to the shop owner. "I must go. Please package that up for me and have it sent to my hotel."

Angeline wove her way down the wide steps of the Royal Ontario

Museum, her jacket draped over her arm. Three months in the sun had bathed her complexion a pale gold, melding into cream. Her blouse was opened at the throat and the tenderness of the skin there was made even more apparent by the crisp white fabric. Clifford Radisson extended a hand to take her arm, but she withdrew it.

"I'm sorry, I can't have dinner with you," she said. "I forgot my father is having guests tonight."

"I'm sure he would understand if you weren't there."

Radisson headed for the subway entrance, to where he thought Angeline was going. She walked past it, forcing him to backtrack. He almost grabbed her arm, almost tripped over a discarded paper cup before he caught up to her.

"Can I give you a lift?" Radisson asked. "My car is just over there."

Angeline declined, and further along the sidewalk, around the corner at a parking lot, she stopped at a silver green Saab.

"I want to apologize for last night," he said.

The lot was half-empty, surrounded by tall oak trees. Her car was parked in the shade, but the sun was moving slowly to the west, and while she stood partially shaded, his head baked.

"Please, let me make it up to you. Let me take you out for dinner. A drink at least. Are you still interested in working for me?"

A breeze caught her blouse at the throat, and he noticed a red mark where the chain had scratched the side of her neck.

She touched the spot with her hand, and he tried not to stare at it.

"If you change your mind, come to my suite Thursday evening after you're finished at the museum. I have no offices in Toronto. I conduct my business there. I still want you to head up my theme park. I have a very important project for you. I want you in charge of the petroglyphs. In fact, I want you to undertake exclusive interpretation of the caves."

Angeline fished the keys from her purse and unlocked the car door. She got in and switched on the engine.

Radisson started to walk to his own vehicle, but the engine to Angeline's car suddenly died. She poked her head out of the window, but before she could say anything, he smiled.

"I have a business trip over the next two days, but I'll be back on Thursday. I'll have a contract ready for you then," he said.

CHAPTER NINETEEN

Angeline touched the red chaffing on her throat, one hand on the wheel. At Rosedale she turned left onto Glen Road and made her way to the four story white-pillared house at the end of the drive. She walked through the front door and dropped the car keys on the antique Chinese bureau in the foyer. Voices came from the kitchen, her dad's baritone, unmistakable.

"I know it's not my place to say, Mr. Lisbon," Teresa, the housekeeper said. "But I've been with this family a very long time. Angeline is only inexperienced."

"Is that *my* fault?" her father thundered. "My wife never hesitates to point the finger at me. Did I give her such a lousy life? Look at this house, her car, her clubs, her clothes, her jewelry. What else does she want that I haven't given her? And now she's taken an apartment hotel that I'm paying for. She won't even come back here to see her own daughter if I'm here. Do you know what she said when she left? That I stole her freedom. Her freedom! What freedom? None of us are free. Does she think I can do whatever I damn well please?"

Poor Teresa couldn't get a word in edgewise. "I want my daughter doing something productive, she's too idealistic, look at her interests. Archaeology, sketching, she spends half her time at the zoo watching the animals. And this volunteer job at the museum. Volunteer work is fine for a woman of leisure, but she doesn't have a husband to look after her. And she won't come and work at my office. Doesn't she know she needs a job?"

Jason Lisbon didn't wait for an answer. "Of course she doesn't. She has me."

Angeline turned toward the staircase, but her father's voice continued to assault her ears. "In order to survive in the world you do what has to be done even if it's unpleasant. My daughter isn't capable of that. She can't make a single decision on her own."

Upstairs in her room, Angeline went to the desk she used to work at as an undergraduate at the University of Toronto. How would he know? Where was he when she was growing up? Most of her memories were of Teresa in the nursery, picking her up after school, taking her to the doctor, the dentist, ballet lessons, French lessons, art classes. Mom was busy with her charities, her benefits, her dinner parties. And *he* was doing whatever it was lawyers did. Even when she left for graduate school, it was Teresa who drove her to the airport.

They had no idea how lonely she was. At fifteen, she had a steady boyfriend, but she wasn't content with that. She wanted attention from *all* the boys. She thrived on seeing their expressions lift simply at the sight of her. *That*, she had thought at the time, was power. She still believed it. It got her adoration, attention. Love. She had used it on Clifford Radisson, thinking it could get her a job. It could still get her a job.

Footsteps sounded on the stairs. A rap came at her door. Angeline's father entered, and stood in the doorway.

"Are you coming down to join us?" he asked.

"I'm not very hungry, Dad."

"I was thinking of inviting Clifford Radisson to dinner one of these nights. He's building an extension at the zoo, but I suppose you know that? I handled a case for the zoo several years ago . . ."

His gaze swept her room, took in the satin walnut dresser, the armoire, and matching desk; her opulently quilted bed and her closet bursting with designer fashions. The window looked out onto the rose gardens, and she got up from the desk and went to move the heavy silk drapes. They matched her duvet, which matched her pillows, which matched the coral upholstered chair in front of her dresser. The roses were in full bloom, huge pink and yellow things, and white.

"I hope you aren't having second thoughts about coming home, Angel. Archaeology can't give you this."

But Clifford Radisson could. And Clifford Radisson had killed the raven with his bare hands.

"You could do worse than marry a billionaire," he said.

Angeline thought about her mother and what she had sacrificed to advance her father's ambition. He sighed, came over and placed his hands lightly on her shoulders. "Don't worry sweetheart. You're doing everything right. I'm sure he'll start to recognize your abilities once he gets to know you better."

***

Jake got back from Seattle around dinner time. He wasn't hungry. So he drove off the ferry and went directly into town. He parked kitty-corner to the museum and got out of his truck. He eyed it meticulously. He hadn't checked it thoroughly for damage that night he'd had that near miss with Tom Jelna. He still couldn't believe he had been driving around in pitch blackness without his headlights on. But when Tom had chided him for doing so he had looked, and lo and behold, the lamps were out cold. He had no idea how long he'd been unconscious, but his battery wasn't dead so his lamps shouldn't have gone out. He still had a bump on the back of the head where he'd landed in the ditch. Other than that, everything else seemed intact.

The museum was still open, but just as Jake walked in the door, the curator warned him she was closing in five minutes. Five minutes was all it would take he told her. He went up to the case housing the masks and searched the display. He scanned up and down, back and forth. Where was it? *Sisiutl* was there, *Dzunkwa* stared back, but where was the Raven?

He turned to the curator who had come up behind him and pointed into the case. A large space was empty on the wall where two masks had once hung.

"Where's the Raven mask?" Jake asked. "Didn't Joe Redleaf return it after the First Salmon Ceremony?"

"The owner wished to borrow it," the curator said.

"What for?"

"I'm afraid I don't know. Mr. Radisson owns it, so I didn't ask."

***

Angeline didn't know if she still wanted to work for Clifford

Radisson. She didn't know if she could trust him. She picked up her phone and pressed the numbers to the lab.

The petroglyphs represented too many diverse styles and legends. Some were common to all of the peoples of the Northwest Coast, but some were specific to certain tribes. The Raven abducting the Salmon Chief's daughter was a Bella Coola myth, and the Samish did not hunt whales.

Something Radisson had said puzzled her. Something about interpreting the cave. Angeline listened to the phone ring and ring. Finally, someone answered. Yes, Josie said, Jake was here. He was just pulling into the drive. Was anything wrong? Was she coming back? Josie didn't know whether to take her off the payroll. By the way, did she intend to write the faunal section of the report? Josie did not sound angry, merely efficient and businesslike. That was the relationship she had always had with Josie. Angeline told Josie she didn't know. She told her she had to speak to Jake. Please.

"All right. Just a minute." Josie put down the phone.

"Angeline?" Josie's voice sent a tremor through to her heart. "I'm sorry, I was wrong. It was only Steve and Carly. Jake should be back any minute though. He went to see Kate in Seattle so unless he decided to stay with her he shouldn't be too late. Can I have him call you back?"

CHAPTER TWENTY

"We need you at the site now." Josie could be annoyingly persistent. "We need your truck to help bring back the gear." She exhaled. "Okay fine. Just give me your keys. Carly will drive it."

Jake dug in his pocket for the keys to his Bronco, then jammed the receiver against his ear and covered the other one with his hand to block out Josie's voice. The phone trilled at the other end, and someone answered. "Lisbon residence."

That was the kind of household Angeline lived in.

"Hello?" the housekeeper asked, when he didn't speak.

Jake snapped himself awake, and asked for Angeline. The housekeeper said she wasn't home. "Can I take a message?" she asked.

Yes. No. He didn't really have a message. "Tell her it's Jake Lalonde, I'm returning her call." Angeline had called him two days ago and only this morning had Josie remembered. Now she would think he was negligent, that he didn't care. Damn Josie anyway. "Do you know when she'll be back?" he asked.

"I'm sorry, no. She didn't say where she was going or when she'd be returning."

The voice sounded a little concerned. Jake looked at his watch. It was six o'clock his time, nine o'clock hers. "Thanks, I'll call back."

He went to the door, then remembered Josie had taken his truck. He stared out at the abandoned shell midden, then returned to the lab. On the table was his drawing of the Fisherman and the Raven. He studied it, then straightened his back and looked around for a place to store it. The phone rang. Jake laid down the sketch, and lifted the receiver, but it wasn't Angeline. It was Jelna.

"It's quitting time," Jake said. "Call back in the morning."

Tom was insistent. "How am I supposed to get hold of you people except after hours at the lab if you refuse to use a cell phone at the wet site?"

"What do you want?" Jake demanded. He did not feel like talking shop with the Regional Archaeologist. He wanted to hear from Angeline.

"Let me speak to Josie."

"Josie isn't back yet. Tell me what it is. I'll tell her."

"It's not that sort of thing," Tom said. "I have to speak to her myself."

Why? Jake was the senior investigator on this project. He hung up. He sat down and stared at the drawing again. Carly had thought it peculiar that he had drawn this picture from out of the blue. He hadn't really. No one could draw things they had never seen before. Especially someone with no particular artistic skills.

***

When the jet touched down at Pearson International Airport, Clifford Radisson sat for several minutes working on a spreadsheet. On a built-in computer on his watch, he recalculated some figures for the development of Otter Cove, saved the new estimates, then looked through the window to the tarmac. He removed his briefcase from the seat beside him and gestured his porter to open the door, and debarked.

Dusk was impending. A rosy glow hovered on the skyline made vibrant by the city's summer pollution. He strolled down the gangway and gave instructions for the porter to collect his luggage and to meet him at his car where he would dismiss him.

With barely a nod from the officials, Radisson passed through customs; he had arranged for clearance prior to his departure so that he would not be delayed with useless questions. Now he walked through the lobby and glanced quickly at a monitor to synchronize his watch to Eastern time. He was not as late as he feared, and hoped Angeline would wait.

He had given Angeline what she'd asked for. The cost of working for him. The cost of freedom, power, position. Everything had its price and it was time she learned what it was. Everyone had a boss, a superior, except him. For the first time in my memory, a woman had defied him, affected his behaviour, distracted him from the corporate side of his life. He had acted too fast. He had frightened her. But she had screwed up his smooth sophisticated social veneer. She had made him angry.

Clifford Radisson stepped through the sliding doors, took the contract his lawyers had drawn up out of his pocket, and opened it slowly. A thoroughly rehearsed image of Angeline sent a charge through his body like an orgasm. He pictured her, as he often did, slender, curvaceous, elegant. She thought that made her untouchable. She thought that gave her power. But it was the one thing that would ultimately be her downfall. He knew things about her she had never told him. She didn't have to tell him because he had other means to find out. He knew she had only slept with one man other than Jake Lalonde, and that was too long ago to matter. Her history did not affect his current interest in her– except as it made her careless. He knew this by the look in her eyes and the possessiveness he had seen in Jake's. He would not allow it. She must come to him. And of her own volition.

***

"Come in. Mr Radisson was delayed in Seattle, but he's expecting you. He called from his private jet to tell you to wait. He won't be long. They were twenty minutes from landing when he phoned."

The air-conditioning hummed against the sweltering summer heat. Sam Smythe appraised her up and down the way he had at their first encounter on the beach, and Angeline gathered her arms around her chest. She was wearing the white raw silk again, but if she had known the contractor would be answering the door she would not have chosen to wear it. Fortunately, she also wore a matching jacket which should keep his eyes from where they weren't wanted. She stepped into the room, despite a warning prickle down her spine, and convinced herself of Radisson's imminent arrival.

"Sit down, take off your jacket, and make yourself comfortable. I'll get us a drink."

"No thanks," Angeline said. "I don't want a drink."

Sam Smythe kicked the door shut with the heel of his shoe and nodded her over to the black leather sofa, then went to the buffet.

"Mr. Radisson might be awhile, depending on the traffic. You may as well relax, and have something. What do you like? Scotch? Cognac? Or maybe a liqueur is more your style." He stooped, took several bottles from a cabinet, and set them on top of the black lacquered buffet.

"I really don't want anything," Angeline insisted.

Above Smythe's head hung a framed print. As he leaned forward to sort the bottles, he bumped the buffet which bumped the wall, jarring the picture. His expression, even from her three-quarter view, was unpleasant, and to divert him from insisting she have a drink, she inquired if the print was new.

His eyes rolled up to the wall and he shrugged. "Guess so. You like it?"

Not particularly, she thought. It was an odd configuration of figures. It seemed familiar.

Smythe smiled, studied the picture a few seconds more, and said, "I never paid much attention to it when Mr. Radisson got it, but now that I have, it kinda grows on you." His tongue flickered out, moistened his lips, and he crouched down. "Sure you don't want a drink? Something long and cool, maybe. It's hot outside, ain't it?" He turned from the cupboard, and a leer curled his mouth. "A Harvey Wall*banger* or Tom Collins or something like that. Let's see what we got. How's about a *screw* . . . driver? There's some fresh orange juice in the fridge, and some vodka."

Angeline got up from where she had been sitting on the edge of the sofa. "Tell Mr. Radisson I'm sorry I missed him, tell him I'll give him a call tomorrow."

Before she could reach the door, Smythe dropped the bottle in his hand, lunged past, and stood like a boulder with his legs apart and his arms crossed, blocking her retreat. A tattoo in black and red flexed on his upper arm. She had noticed it once on Cedar Island, but had not identified what it was. Now she saw it was a pair of eagles.

"Mr. Radisson specifically asked me to keep you here. He wants to see you tonight. He promised he would be here– And he *will*. You wouldn't want to disappoint Mr. Radisson, now would you?"

"It's getting late. I think I should come back another time when it's more convenient for him."

Smythe's hand went to the deadbolt on the door and slammed it down. "It's convenient now."

She stared. "Unlock the door. Please. I have to go."

When he didn't, she stepped around him, and positioned her fingers on the bolt. His hand came onto her shoulder and stopped her in mid motion. "Sweetheart, no one disappoints Mr. Radisson. If you leave now, he'll blame me."

She swallowed, turned her head slightly aside. "He'll understand. It wasn't anything that can't wait anyway. Please remove your hand."

His fingers traced her shoulder to her back, then glided deftly around her jacket to her waist. She swung sharply around, but he gripped her wrists with both hands and sneered. He smelled like he had already had a drink or three too many.

A brisk knock came from behind them. Angeline started, and to her horror, landed right in Sam Smythe's arms. He grinned, held her, and she felt a hardness stir in his crotch. She struggled, cried out, and the knocking ceased.

"Be quiet," he said. "Mr. Radisson *will* be here. He never goes back on his word. Even if he has to land his plane on top of this building, he'll be here."

She was roughly flung from him, and she fell on her side, hitting the sofa. The knocking at the door began again. Smythe opened it.

"Oh, excuse me sir." The chambermaid paused. Angeline struggled to her feet and felt her ankle give out on her; the same one she'd hurt before. "I've brought Mr. Radisson's linen. He always wants fresh towels in the evening."

Smythe extended his arms to receive the stack of neatly folded fluffy white terry, then turned to close the door.

"Mr. Radisson likes for me to make him a . . . a nightcap before he goes to bed." The maid had one hand on the door and peered into the room to the buffet where the developer kept his cognac. Angeline sprinted toward her.

"Don't worry about the drinks. We'll help ourselves." Smythe shut the door and slammed down the bolt. "Don't try that again," he warned Angeline.

There was silence on the other side of the door.

At the buffet, he poured himself a hefty scotch, swallowed three-quarters of it, then refilled the glass. "Sure you won't have anything? We serve only the very best."

"Does Mr. Radisson know you help yourself to his expensive liquor?" Angeline asked.

"Oh fuck you princess." Smythe's leer was ugly. "Get off your prissy high horse. Don't you know *that's* exactly what he wants to do to *you*?"

She darted for the door, but Smythe dove after her, almost fumbling his glass.

"I told you not to do that again." He grabbed her by the arm and spun her to face him. "You think you are really something don't you? Too good for someone like me, eh? You in your white satin dresses, and your perfect hair and skin. Look at you. Are you even real?"

His thumb jabbed under the lapel of her jacket and yanked it down.

"Such a fine pretty girl, aren't you? What are you made out of sweetheart? Ivory? *Ice*?" He hurled her from him, swallowed the rest of his drink in one gulp, and advanced on her.

Angeline lay sprawled on the floor, her shoulder exposed where her jacket was torn. Suddenly a crash from the buffet arrested Smythe in mid lunge. The scotch bottle had splintered into two sections where the picture had fallen off the wall onto it, and dark amber fluid spilled over the lacquered surface onto the plush cream carpet.

Smythe straightened from where he hovered over her, and rushed to rescue the print. As he wiped it dry with one of the towels the maid had brought, Angeline lurched to her feet.

"Where do you think you're going?" Smythe asked, abandoning the picture.

She sprang for the door, but too late. The contractor beat her to it.

***

Angeline stumbled backwards into the room as Smythe's hand shot out. "I *said*, he wants you to wait. Would you rather wait in there?" Smythe's head jerked toward the bedroom. "I could tie you to the bed. That's where you're going to end up anyhow."

Angeline gave no reply. She let him drag her to the sofa and sling her down on it.

"Now, about that drink." He went back to the buffet and righted the scotch bottle. The neck had cracked off and he waved it in the air. Bits of glass were shattered over the top of the lacquered surface, but the base of the bottle still held a few ounces of liquor so he poured that into the glass he was drinking from before, and brought it to her.

"No thank-you," she said, trying to sound firm.

"When your host offers you a drink, you take it. Isn't that what you prissy girls do?"

"It might have glass in it," she said, her voice a dry whisper.

"It might . . ." he drawled, menacingly. "Orrr . . . it might not."

She didn't take it. It was deep gold. Clear. And she could see no slivers in it. But glass wouldn't show up in liquid. And even if there was none, she would never drink out of anything he had touched.

"Drink," Smythe said.

"I don't want any." She tried to move, but his hand struck out and blocked her in the chest. "Why?" she whimpered.

"Because I want you to."

The man was drunk. He did not know what he was doing. If she did not play along, showed no fear, maybe he would leave her alone.

"Don't try it," he said, as she braced a hand on the cushion to push herself up.

Angeline could smell his foul breath. His tongue slipped out and touched his lower lip, leaving a wet glistening shine. His mouth was red, his eyes black, his expression crude, spiteful.

"Let's play a game," he said, the lines deepening on his face. He looked long into her eyes, and rested one hand on her knee. "For every sip you take, I don't rip off a piece of your clothing."

She flinched. His fingers gouged in. He sat closer to her, and moved his hand slowly up her thigh. He handed her the glass. She stared at him and he stared back, waiting.

His free hand whipped down her shin, grabbed her foot, and thrust it up. She winced, fell backwards against the sofa, the scotch splashing wildly as he tore off her shoe.

"That's one," he said, tossing the white pump over his shoulder to the carpet.

He leaned into her face, and she turned her head aside, repulsed. His lips curled in a deep smirk, then his head came forward and he licked her cheek where the liquor trickled to her chin.

Angeline pushed Smythe away, pitched the glass at his head. With only one shoe on, she ran and tripped. He seized her from the rear. The act collapsed them both to the floor.

His hands were rough, gripping like vices, tearing at her clothes. He rose slightly to his knees, and grabbed at her jacket. She rolled back her shoulders, let the fabric peel away from her body, leaving her arms free; then before he knew what was happening, she kicked off her other shoe, crawled out from between his legs and blind to any pain, dashed across the room.

She didn't look back. Not once. She rammed back the deadbolt and yanked opened the door.

CHAPTER TWENTY-ONE

If Angeline thought about what had happened she would die. She could not tell Dad. Or Teresa. This kind of secret Teresa couldn't keep. Somehow, it was her own fault. Just dress, and get to the museum. The Northwest Coast exhibit opened in two days and they were counting on her. A knock on the door, and her father walked in without waiting for an answer. She almost screamed at him. Didn't he know she was getting dressed?

"Good morning, Angel."

Trembling, Angeline finished buttoning her blouse, and bent down to take a pair of sandals out of her closet. She rubbed her ankle. Thankfully, last night's ordeal had left only a slight bruise. There was no swelling.

"Have you had a chance to see your mother much, since you got back?" her father asked.

She nodded, and clipped the straps over her feet, one at a time.

"I'm sorry she refuses to stay in this house while you're here. She's afraid we'll get into an argument in front of you. I want you to know I'm trying to work things out, I've been trying for a very long time. I think if she'll just talk to me, we can fix this."

Mom's version of their marriage made Angeline desperately sad. Dad was the best lawyer in the country with a reputation extending even into the United States. He knew how to talk, but *not* how to listen.

"I want you to know how pleased I am that you're seeing Clifford Radisson," he said. "We spoke this morning, he says you have a date tonight, so I took the liberty of inviting him to dinner this weekend."

"Without talking to me first?"

"I talked to you; you didn't object. Besides I thought you liked him."

Angeline yanked angrily at her hair with a brush. Her father reached out and snatched the brush away. "You're shaking like a leaf. I know what's happening between me and your mother is upsetting you, but you can't resolve anything if you don't talk."

"I talk," she snapped. "When there's someone to listen to me."

"I've done nothing but listen to you for the past twenty-four years," he said. "Didn't I have this room custom-designed to your specifications, didn't I plant that rose garden outside your window, didn't I give you your own phone, your own car, your horse? People make mistakes, Angeline, and God knows I've made plenty. You don't know this, but when I bought you that horse when you were nine years old I sold my Ferrari in order to have it stabled properly. I wanted you to have the best. All I'm asking in return is that you listen to me. Clifford Radisson can give you the life you deserve."

***

Angeline was in the Special Exhibits gallery, un-boxing some carvings and prints for the display when Clifford Radisson came to see her at the museum. She did not want to discuss what had happened in his hotel suite.

While driving her home last night, he had apologized profusely. "I feel like it's my fault," he had said. "It wouldn't have happened if I wasn't late. I had no idea I'd left you with a scoundrel."

Radisson had been so incensed that Angeline had found herself having to calm *him* down. Outraged by the conduct of his contractor, he had sworn to support her in whatever action she chose to take.

Angeline did not know what action she should take and so, took none. The whole thing was like a nightmare. Even Radisson's sudden appearance outside the door had frightened her out of her wits. She should not have gone there.

Clifford Radisson stood at the far wall, examining a large Haida print. It was silk-screened in black, red, and white, depicting a two-headed eagle. Just like his company's logo. Just like his contractor's tattoo. His eyes moved to the right, and she followed them. Another print hung beside the first, and the title read: *Eagle with Salmon*. Inside the fish's body was a human figure, a reminder that salmon were people in the form of fish. She had not taken much notice of it before, but now as she looked at the eagle with its claws hooked into the salmon woman, her chest ran cold.

"They work you like a slave, Angeline. When my plans are firm, you'll have a real job."

Angeline swallowed. Smiled. She wished Radisson had given her another few days to compose herself.

"Let me help you with that," he said.

From a cardboard box she pulled out a large wooden pestle exquisitely carved in the image of an upright wolf baying at the moon.

"It's on loan from the Rasmussen Collection from the Portland Art Museum," she explained. Her fingers fussed, removing bits of tissue paper to mask their nervousness.

"May I?" he asked.

She hesitated. "You'd better put these on first."

He willingly donned the white cotton gloves she handed to him and lifted the statue to the light.

"It says here the piece is a wooden pestle that was used for mashing fish eggs." Her voice came surprisingly light. "It's so beautiful; I can't imagine it had a domestic function."

She could not concentrate. She should have taken the day off, should at least have postponed their dinner engagement to another evening. But Dad's words kept ringing in her head. Her distraction did not go unnoticed, and Radisson gently took her hand and led her to a table banked with chairs.

"Sit down," he said, quietly.

She did and realized her breathing had grown extremely shallow.

"What exactly happened, Angeline? Why don't you want me to call the police?"

She could not answer that. "I don't know what I would say to them."

"Just tell them the truth."

She shook her head.

"All right, have it your way then. But I hope you realize how sorry I am that I trusted that brute to take care of you in my absence."

She rose. She had to finish unpacking these things. He followed her to another open carton and looked down. He had not removed the gloves, and carefully picked up an object from its nest of acid-free tissue. The frog bowl was carved from yellow cedar and its ovoid eyes and decorative curvilinear shapes were painted green.

Angeline's supervisor walked in. "I can't leave until I've finished here," Angeline apologized to Radisson.

"Don't be silly." Mrs. Korenski chuckled. "Go on, both of you; and have a good time."

All through dinner Angeline couldn't bring herself to agree to Radisson's terms. He had brought the contract with him, wanted her to commit to him there and now, but she wanted to read it first in broad daylight, to examine the small print.

He was impatient. "Isn't this what you've always wanted?" he asked. "A job in your own field. Archaeology, Angeline. Think how proud your father will be. How many people, even with PhDs, can say that?"

She didn't answer, and when she looked at him, she noticed something she had never noticed before. His expression almost exactly resembled that of a bird of prey.

"Why do you hesitate?" he asked. "If you're worried about that rogue, Smythe. Don't. He won't be troubling you again."

Angeline's hand shook as she lifted the pen. She paused over the black line beneath the last paragraph. He had stopped something unspeakable from happening. He was ready to give her a wonderful job. What was the matter with her?

It was dusk when they finished dinner. He insisted on going for a drive along the lake. Around a quarter to twelve she asked him to take her home. Her father would be waiting up. He drove to his hotel and under the yellow lamplight, she declined going up to his suite for a drink.

"I would like to go home," she said.

He looked coolly at her. "You have to put this incident behind you. The Sam Smythes of the world are the kind of people you will have to learn to deal with. If you aren't up to it, *get* up to it. If you want to be part of my world, then you have to lose the little girl act."

Angeline gaped at him.

"I think you *can* do it, Angeline. I know you *want* to. All you have to do is decide. So come up to my suite, sign the contract, and we'll celebrate. There are great things waiting for you."

How dare he? *How dare he?* She opened the car door.

He taunted her as she stepped onto the curb. "I *want* you, Angeline. You might as well give up."

She stopped on the pavement and spun around. Radisson left the car with the valet and walked the few paces to the Four Seasons Hotel. He stood perfectly still, turned his head, and asked, "You know, you never did tell me what you saw in the cave. What were the petroglyphs like?"

She didn't answer.

"I see. It's like that, is it?"

He smiled. "I always get what I want, Angeline."

Then he turned away, swung the glass doors to the hotel lobby shut, stranding her in the middle of downtown Toronto in the middle of the night.

CHAPTER TWENTY-TWO

Angeline shuddered as the words echoed in her ear. Had she made a mistake by offending Clifford Radisson? She studied the map she had received at the admission gate of the Metro Toronto Zoo this morning. It was the one place where she wouldn't run into him.

At the North American section, she stood in front of a large wire enclosure where eagles peered down from artificial eyries on top of a concrete cliff. A white panel hung from where she gripped the steel mesh. Future Site of the P. Clifford Radisson Rehabilitation Centre for Predatory Birds, it read.

A few dead branches mimicked a live tree and below them, small mice carcasses littered the floor. The air reeked of guano, and something ran by inside the cage. One of the birds swooped down. Blood spurted, darkening white fur, and the fleshy feet of a rat pummelled the air. Another eagle lunged, but in defence of its kill, the first slung back, riding its tail, hissing like a snake, and struck with hooked claws. The would-be thief backed off and the first eagle tore into the rat.

Someone came up behind her and placed a hand next to hers. Her eyes travelled up his arm to the sleeve of a black T-shirt and khaki vest.

"Hot enough to fry eels out here, eh?"

Angeline glanced from the birds tattooed near the speaker's shoulder to the face of Sam Smythe.

"You *do* like eagles, don't you?" he asked, and gave her a droll wink. His lips turned up, simpering. "It was nice the other night, just you and me. I *liked* it."

He couldn't hurt her in broad daylight. There were people everywhere. Couples, families, zoo officials. She scanned the area to confirm this, then saw a discarded McDonald's wrapper lying on the ground.

"The only food service here," he said. "It'll be the same at RAVENSWORLD."

Angeline did not reply.

She hurried out of the simulated Pacific rainforest. She felt stupid for being so afraid of him, but that didn't stop her from speed-walking, then running down the long winding path until she arrived at the zebras, where she hustled on past to the rhinoceroses and the gazelles and so to the heart of the African exhibits.

In front of her was a large concrete enclosure. No vegetation grew here, and her view was perfectly clear. Her tormentor was nowhere to be seen. How did he know she would be here? She stopped to catch her breath, to ease her lungs and her legs; then she peered down over the cement wall onto a low grassy hill, surrounded by a deep moat, into the lair of the lions. Radisson was building an extension to the eagle aviary–

A sound came from behind, and she spun around. Before she could act, a pair of hands shot out and lifted her onto the concrete wall. Her knees shook, they were shoved apart, and Sam Smythe jammed his hips between them.

"Now I have your un-*divided* attention," he said with a smirk.

Angeline clutched the cement ledge, reeling from his smell. A snarl from below reminded her what was in the pit.

"I don't think they've been fed yet," he said lazily, and craned over her shoulder, forcing her to lean back too.

The odour of tobacco was stiff in his hair, and the brush of his coarse whiskers on her cheek made her want to retch. "Lions are fascinating. Like sharks. They go for days without eating, then some prey comes along, and *wham* – they go into a frenzy."

She did not speak. Couldn't.

"I got something for you to look at," he said.

Her head swam, he was too close, and whatever it was he was reaching for in his pocket, she did not want to see it.

A zoo official on the far side of the enclosure waved her arms, yelling at them. "Hey sir! You, sir! Get her off that wall!"

Angeline dropped to the ground, hands out-thrust, knocking the startled contractor backward, and ran. The official sped off in her jeep.

Headlong down the winding path, Angeline raced until she came to a concrete building with a double glass door. She ducked in and stood gasping, waiting for her lungs to catch up. When her eyes adjusted to the dim interior, she followed a man and his sons up a set of steps to a platform overlooking a large arena which plunged twenty feet and domed at the ceiling. Behind a wall of glass, a tree and a metal jungle gym rose from the ground. Eight orangutans were there – a large male, four females, two juveniles and an infant.

She sat down on a bench facing the glass, and waited. A few minutes to catch her breath, then she'd make her way out of the zoo back to the parking lot and escape. But what if Sam Smythe had a car?

She scanned the stairs, the windows, every post and partition where someone could hide, but the contractor did not reappear.

A screaming came from the orangutans, and the father sitting beside Angeline got up and went to look. Two females were tugging at an infant, one hanging onto either arm. The male orangutan rose from the tree, hung by one arm, then swinging slightly, dropped to the ground. He roared, bared his fangs to the squabbling pair, and swatted them each in turn; then the aggressor released her grip and went skulking under the tree while the mother cradled her infant and climbed to a concrete ledge.

"That was quick. If only humans could solve their problems so easily," the man said.

He winked at Angeline, signalled his sons it was time to leave, and Angeline smiled. She sat back on the bench and looked around. She was calmer now, calm enough to drive home.

She clutched her purse to her side and started toward the stairs. Sam Smythe appeared on the landing holding a styrofoam cup. The gallery was deserted. Angeline stepped to one side and he sidestepped to block her. She stepped to the other side and he stepped back.

"I know you like these little love games," he said. "But I'm getting a wee bit tired of it. Stand still and listen."

He brought the cup to his lips, but the coffee was too hot to drink.

"Do me a favour, honey. Accept Mr. Radisson's proposal. It's the best job you'll ever have and if you play it right, you won't even have to work much at all."

Angeline pushed past, vaulted down the steps with Smythe at her heels. At the foot of the stairs, he seized her arm and she yanked it back.

"Relax sweetheart. I have no intention of makin' love with you here."

He backed her toward a bench near the gibbons, and ordered her to sit. Then he put his styrofoam cup beside her though he didn't sit himself, and stood hovering, his sharp black eyes studying her. He removed a piece of paper from the breast pocket of his khaki vest and placed it on her lap.

"When Mr. Radisson is happy, I'm happy," he said.

Angeline picked up the sheet of paper and unfolded it. She recognized the contract.

"Mr. Radisson and me had a bit of a misunderstanding. He said he wouldn't be needing my services anymore, but I beg to differ. Sign the contract. Then we can all go back to being happy."

"You deserve to be fired!" she spat.

Smythe lifted the paper from where she had hurled it, and fingered it impatiently. His other hand came toward her, and Angeline slunk aside. The cup was frothing from a small slit in the top of the lid, and she almost knocked it over. He picked it up, blew on it, and watched her.

"Coffee?" he asked, thrusting it out.

"No, thank-you."

"Damn, that's hot," he said as he took a sip. "Why the hell do they have to make coffee so hot you can't even drink it? No wonder people sue restaurants for serving drinks too hot."

He held the cup in front of him, tipping it slightly. He stooped, jostled it deliberately in her face as he waved the contract with the other. The steam singed her chin and she recoiled. "I have a pen. You sign this, and you'll be set for the rest of your life."

Angeline flinched, startling him, and a splash of boiling liquid geysered over the lip of the cup almost landing on her lap. Sam Smythe stood up, teetering the cup dangerously. His eyes were piercing, black. He looked down at the plastic lid and removed it.

The contract had been prepared by an eminent law firm, a rival of her father's. It reminded her of what Dad had said. *Clifford Radisson can give you the life you deserve.*

She did *not* deserve this! Her fist shot up, splashing coffee into Sam Smythe's face. Then she bolted, startling the gibbons who set off a chain reaction of primate screams that sent the keepers rushing from all directions to see what was the matter; and sprinted through the glass doors, and didn't stop running until she exited the admission gates and found herself among rows and rows of multi-coloured vehicles.

Cautiously, Angeline searched for the silver green hood of her Saab.

She paced up one aisle, then down another. Why couldn't she remember where she'd parked? On Cedar Island the contractor had driven a bright orange truck with a black logo painted on the doors.

Was that what he had driven here? She scanned the horizon for anything orange, then lurched.

"It's not so easy to lose me, sweetheart." The voice had come from her right, and as her heart did a triple flip, Smythe emerged from between two cars.

Frantically, Angeline glanced around for help. She wanted to scream.

Smythe fished a package of cigarettes out of his breast pocket, took one out and lit it. He gazed at her, puffing smoke rings into the air.

"You forget," he called out, as she walked away fast. "I have something you need."

She turned around and he leaned into a car and winced as his sneer creased his burned cheek. He was ten paces away from where she stood. He caressed her silver green Saab with one hand, while resting the other arm on its roof. "You can't drive without these."

Angeline's keys dangled from Smythe's upraised hand, then slid noisily to the ground. Angeline shot forward to retrieve them, but Smythe got there first. Now his cigarette was burning an inch from her face. "You have such nice baby skin. It would be a shame to see it end up like mine."

Angeline rose, stumbled backwards. The air in her lungs looped short and fast. Still no people. No help. She could run, if she ran . . . His hand moved to his chest–

Smythe pulled her purse out from beneath his vest and dangled it in her eyes. "You were in such a hurry to leave those overgrown monkeys, you forgot this."

A family came sauntering over the asphalt looking for their vehicle. The father from the orangutan's enclosure beamed at her.

"That man is trying to steal my car!" she cried.

CHAPTER TWENTY-THREE

"Angeline! Over here!" Jake waved his hand and she came toward him, dragging her suitcase by its wheels, a flight bag in one hand, and a backpack on the opposite shoulder.

He bent down, kissed her lightly on the cheek. She stepped back and smiled at him. He took her suitcase and flight bag and followed her out the exit. Two hours later they reached the ferry at Port Angeles.

The sky was clear, a deep azure, and low clouds, tinged with grey, hovered along the horizon. Foot passengers gathered on the pier and the ferry was thirty minutes away. Jake picked up a booklet that lay open on the console of his truck and skimmed the page, then looked through the window. People were moving sporadically in and out of the glass doors of a low building. Angeline had not come out from the washrooms at the ferry terminal yet.

He turned the page of the book. The petroglyph drawings looked familiar.

Angeline exited the passenger lounge and came toward the truck as wind fluttered her hair and her red nylon windbreaker. She opened the car door and slid in beside him.

"Feel better?" Jake asked.

She blushed very slightly and grumbled, "I hate men. You never have to go to the bathroom."

He grinned and closed the booklet on his lap. The cover read: *Indian Rock Carvings of the Pacific Northwest Coast*, and he had picked it up in the souvenir shop while he was waiting for her. Now he passed it over and she propped it open in front of her face.

She thumbed through the pages. Her hair was tousled from walking in the wind and she smelled faintly of ferry soap. Her long lashes flickered up to the top of the next page and slowly lowered. Something troubled her. Did it have anything to do with him? She had been solemn like this since he had picked her up at the airport in Seattle.

She squinted through the side window to check on the progress of the ferry.

"I've been thinking about what you said about the petroglyphs," he said.

"Did you get a chance to go back there?"

"No. I thought I would wait for you."

Jake hoped if Angeline went back there with him it would remind her of what they had done there, what she meant to him. "If those rock carvings are fakes, I can use them to stop the theme park. I won't have to try for a UNESCO World Heritage Site designation after all."

"You were going to do that?" She seemed surprised. "Wouldn't a UNESCO designation just bring more publicity and encourage them to develop it for public use?"

"It might, but the sites would have to remain in their natural state with just some didactic panels or something, or maybe a visitor centre, but no theme park."

Angeline met his eyes. "I think Radisson *wants* a UNESCO designation, just not yet. Not until the property is legally his, then he can do whatever he wants with it. He's holding something back. When RAVENSWORLD opens to the public, he'll reveal it just as you said, like the greatest show on earth."

Now this was odd. He had detected a change in her attitude when she'd called to tell him she was coming back. She hadn't said why. Just that she wanted to stop the theme park.

"He's always had an interest in that cave," she said. "He should have a much stronger interest in the wet site, don't you think? That's where all the interesting things are coming from, but he keeps harking on the petroglyphs."

"Well he does have an interest in Native art," Jake reminded her. "He's a collector."

"But petroglyphs aren't mobile. You can't take them with you." Angeline turned away and Jake could feel her agitation.

"When did you change your mind about the theme park?" he asked. She partially rolled down the window and placed a finger against the glass where droplets of rain clung from a brief shower. "What happened in Toronto, Angeline?"

He wanted to know what Radisson meant to her. She didn't answer. She pointed to where the boardwalk flanked deep water, leading to the pier. "Isn't that Connie?"

Among the people waiting for the arrival of the ferry, was an elderly woman in a yellow dress with a long braid over one shoulder.

Jake unlatched the door and poked his head out over the roof of his truck. A gust of sea air slapped his face as he slammed the door and walked around the hood. Halfway to the board walk Jake called to her. It *was* Connie, and she turned and came toward him.

The ferry arrived and Jake offered Connie a lift in his Bronco. As the ferry left the dock, she noticed the booklet on the dashboard and asked what they were reading. Jake gave the booklet to her.

"We think some of the petroglyphs at Lookout Island are fakes," he said. "And we're going to go back to the cave to see. Will you come with us?"

Connie looked uncertain. She was not sure she was the right person to go. "Joe Redleaf certainly would help you if he wasn't so busy making arrangements for his betrothal potlatch," she said.

Angeline's eyes widened at the news and Connie smiled. "Didn't you know? Joe and Marina are getting married."

***

The cave was just as black and damp as before. The odour of the sea lingered, and the remnants of their fire sat by the entrance. The pale nodes of sandstone rose and fell in short, broken, rolling hills. The eyes were there, looking as though in a single direction toward the towering pillar.

The air was cool, and somewhere deep inside the rock, water resonated. Jake turned, went back outside, and walked a few short paces to the side.

He didn't understand it. He didn't understand the crippling feelings he got every time he went inside that cave. He waited, exploring the large flat stone he sat on, trying to overcome the helpless sensations.

Connie had followed him and now looked down to where he scraped away at moss and deadfall.

A large beaked head attached to a man's enormous shoulders peered back at him from the stone. It was familiar– a mask of the Raven, opening to reveal the face of the moon.

"He was here," Jake said. "The shaman was here."

Connie studied the petroglyph. "I thought you believed the petroglyphs were faked."

She turned, leaving Jake puzzled.

The dancing beam from his flashlight washed the chamber with a yellow glow, and the spirits of day and night, forest and sea, sprang from the walls. Angeline's voice rang falsely light as Jake and Connie approached. "Do you see what I mean, Connie? The Samish didn't hunt whales, did they?"

"Not as far as I know, but some of our close neighbours did," Connie replied.

Jake gazed at the Raven abducting the Salmon Chief's daughter. The figure of the bird was grotesque compared to the delicate rendering of the princess. He perched inside the long canoe lined with small circles. In front of him the smaller figure sat poised to spring. Below and slightly behind them were the oval fish-like drawings – the Salmon People with their human faces.

Something was different today. Closer to the floor, red pigment had been rubbed into the complex grooves of another image of the Raven.

"That wasn't here before," Angeline said from behind him.

The space below the swimming Salmon People had been blank yellow stone, but now the Raven lay curled within the stomach of a giant killer whale, and beside it lay a long sharp object like a beak. Above the drawing of the whale dangled the tentacle of a squid.

The granite stones where Angeline had chipped off the iron pyrite were on the floor beside a scattering of dry wood just below the scene. Jake lifted a cobble and held it like an offering. It glittered.

Angeline was studying the cave where it curved away from the Raven etchings and Jake slowly lowered the cobble to the floor. His eyes followed her movements as he rose. Nothing marred that wall except the tall pillar of stone.

A current, a draft, blew from somewhere by that spike of stone.

Jake swallowed. He touched Angeline's hand and she didn't flinch. They had both behaved uncharacteristically in this cave. Like some power had played with them, played with their bodies and their emotions.

Connie was watching him. He knew she was watching him. She knew something, not exactly what, but she knew that something happened to him every time he came inside this cave.

She suddenly went limp and fell to the ground.

Jake ran to her. He flashed his light down, but she did not move. Her eyes were wide open, glazed like a film had come over them. Jake touched her forehead, ran his hand over her crown to the nape of her neck. He held her chin, and shone his light into her eyes. Gently, he arranged her limbs more comfortably, resting her head against a sloping plane of sandstone.

"Is she hurt?" Angeline asked.

"I don't think so. I couldn't feel any bumps on her head and there's no blood. I didn't know she was claustrophobic. I would never have asked her to come here had I known," he said, unhappily

"What should we do? Shall we try to take her outside?"

Jake shook his head. "I think we'd better wait. If it's only a fainting spell, she should revive on her own."

The minutes passed and still Connie didn't stir.

An icy gust of air breathed around Jake's ankles. He told himself that this was just a cave. A dark, miserable cave.

The image of the Raven danced in denial and he knew, just as his reason told him otherwise, that this was a place he had known before.

The tingling again. A weakness in his hands and feet. A brief wave of vertigo. For Godsake, what was the matter with him? They were inside a bloody cave. Nothing more.

"This cave must have something to do with the shamans," Angeline said. "I wonder how old these petroglyphs are."

Jake moved to some pictures further away. He was trying to act more calm than he felt. He jumped as a clear voice broke the silence.

"*Stay with me my mother, stay with me, O my mother, 'til the night shadows fade; 'til the fish come to welcome the dawn, stay with me until I am grown . . .*" Connie was singing.

"Thank goodness, you're alright," Angeline said, and went to her.

"Our culture is dying. Soon all of the Elders will pass into history, taking with them the old ways and the old stories. The Raven will die unless . . ."

Jake glanced at Angeline. Connie stared across the cave to the images of the Raven.

CHAPTER TWENTY-FOUR

It was late afternoon the following Saturday when the crew drove off the ferry to a cool sea breeze and menacing clouds. They had reached Port Angeles where the potlatch was to take place, and while Steve went immediately toward some men who were unloading furniture from a van, Angeline, Josie, Carly, and Erika went inside the large house.

Jake detained Connie by the side of the Bronco in the large parking lot. Across the stretch of lawn, the Native cultural centre - a big cedar shingled house spacious enough to hold a crowd of several hundred - stood silhouetted against the sky. People entered the stout wooden doors loaded down with boxes of food, pots and pans, dishes, and utensils. Some of Joe's and Marina's relatives had arrived early to help with the cooking and other preparations. Joe was marrying his long time sweetheart and had insisted on a traditional announcement of their engagement. When Connie was Joe's age, social upheaval had almost eradicated their culture. Now he and Marina were celebrating their forthcoming marriage with a potlatch.

Perhaps now wasn't the most appropriate time to dig into Connie's personal history, but Jake couldn't wait any longer. In the cave, Connie had sung the lullaby he remembered from his childhood; she had mentioned the Raven. He zipped up his rain jacket as the sky darkened and wondered how to broach the subject. He suspected she knew something about his background that he didn't.

"Last week, what did you mean when you said 'the Raven will die?'" he asked, though what he really wanted to know was how she knew that song.

Connie removed the nylon cover from a compact umbrella and glanced from the clouds to the swaying trees behind the house, then to the porch where Joe held a storm door open for two men who carried a folding table into the house.

"I don't remember saying that, exactly. I think I only meant I didn't know where our traditions had gone. The Raven is symbolic, Jake. You know that."

Jake started at the sudden revving of an engine and turned to see an orange pickup truck idling in the parking lot. The driver was squirting soap on the windshield and had turned the wipers on. The twin eagles on the front doors were unmistakable. He dragged his thoughts from Clifford Radisson and looked at Connie.

Several things about her intrigued him - the ritual paraphernalia in her home, the huge gap in her past between losing her husband and now, and her animosity, unshared by the rest of the community, toward Clifford Radisson. He tried to remember what Joe had told him about Connie, and if he thought carefully, he could see how those things made perfect sense now. For one thing, he was pretty sure she was *not* claustrophobic.

"You came to the San Juan Islands with your husband after you married," Jake said. "When he died, you fell ill and thought you were going to die too, so you gave up your son. You were sick for years and when you got well, you became a healer for the Samish." Here he paused to formulate his next sentence. "You're a shaman."

Connie's face showed no emotion and behind her the pickup truck rolled out of the parking lot, onto the road.

"You *aren't* Samish are you?"

"No," she said. "I'm Haida."

There was one last thing he had to know. He was partly Haida, and if the surname, Lalonde, meant anything, he was also half French. Connie had given up a baby *boy* when he would have been too young to remember. Her husband was French.

"Are you my mother?" he asked.

***

The Haida were divided into two main social groups: the Eagles and the Ravens. If a woman was of the Raven side, she had to marry an Eagle man. At birth, their children were automatically part of their mother's group. They had to belong to the Raven.

Connie unsnapped the thin strip of fabric holding the umbrella closed. A drop of rain hit her brow and Jake raised his hood over his head.

He asked her again. "Are you my mother?"

"My family crest is the Eagle," Connie said.

She unfolded the umbrella as the sky ruptured, releasing a torrential downpour. Jake ducked as the waterproof fabric ballooned over their heads. They walked over the slick green grass to the house. Rain drummed on the outer sleeves of their jackets and on the nylon dome above.

"It was over forty years ago."

She was not going to explain about the Eagle crest because Jake must know. And even if he didn't understand right now, she was not going to explain it. Soon she would return the photograph to him, and maybe he would recognize the totem pole, but for now, she would explain only why she did not practice shamanism anymore.

She had come to Cedar Island with Paul when they were married. And yes, when he died, she became very ill, so much so, that she felt compelled to give up her son. When she recovered she repaid her community for their kindness to a stranger, and nursed their sick for many years. She adopted the Samish as her people, but as time passed she saw she no longer had any effect. People stopped coming. A clinic was set up especially for indigenous peoples. Conventional medicine was quicker and required no effort from the patient. There was no need to believe.

"If healing the sick is a shaman," she finished, "then that is what I was."

Jake stopped, and faced her beneath the pattering rain. "Why didn't you ever look for your son?"

By then it was too late. His foster parents had given him a better home than she ever could. The rest she couldn't tell him.

Jake seemed to take it all in, and accept it. She listened to the rain.

"What happened in the cave, Connie?"

"Among our people, some of us have a special ability to know the past."

Jake's expression flickered noticeably and his voice rose in anticipation. "Then you have feelings of familiarity when you're in certain places. You see things. Have dreams."

She nodded. "Yes, like you."

Connie handed the umbrella to Jake and linked arms with him. Drumbeats boomed from the large house while smoke and sparks billowed from the chimney into the grey sky.

He searched her face, eagerly. "What do my dreams mean?"

Connie turned away. "I think, perhaps, we should leave that cave alone."

"But you saw something in the petroglyphs," Jake said.

"I saw the clash of two wills. I saw the Eagle and the Raven."

***

The Great Hall was enormous, spacious, with empty panelled walls, small windows, and wooden floors. Jake stacked the last of the folding chairs against one wall. Connie was at the other end of the room now, greeting Chief Graeme Redleaf and Shaman Moon.

The crowds were beginning to stream in, and this room, set up to hold a hundred and twenty people, was beginning to shrink. The extra seats Jake was laying out were to accommodate any unexpected guests. Joe joined Marina at the head table and two young men stood in the corner banging on skin drums.

It was a privilege to have been invited here to one of the most important of all identity affirming ceremonies. Everyone had come to witness the betrothal of Chief Graeme Redleaf's son, Joe, to Shaman Moon's daughter, Marina.

Jake walked to the foyer and watched the people pouring through the front doors. Outside, the squelch of wet tires and the slamming of car doors announced the arrival of more guests. Men and women filed out of cloak rooms having rid themselves of rain jackets and umbrellas. Babies cried in their mother's arms and children behaved like children everywhere, running and screaming and having a grand old time.

"Have you seen Angeline?" Jake asked Carly and Steve who had just come in through the door.

"She's outside with Erika, bringing in some more food," Carly said. "Want me to get her?"

Jake looked around at the milling people and shook his head. "No. Don't bother. It looks like things'll start any minute now."

They went into the Great Hall where long tables were arranged in rows around the room. The centre of the floor was bare and a fire smoked in the modern brick fireplace against the wall beyond the chief's table. Angeline and Erika appeared in the doorway and wound their way to where Jake had claimed a table for his crew.

As the room filled with people, the air turned thick and stifling. The smell of tobacco mixed with the wood smoke from the fireplace and the aroma of roasting meat. Chief Redleaf rose and asked everyone to acknowledge the upcoming nuptials of Joe and Marina. He offered a toast, then Shaman Moon spoke to honour his future son-in-law. The speeches were short. After Joe's uncle spoke on his behalf, Shaman Moon offered a prayer of thanks for the food they were about to receive.

The feast was mostly seafood – halibut, salmon, and clams, as well as eulachons. There was a haunch of venison for those who had a penchant for meat. Some traditional vegetables were offered: riced chocolate lily bulbets and the soft brownish and very sweet Blue Camas roots. There was baked Wapato or Indian potato with their light fluffy texture and sweetish chestnut flavour, cow parsnip which tasted like celery with regular celery beside it, and carrots and peas, crab apples, blueberries and oranges.

Jake sent a wary eye around the room on the lookout for Clifford Radisson, and as he brought a last forkful of halibut to his mouth, their eyes met.

Music boomed. The entertainment began. Dancers lunged out of the dark, swaying and weaving between the tables, ending up on the centre of the floor. Cloaks and sequined floor-length dance robes caught the light from the blazing fire. Button blankets twirled and billowed to the beat of dance steps. Drums exploded and the spirits of Wolf, *Sisiutl* and Raven permeated the room. The costumed people performed dances symbolizing land, water, and sky. A scream lanced the night as *Dzunkwa* leaped out of the shadows to grab an unsuspecting child.

"Oh God," Carly gasped. "That was planned wasn't it? I mean that little girl was in on it, wasn't she?"

"Don't worry. It's just performance art," Josie said.

In a human wave, Joe's entire family – aunts, uncles, cousins and siblings, even babes in arms, circled the centre of the floor. In a dance of giving, each held out a scarf, a towel, or other such item, as they bobbed and swayed and whirled in time to the rhythm of drums and the chanting of singers.

The swirling dance ended. Some men unfolded a huge canvas tarp and spread it onto the centre of the floor. Several members of the Redleaf family carried gifts from behind a beautifully painted screen.

Brightly coloured cushions were piled in one corner of the tarp and crocheted blankets in clear plastic wrappings were stacked in another. A girl in braids, Joe's youngest sister, opened a wicker basket full of quilted potholders. Cousins stacked scores of plastic storage boxes and their lids at the remaining corners of the tarp. Spaces between these items were filled with tea kettles, coffee pots, vases, china dishes, copper trays, pottery cups, acrylic tumblers, ashtrays, appliqued wall hangings, oven mitts, balls of yarn, and wool sweaters.

Chief Redleaf's family continued to hand out gifts. Everyone must be paid for witnessing the dances, hearing the songs and listening to their host's proclamations. By accepting the payment, they affirmed all that was said.

"Are we supposed to take that?" Angeline asked as a young boy thrust a crisp ten dollar bill into her hand.

Jake looked to Connie for confirmation and Carly shook her head, astonished. "Doesn't all this gift-giving put them in the poorhouse?"

Josie shifted in her seat to pat the little boy on the head who was also handing her a ten dollar bill. A kind of break in the ceremony occurred. The coffee pot came around and Jake poured. More food was offered, regular desserts like chocolate cake and apple pie and sugary pastries.

The empty tarp was rolled up and put out of sight. Music rose and the drums beat again. A puff of smoke exploded; thunder rumbled from the skin drums. From a trap door in the centre of the floor the Thunderbird leaped out.

"I thought the Samish only used the two-headed serpent, the *Sxwaixwe* mask, at potlatches," Angeline whispered.

Maybe the dancer had decided to do something non-authentic, Jake thought. After all, it was just a show. But he was perplexed. Thunderbird masks were not a traditional part of Samish dance.

The bird figure rose above them suspended from invisible lines. He dropped, hovering over their table shaking a perforated rattle filled with smouldering bark. Jake recognized the dance as Haida, *Nuxalk,* or *Kwakwaka'wakw.* It was not Samish.

Why were they performing another tribe's dance?

The dancer circled the floor and rose again, haunting, menacing. Sparks flew and smoke puffed into their eyes. A sudden flash of light illuminated the dark. Thunder clapped and rain fell. Jake smiled. Rain. A spray of water had come from hidden squeeze bottles inside the dancer's costume.

"That's not a Thunderbird, Jake," Angeline said. "It's the Eagle. The Haida Eagle mask. The one that Radisson bought from the museum."

As the dancer stopped moving he could see it clearly. The square tufted ears, the evil raptor eyes, the sharply down-curved beak. What was it doing here? He looked across the room at Radisson, who looked back.

"Ask Joe," Angeline said. "I think he's going to the john. Catch him and ask him."

Jake wove through the crowd, aware of Radisson's eyes on his back, and caught Joe at the doorway. "Congratulations. Marina's a beautiful girl," he said.

"Not doing so bad yourself." Joe grinned and gestured at Angeline who was rising from the table with two raincoats in her arms.

"I wanted to ask you something. That Thunderbird dance. Who authorized it? It's not traditional, is it?"

Joe shook his head. Mr. Radisson had paid his Uncle Charlie two thousand dollars to do the dance. He hadn't wanted to at first because it wasn't traditional, but then after talking it over with his father, he'd thought why not? It was only entertainment and it was a beautiful mask.

But why the Thunderbird dance? That mask was an Eagle. Joe shrugged, then grinned again. More dramatic? Mr. Radisson had wanted the Thunderbird dance. In fact, he was here.

Jake already knew that. He looked around at the hundred plus people in the room. It was not unreasonable, he decided, for Joe's family to share the mask with the whole community so that the young people could see how masks were traditionally used. "Your uncle took the money?"

Was there something wrong with that? Joe seemed a bit offended. Radisson had meant it as a wedding gift, and his uncle had put it into the gifts for the potlatch. Well, it was interesting to see it in use. His uncle had done an excellent job. How did he know the dance, by the way?

His sister married into the *Nuxalk*. She lived in Bella Coola.

Jake congratulated Joe again then turned back to the crowd. Radisson was no longer seated at his table. The Eagle at a betrothal potlatch, Jake pondered. What was the significance in that?

Joe left, and Angeline slipped up beside Jake and passed him his jacket. "I heard what Joe said. I think Clifford Radisson wants you to know he's watching you. He's worried you'll stop his theme park. That eagle is a spirit mask for his RAVENSWORLD collection. It's a warning."

She glanced over her shoulder, eyes darting nervously around the room.

"Shit."

This was the first time Jake had ever heard Angeline say anything like that. He looked to where she was staring, petrified.

"Let's go outside, get some air," she said urgently.

Out on the stoop, rain slickened the untreated cedar boards, and the roof over the porch caught most of the downpour. They sucked in the smell of damp wood.

"Angeline what's the matter? You look like you've seen a ghost."

What she had seen was only Radisson. Jake frowned. Had Radisson done something to harm her?

She covered her mouth, like she felt sick.

"What happened?"

"Nothing."

She swallowed hard, but had trouble looking him in the eye. He was not buying that. The developer had done something, and Jake was going back in there to confront him. He turned to leave but she grabbed his arm, shaking badly. "Please. Don't."

He stayed where he was. She took a deep breath controlling herself as drops rattled inside the eaves and onto the steps.

"I found out something from Connie," she said.

He pulled his hood over his head. Across the lawn the sky was black. "What?"

"Radisson thinks he's distantly related to Shaman Moon."

"What!"

Angeline stepped backwards into the wall as wind brought a flurry of rain into their faces. Her hood blew off and she didn't bother to replace it. Her hair glistened with the sheen of mist. It seemed Jake and the developer had a common ancestor. A white sea captain who married a Native girl. That, Radisson thought, gave him ancestral rights to the Eagle mask.

Jake blotted a drop of water from his nose and inched into the wall next to her. "What are you talking about? Radisson is a *Blanco* if I ever saw one."

Angeline wiped rain off her cheeks and told him about the photograph in Connie's bathroom. "It's a totem pole with a crest figure of the captain. He thinks he's descended from that captain."

***

Radisson coughed from behind Angeline and her face went pale.

"What are you doing here?" Jake asked.

"I imagine the same thing you are . . . Angeline." The developer smiled.

She had turned around on his arrival and now moved back as though he terrified her. Jake placed a hand on the wet sleeve of her jacket, stepping between them.

"I was talking to the lady," Radisson said.

"I don't think she has anything to say to you."

"Shouldn't we leave that up to her?"

Angeline's breath escaped in short misty puffs. Jake looked sideways at her, waiting.

"We have some unfinished business, Angeline."

Jake watched her hesitate, swallow under the throat guard to her jacket. Anything Radisson had to say to her, he could say in Jake's presence.

"This has nothing to do with you, Dr. Lalonde."

Jake felt the adrenaline surge from his gut. His breath was wheezing. He clenched his fist, grinding his jaw. One more snotty remark, he thought.

Angeline looked up, sensing his outrage and calmed him with a look. He wondered what she planned to do because he was not leaving her alone with Clifford Radisson.

"I think we owe each other the courtesy," Radisson said to her.

Jake didn't know what the developer was talking about or what had suddenly come over her, but she touched his sleeve in a dismissive gesture and told him to leave them alone.

He was not leaving them alone. What could Radisson possibly say to her that *he* shouldn't hear? Now she was angry. It was none of his business.

"Jake, leave us alone."

If she didn't want him to protect her, he had to respect that. But he couldn't. He paused, fidgeted, and Angeline asked him again to leave.

Radisson smirked, victorious. Why couldn't she make up her mind? Jake walked back to the doorway, hesitated before opening it. They were both watching him, so he stepped inside and gently let the door fall. Fortunately it stuck, and if it hadn't, he would have made it stick, leaving about a two inch gap. He moved back slightly from the window in the door and stayed there. Rain pattered overhead and pounded onto the porch where the roof didn't reach. He could see the side of Radisson's face and most of Angeline.

"Why are you afraid of me?" Radisson asked. "What have I done?"

"You– " Angeline was stumped for words. Her eyes looked huge, distressed, and any minute Jake was going to step out there and break this up.

"What did I do?" he repeated.

"You left me in downtown Toronto in the middle of the night!"

"As I recall, you wanted to be left."

"What do you want?" she demanded.

"I want you to tell me something about the petroglyphs."

"Why don't you ask Jake!"

He laughed. "I'm asking you. Are you telling me he's more of an expert on the subject than you?"

"I think you know," she said and her eyes grew dark.

"Know what?"

She couldn't say it, and Jake willed her not to. If there was a reason Radisson wanted them to know the petroglyphs were fakes this was not the time for her to let the developer know they suspected him.

"I still want you to work for me," he said. "I still want you in charge of my caves."

Water poured over the eaves in a sudden gush as the rain thundered down. For several seconds neither of them spoke, then Radisson said, "Tell me what it is I don't have that you want."

He moved over toward her and she tried very hard not to step back.

"You know what you did."

He shook his head, patronizingly. "You are such a child. *This* is what I did– "

He dipped forward to kiss her. Her hands flew out. Jake smashed open the door, seized the developer by the neck of his jacket, and swung him against the wall.

"Stop it!" Angeline grabbed Jake's arm as he went to punch Radisson in the face.

"Don't you ever fucking touch her again," Jake said.

CHAPTER TWENTY-FIVE

Angeline shot wide awake. Her breathing was ragged, her sleeping bag damp with perspiration. His face leered at her – the piercing black eyes, the twisted lips, the coarse red beard. She could see the broken bottle of scotch, her shoe flying though the air, hands tearing at her dress. Then the lions, boiling coffee, and a burning cigarette.

She ran through the living room to the bathroom, tripping over something in her haste. She reached for the toilet paper and dragged at the roll until it started looping on the floor. She wiped her tearing eyes, stood up, turned on the tap and splashed cold water all over her face. Then she stopped, blinked, and mopped herself dry.

Why was Sam Smythe haunting her sleep? Why this feeling of imminent doom?

She swallowed, inhaled. Almost whimpered as Radisson's voice resounded in her brain.

I always get what I want, Angeline.

An icy chill shivered from the base of her spine to her neck, and she stared into the darkness. She touched her throat where the memory burned, and let her fingers slide down to her chest.

She left the sink and stumbled into the dark. Caught her breath. A shadow was standing there.

"Angeline? Are you all right?"

It was only Jake. He came to her and touched her gently on the arm. "Something you ate?" he asked softly.

Angeline shook her head, clenched her fist. "Nothing like that."

"Nightmare?" he asked.

She nodded. He put an arm around her and she stiffened. "Do you want to talk about it?"

She willed the anguish back and gently pushed him away. No. She could not tell him. Not yet.

"Is something wrong?" Josie whispered from their feet.

Angeline looked down as Josie slowly rose from where her sleeping bag lay rumpled beside Jake's.

No. *No.* Everything was fine. The words wouldn't come out.

"It's all right, Josie," Jake said. "Go back to sleep."

Angeline returned to her room. At the far corner of the den a dying fire glowed in the grate surrounded by ceramic tiles. Two people lay on the floor, their chests peacefully rising and falling in sleep. Carly, Steve, Erika and Jason were staying at the shaman's house that night, while she, Josie, and Jake, and some of the other crew were staying with Joe at his father's home. She tiptoed past the two crew members and lay down on her sleeping bag on the sofa.

Radisson was relentless, he refused to take no for an answer. But that wasn't all. Something else was going on here, something that went beyond mortifying her. She pulled the covers up to her chin and huddled down. She had messed things up. She had not signed his contract. She did not want to work for him or be his lover. That infuriated him, but it did not explain his interest in the petroglyphs.

Why did Radisson care that she knew the petroglyphs were fakes? Angeline rolled onto her stomach, unclenched her fist, and opened her eyes.

She rose and walked to the embers glowing in the grate. To keep her away from Lookout Island? To keep Jake away? She stared into the red hot coals and felt the heat on her skin. What had Radisson said when he'd offered her the job?

She had thought it was just a slip of the tongue the first time. But every time since, whenever he mentioned the petroglyphs, he had said *caves.*

***

Jake couldn't go back to sleep because he had just had a nightmare of his own.

Time was running out and there was nothing standing in Clifford Radisson's way. Lookout Island was for sale and he could buy it because the petroglyphs were fakes.

Jake wasn't sorry for what he had done. He only wished Angeline had let him finish it, pummel him, pulverize him, beat him to a shivering, quivering pulp. He would do it again. And again to keep him away from her.

He heard once more their conversation. He would have to go back to the cave and look at those petroglyphs. Radisson wanted that cave even if the carvings were fake, and that didn't make any sense.

Jake moaned. They had flickered, the lights had flickered, the glitter from the stone cobbles. Marten Lake. Josie. Twelve years ago. Holding a glittering stone cobble in his hand. Sitting on a hard stone floor with Josie nagging at him, telling him it wasn't an artifact.

He stared up at the darkness of Graeme Redleaf's living room, at the ceric white moon glow – and saw the skeleton of a raven.

CHAPTER TWENTY-SIX

Jake rolled up his jeans and removed his socks and running shoes, picked up a trowel and a hose, and went to the edge of the pit where Joe had dug up the Raven rattle at the beginning of the summer.

He hadn't written the report for the Heritage Advisory Board yet, Kate and Tom were on his case, and the theme park was looming. He had to find something to stop it. If Josie saw him–

So what? She wasn't interested in what he was looking for anyway. They had been digging in the wrong place. After three and a half months of excavation, nothing else of the shaman's had appeared.

On the bottom, four feet down, he crouched. Only the slightest traces of stratigraphy showed. Most of the matrix was grey and yellow clay, the results of an ancient mud slide, and stones stuck out everywhere. He raised the hose and switched the regulator on, sending out a gush of water.

"Just what do you think you're doing?" Josie asked.

Jake stood up to see her hovering over him. "I've pumped all the water out, that's what I'm doing."

She pointed to where the excavators were working in what was now a very large and wide depression twelve metres away. "The main village is over there."

"Shamans didn't always live in the heart of the village," he said.

"Shamans?" she asked, caustically. "Since when did we start looking for shamans? We have to do this systematically, Jake. We can't just dig holes on a whim."

He hunkered down again and aimed the hose at the side of the pit. Water washed over something just below a projecting stone on the floor. A root? No trees grew in the bog. He sent off a strong jet spray, splattering mud.

"Josie!" someone called from the trenches, "Can you come here for a minute?"

"You're wasting your time," she said, and left.

Whatever the thing was, it was made of wood, long and thick and soft from being waterlogged. A shadow suddenly fell over him, blocking the sun and shading the object. Jake looked up to identify its source.

He smiled. Angeline smiled back.

"Come down here and see what you think," he said.

He gently pried the object from the mud. It was two joined pieces of wood, forming the upper and lower portions of an object measuring more than a foot long. The hinge where the two pieces met wiggled to the touch. He passed it to Angeline, adjusted the pressure on the nozzle of the hose, and aimed water just beyond his feet. Then he picked up the trowel and gently scraped.

Here was more wood, a portion of a circle the diameter of a basketball faintly stained black and red; and in the centre of it was an eye, part of a nose, and the corner of a grim mouth.

He rose, and placed the circular section above the pit on the grass, took the other part of the mask and reached overhead to place it beside the first. Bracing his palms on the ground beside them, he heaved himself over the edge.

The two sections fit together. Just as he knew they would. Just as he had seen them etched on that petroglyph stone outside the cave. With the beak portion closed, it was the head of the Raven; with it opened, it revealed the moon.

"Do you know what this is?" he asked Angeline.

He looked down, realized she couldn't see it from there, and dropped back into the hole to hoist her up.

"This must be where the shaman lived," she said. "It's a transformation mask, isn't it?"

Jake hosed mud off his feet. There was no house here. No wooden planks. He hunkered over the two pieces of the mask. When he looked up, Angeline was staring at the far wall of the pit.

"What's that?" she asked, pointing to something projecting from the dirt.

Jake went over, then lowered himself to stand where part of the exposed surface of a stone glinted in the sun. His pulse quickened again. Little flecks of gold shone from the granite. Jake dropped the hose, drove his trowel in, wiggled until it loosened, then grabbed the stone with both hands and hauled it out.

It was another one of those cobbles like they had found in the cave where Angeline had chipped off the iron pyrite, and that he had found in the rock shelter at Marten Lake.

***

Almost everyone was downstairs in the pub. Angeline had waited until most of the crew had had their showers before going up to have hers. She shoved the key into the lock, but as she did, the door eased opened.

The room had a double bed, twin night stands, a dresser with a chair, an armchair in the corner and a large curtained window at the far end. The bathroom was by the door, and the fan whirred from within.

A whole assemblage of clothing was draped on the furniture and on the floor because some of the crew intended to spend the night in town. Angeline pulled off her sweater and sat at the foot of the bed.

In the mirror, she recognized Josie's purple fleece jacket sprawled out behind her. Josie was probably still in the bathroom. She undid her shoelaces and kicked off her Nikes, then yanked off her socks. She was just about to remove her jeans when the bathroom door opened.

Jake came out in a puff of steam, wrapped in a light blue towel from the hips down with nothing else. His tan line came just below his waist, and the dark hairs on his belly crept up to meet the curls matted on his chest. The towel slipped.

"Hey, you forgot this." Josie appeared in the doorway behind him. Dressed only in an over-sized T-shirt, she handed Jake a plastic bottle. She noticed Angeline. "Did you want the shower? We're done, you can have it."

Angeline forced herself to rise and went into the bathroom. She shut the door and locked it. Then she undressed, yanked the plastic curtain closed, and turned on the water before getting in. She sat at the bottom of the tub and drew her knees up to her cheek.

What was Josie doing in the shower with Jake?

Josie was gone when she came out, but Jake sat fully clothed at the foot of the bed.

"I want to talk to you," he said quietly.

He watched her in the mirror. She remembered the day she had seen him inside Josie's tent. His chest was bare then too, and Josie had worn the same over-sized T-shirt she wore today.

Angeline leaned into the dresser and ran her fingers through her hair. She searched her pockets, then crouched to rummage through the front pouch of her pack.

"What are you looking for?" he asked. "I've got a comb."

She rose, looked into the mirror, lifted a fingerful of hair, and let the strands fall softly to her ears.

He grinned. "You think I have lice?"

No, she thought. Worse. She took the comb and parted her hair.

"What happened while you were away, Angeline?"

She didn't answer.

"I know I said some things and I'm sorry. I have a tendency to open my mouth before I think, but then you started going out with Radisson. What did I do to make you do that? And why did you bolt for Toronto so abruptly?

"Aren't you going to say anything at all? Don't you owe me some explanation?"

Angeline didn't know what to say. He may think nothing of sleeping with several women at the same time, but she did.

What was Josie doing in the bathroom with him? Who was he sleeping with while she was away? She was pretty sure he had stayed with Katherine in Seattle that night she had phoned.

"I'm sorry I called you an ornament, I'm sorry I called you mercenary." He stopped. "I didn't mean it in a bad way." He sighed. "If you won't tell me what happened between us, the least you can do is tell me what happened to you in Toronto. Why did you suddenly decide to come back?"

She was not expecting this. He couldn't guess and even if he did, she could hardly believe it herself. It would make her look *so* stupid.

"I had to do some research. U of T has the most comprehensive collection of Northwest Coast references," she lied.

"Since when? And don't tell me you went back there to look up something for your thesis."

"And why not? If you thought of me as a colleague you would want to know what I was doing." She decided to let him know anyway. "Marine foods were eaten as early as 9,000 years ago in B.C., Alaska, and Siberia. And though that's no proof Siberians followed the fish runs to the New World, why would people, dependent on a marine diet, follow bison to somewhere they didn't know? Fish were the reason people came this far south and decided to stay. To prove it, I'll have to go north."

"This is not about your thesis," he said.

"It'll take at least six more years of graduate school to get my PhD, another few more to get some kind of job. Even after all of that, I might not find anything in Seattle." She paused. "Hypothetically speaking, would you just drop everything and follow me wherever I went?"

Jake stared. "Oh, I see. Clifford Radisson could just give it all to you so you would never have to leave. Is that why you started seeing him?" She didn't answer and he didn't stop. "So, what happened? If he's so right for you, why did you leave him? What's going on between you now?"

He glared at her and shook his head, then got up and went to the door.

"Just tell me which one it is," Angeline said, feverishly. "Katherine or Josie? Or both?"

He started, suddenly realized what she was thinking, and turned around. "Who have you been talking to?"

"Nobody – *Everybody*. You have quite the reputation."

Jake threw his hands up in despair, then massaged his left shoulder like it hurt. "You can believe what you like. Nothing I say will change what you think because you've already made up your mind. But that doesn't change how I feel about *you.*"

"If the Raven *was* a real person, if he really was as oversexed as myth makes him out to be, then I wouldn't be surprised if you were directly descended from him," she said.

***

They went down to the pub and joined the rest of the crew. Jake suspected there was something more upsetting Angeline than just her thesis or even his history with Kate and Josie, but she obviously had no intention of telling him what it was.

"Twelve forty-five," Josie said. "I'm beat. I'm going to bed. If anybody wants to know, I'll be in room seven. Kate!" she yelled across the room. "See you tomorrow."

At the far end of the pub, Kate was drinking with Sam Smythe.

Josie turned back, rolled her eyes in disgust and left. No kidding, Jake thought. What was she doing? Sleeping with the enemy? Angeline had seen them too, and her eyes opened wide.

Kate was smiling. God was she nuts? Desperate? Or just indiscriminately horny.

"Angeline, what's the matter?" he asked.

"Let's get out of here."

She got to her feet but he hadn't finished his beer yet. He put out a hand to stop her and she suddenly dropped back to her seat.

Sam Smythe hovered over the table grinning at Angeline. She looked like she wanted to disappear.

"Hi Jake," Kate said.

"What are you doing here?" he asked.

"I had a meeting."

"With whom?"

She fussed with a loose strand of hair and the rings on her fingers flashed as she smiled at Sam Smythe. Jake thought he would puke.

"What are *you* doing here?" he asked the contractor. "I heard Radisson had let you go."

"Oh quit being such a wind bag," Kate said. She planted a peck on his cheek and he yanked away. "'Night Angeline."

Without acknowledging Jake's question, Smythe wrapped his arm around Kate's waist, cocked a brow at Angeline, and strolled to the door.

"Jesus, I can't believe she's going to sleep with that worm."

Angeline stared at Jake's half full glass. Hers was empty. He had consumed five beers to her two. She looked like she needed another.

"Last call," the waitress said. "We're closing in fifteen minutes."

He ordered a half pint of Redhook Ale for each of them.

"What's the matter, Angeline?"

"Nothing."

Something, he thought. Had that creep said something to her? The contractor consistently made crude remarks about women. Kate obviously liked it. Either that or she was insane.

Jake reached out, wanting to take her hand. Something had happened since she had gone home to Toronto. He wished he knew what it was.

"I won't let Smythe hurt you," he said, knowing how patrician he sounded.

She looked like she was about to burst into tears.

"Angeline, what's the matter? Did he do something?"

She shook her head.

"I can't believe Kate is that desperate."

Jake tipped the glass to his lips and swallowed. He scanned the room while Angeline composed herself. They were alone. The kitchen door opened, and the smell of grease and french fries wafted over with the waitress. She set down two glasses of beer.

He took a slug and watched Angeline. She seemed to have developed an irrational fear of Sam Smythe.

"Jake, we have to go back to the cave."

He thought so too.

Cobbles, so many cobbles, all filled with fire. They reminded him of the cave, the petroglyphs, the Raven. And the last reminded him of what she had said upstairs. It was an absurd thing to say that he was descended from the Raven. Yet, he believed it.

The Haida system of belief and their social organization had two moieties, the Raven and the Eagle. But that wasn't what she had meant when she'd said he was descended from the Raven. She didn't mean from the Raven line. She meant from *the* Raven.

"I've been having these dreams," Jake said.

Angeline looked up, not exactly up, since she barely raised her head, but he could sense he had her full attention.

"They've been driving me crazy. I keep seeing familiar things." Some really disturbing images, and some of them had her in them, but he didn't say so.

"It's dark, and someone is crying. I can't move, can't help. It's like I'm drowning. I'm . . ." He didn't finish the sentence. He remembered stealing another man's woman. "There was fire and these cobbles. Like the one we found today."

A light went out over the bar. Some glasses clinked as the bartender tidied up.

Angeline looked frightened. He hadn't meant to frighten her. But the dreams *were* frightening. If they were memories and not merely dreams.

"Like the images in the petroglyphs," she said. "Like in the cave."

The thought had occurred to him too. The whole incident in the cave had seemed like a dream.

He shook his head. He'd known exactly what he was doing then, just as he did now. So had she. It was just a cave. Rocks and dirt and some ancient stone carvings. There was *not* some power controlling him in there.

He reached over almost taking her hands, but left them lying in the middle of the table on either side of her beer glass.

Connie was right. They should leave that cave alone.

His face darkened. He had drunk too much, and his hands pressed into the table. Clifford Radisson was going to win.

"I can't save the world," he said viciously. "I can't save the *Indian*. I can't even save this little goddamn piece of real estate we're sitting on."

Her eyes flared. "Don't be so derogatory. And don't you give up! I won't allow it. I won't allow Clifford Radisson to destroy these islands!"

Jake was startled by the outburst. What could she do? What could any of them do?

"He's a fucking asshole and I won't let him do this to me!"

To her? What was she talking about? She clammed up. He frowned. "Angeline . . ."

"Jake, listen to me. We have to try for a UNESCO World Heritage Site designation, now. There's no other way. We have to find the burial of the Raven. If we do, if we find it before he buys up any more land, we can protect the islands. Think! Isn't there anything we've found that makes these sites important?"

"I'm afraid my theory of a prehistoric shaman is nothing more than the product of a desperate imagination," he said. "You know what? Thanks for doing that for me. For opening my eyes to the futility of what I'm doing. There is nothing gonna save this place from being bought."

"The Raven came down from the north," she said, fiercely, "from Alaska or *Haida Gwaii*. He was selfish and greedy and irresponsible, but he also did good. He was a trickster, a magician, a creator . . ." She threw his own story back in his face. "Somewhere along the way his actions became magical, unreal. Myth!"

Jake raised his glass to her when she had finished. "I have an idea. Instead of producing a thesis, maybe you should write a novel. I'll give you all my notes."

"But it makes sense!"

"It doesn't." He grinned crookedly at her.

Angeline took his glass away and caught the eye of the bartender. "It's time to cut you off. Can we have a cup of coffee here?"

The man behind the bar grinned and said, "Sorry, there's none left. You two will have to scoot. I gotta lock up. Do you have a room? If you don't, I can give you one. Your fella there looks like he could use a nap."

Jake leaned on his elbows chuckling into his arms. Angeline got to her feet and slung her backpack over one shoulder. "Come on Jake, let's go. I'll drive."

They walked out into the night.

"Time's it?" Jake asked.

"Well past your bedtime."

Behind the dark buildings, the sky was a deep, violent purple. The street lamps sent a fuzzy pink light over their heads. Jake's Bronco sat solitary on the side of the road. He went to the driver's side and fumbled around in his pockets.

"I don't want to end up a permanent fixture on some tree trunk," Angeline said. "Or a human example of flattened fauna. Give me your keys."

Jake cocked his head at her. "You have a sense of humour when you feel like it."

She got in behind the wheel, then opened the passenger side. She found the ignition, fastened her seatbelt, and stepped on the gas.

"Angel, were you serious about what you said inside? You don't think I'm crazy? You think maybe the Raven was a person?"

"Why not? What is mythology based on anyway? Somebody had to make it up. It's just that the stories were invented so long ago, nobody knows where the inspiration originated. The Raven could be a thousand years old."

Or ten. Jake wasn't positive of that, but the raven skeleton at Marten Lake had been that old.

She shifted as the road graded up a hill.

"You don't think it's inconceivable he could have ended up here?" he asked.

"Maybe we have him already, Jake. Maybe he lived in that shaman's house, and Connie's rattle and the transformation mask belonged to him."

"It'd be pretty hard to prove, seeing there is no house in that pit."

"Then we just have to come up with something else."

But what? What was the evidence? The Raven icon was the most important among the Tlingit, Tsimshian, and Haida of British Columbia and Alaska. By the time you got to Washington and Oregon you really had to search to find some mention of him or some physical representation. They needed a time perspective. They didn't have archaeological evidence. Wood didn't survive in most sites and the Raven didn't appear on many stone artifacts.

But at their site, Angeline reminded him, he did. The Raven's influence was strongest in the north because people were exposed to him sooner. They had time to develop the lore around him. In the south he spent less time and therefore had less of an impact. It was evident in the myths.

"They don't prove a thing. They don't prove he was born in Alaska and died, assuming he was a person, here, in the San Juan Islands."

Jake stretched out and yawned.

"We have nothing but a circular argument," he said.

"We are not talking in circles. We are following the lines of evidence and allowing for creativity – as you so eloquently put it in your most entertaining and enlightening graduate seminars."

He snorted, almost a laugh. "I don't do that. I just don't want you to be fudging it. Making the data fit the theory instead of the theory fitting the data."

"Am I doing that? I didn't think I was." She yawned and lifted her foot from the gas pedal. "How'm I doing?"

"You haven't hit any trees yet. Do you wanna stop?"

"I think I made a wrong turn somewhere. We're on the other side of Berry Point."

The dark purple of the sky was lightening in a thin line above the sea. Angeline pulled over to the side of the road. They got out of the truck and stood on the asphalt above the rocky beach. It was cool. It was the dead of night, early morning. No creatures stirred, just the slapping of the waves. They walked toward the sound of the water.

The moon had appeared from behind a cloud, a sharp fingernail arc. They sat on the hard sandstone beach and listened to the tide.

He could hear his own breathing. People breathed differently when they drank. It was like breathing became a controlled, rather than a natural, involuntary, response.

Angeline wrapped her arms around her knees. A light breeze kicked up. Jake gazed out at the glowing horizon, then up at the stars. He suddenly fell into a fit of derisive laughter.

"That damn cave."

Angeline dropped her arms. She shivered. Whether it was from the cool breeze or something else, Jake didn't know.

He jerked his head up. "Did you hear that?"

Something had made a sound on the road. He stood up and looked toward the Bronco.

"What is it?"

"I don't know. I feel like we aren't alone."

Angeline rose, glanced around and started to walk away.

"Angeline come back here."

"Why? What's the matter?"

He didn't know, but he felt funny. Edgy. Like something, someone was watching them. The wind blew in from the sea. The trees jutting into the water from a spit of land were darkly outlined against the luminous sky.

They went back to the Bronco and he begged her to let him drive. She examined her watch. It had been hours since he'd had a drink.

He looked cautiously about, peered into the backseat, then watched her get into the truck, and slammed the passenger door shut. As he drove he had a niggling thought. Just what was Sam Smythe doing back here?

"Where are we going?" Angeline asked. "We've passed the turn off."

The truck sounded funny. Jake geared down, listened. He took the centre road through the island and drove to Otter Cove.

CHAPTER TWENTY-SEVEN

Jake stared. Most of the forest that led to the beach had been clear cut and trees lay felled all around the base of the cliff.

He shifted into park and opened the door. Angeline got out on the other side. If it wasn't for the fact that he knew they were the only archaeologists on this island, he would have thought someone else had set up an illegal excavation.

The land was barren of vegetation, stripped to the raw earth; a huge gaping hole yawned where towering trees used to be; and beside the road, in front of the truck, a trailer was parked.

Jake walked over. What he saw there made a knot tighten in his stomach. Twin eagles, back to back, fenced on the aluminum siding.

The crew had been busy the last two weeks and hadn't been away from the bog much. He had gone to Seattle to meet with Kate, then to Lookout Island the following week. Joe's betrothal potlatch had kept the crew in Port Angeles for the weekend. The contractor must have been hard at work, and he must have done this in the last few days. An ugly thought occurred to him. What had Josie been doing through all of this?

"Who does this beach belong to?" he asked Angeline.

"It's a government park, isn't it?" she said. "Wouldn't it be under the jurisdiction of the County Parks Service?"

Jake started toward the Bronco, gesturing her to follow. "I've got to find a phone."

"No one'll be at the office yet. The sun's barely up."

He went back to the edge of the depression. Jumping down, he hunkered to his knees. If there were any signs of a midden he could charge Radisson with desecrating a historic site. He sank a finger into the charred earth and felt its ashy texture. Sandy soil, burnt wood, and pebbles. But no bits of crushed shell or flakes of stone. Not even a fragment of bone.

"There's no site here, is there, Jake?"

No. He poked at the charred, crumbling remains of a tree root. Had Radisson's men used dynamite? How else could they have levelled these trees, roots and all? He rose and climbed out of the ash to stand beside Angeline. From the crater where firs had once stood, to the yellow sickle of sand behind, the land looked like a strip mine.

Jake went to the aluminum trailer and peered through a dusty window. Inside, were a desk and several chairs, a filing cabinet and hooks on the walls holding orange fluorescent vests and hard hats. A large table at the rear was covered with rolls of blueprints. One was laid out flat, held down by a book, a coffee mug, and one of those tacky snow-filled paper weights.

He grabbed the handle of the door and shook it hard. The whole trailer rattled.

"That won't help," Angeline said. "Radisson must have obtained the permits he needs to start building."

If he could get inside, he could tear up the permits. But the door was stronger than he'd thought.

They got back in the truck and Jake made a U-turn in the middle of the road. The road slipped under them, the scenery dashing by. Angeline glanced at the speedometer as Jake cranked the wheel to the left to meet the next curve. He compensated and jerked to the right. They were going downhill. Fast.

"Oh shit."

"What?"

"I can't slow down, the bloody thing won't stop!"

"Step on the brake!"

"I am!"

His foot was to the floor, but with no results. They were rushing full speed directly toward the town.

He yanked on the emergency brake. Nothing happened. Thank God there was no traffic. He twisted and turned following the S-curves in the road.

Oh shit, oh shit, oh shit. Houses were rushing up at him, trees, and parked cars. Angeline shut her eyes. He gripped the wheel, hunched over, and swerved to the right, to the left, past the Surf Lodge, and dead on into town. Main street was straight as an arrow. Steady, steady, steady. They zipped past the stores, the Laundromat, and gradually coasted, rolled, as the road angled up to the Innis Hotel.

And stopped.

Jake unfastened his seatbelt and opened the door. He got out, looked under the hood, then peered under the truck. Fluid dripped, leaving a dark wet splotch on the road. What the hell was wrong with this thing? He had serviced it three months ago and there was nothing wrong with it then.

He slammed the hood down. Nothing to do about it now. He had more pressing things on his mind.

The windows to the rooms and the pub were black and the lobby was empty when they entered the Innis Hotel. They walked past the reception desk and no one was there either. Jake grabbed the knob to the stairwell, opened the door and flew up the stairs. A few doors down the hall, he found number seven and banged his fist on the wood.

"Josie!" he hollered. Angeline came up behind him, breathless from racing up the stairs. "Josie! Wake up! Get your pimply ass up off that bed and open the door."

Sounds stirred behind the door, the creaking of bedsprings. Then came the pad of bare feet as Josie approached the door.

"What is it?" she asked, an eye darkening the peephole. He frowned, wiping hair out of his face. "Is that you Jake? Don't you know it's five o'clock in the morning? The birds aren't even up yet."

"Open the door," he said.

She did, in all her scraggly just woken up manner, and scowled at him. "Jesus, I had to get my clothes on so fast with you making enough racket to wake the dead, I've got everything on backwards."

"Sorry we woke you," Angeline said.

"What's this about?"

"Otter Cove. Did you know about it?" Jake demanded.

Josie yawned and rubbed at a weepy eye. "I don't know what you're talking about."

"There's a fucking blasted hole in the beach, that's what I'm talking about."

"Will you calm down? They are just clearing some land."

"It's Otter Cove! For Godsake Josie, that beach is a sanctuary. It's a wildlife preserve. What the bloody hell has gotten into you?"

Josie pulled at a brown curl that had crossed to the wrong side of her part. "Listen, it's not my fault. I didn't sell it. If you should be yelling at anybody it should be the Heritage Advisory Board."

"What the hell are they doing giving Radisson the go-ahead to start work for? We haven't even submitted an assessment yet. How does he know all the residents will even sell? He can't just build around them."

Angeline interrupted. "I think that's part of his plan. He thinks if he starts clearing land people will see that it doesn't make any difference how they feel. They'll have to sell because who wants to stay with a theme park in their backyard?"

Jake had almost forgotten Angeline was there. She stood with her hand on the doorknob, still breathing hard from climbing the stairs two at a time.

"You can't do anything about it," Josie said. "Whether or not Radisson gets all the property on this island doesn't make any difference. He's going to do what he's going to do."

Jake went to the rumpled bed and reached for the phone on the night stand.

"Who are you phoning?" Josie asked. "No one'll be at the office yet."

Impatiently, he depressed several buttons. He waited, replaced the receiver. "Why the hell didn't Kate tell me Otter Cove was for sale?"

"Because it wasn't an archaeology site, and she knew you'd give her a hard time. Radisson owns that property now, and what he does with it is his business."

He picked up the receiver again. "What room's Kate in?"

"How should I know?" Josie scratched the back of her neck and came and stood in front of him. "What's the matter, Jake? Jealous?"

Angeline hadn't moved from where she stood by the open door. Her eyes had darkened just a bit after Josie had spoken.

He could ask at the front desk. But the repulsive memory of Kate with Sam Smythe suddenly changed his mind.

Angeline looked away when she noticed him watching her. He glanced down at the buttons on the telephone.

"What's with Kate anyway?" he asked, replacing the receiver.

Josie made a face. "God only knows."

"She's still pissed off at me. It's been over a year. It's not my fault Tom was made Regional Archaeologist over her."

"You were living together then."

"All the more reason I couldn't help her. Do you think anyone would have taken my recommendation seriously? They would have been screaming nepotism all over the place."

Josie sat down on the bed next to him. "Let that be a warning to you, Angeline. A man is a woman's greatest impediment if you want to have a career. And even though he's cute as a teddy bear, and waves that magic wand of his like there was no tomorrow, he isn't worth it."

Jake scowled.

"Okay," Josie said. "I'm sorry. But I'll thank you to stop blaming me every time Radisson makes a move you don't like. I just work here and not for *him* I might add."

Jake felt like kicking her.

"I'll phone Tom from the lab," he said, going to the door. He suddenly remembered his truck. "Give me your keys. There's something wrong with my brakes. I nearly killed us getting back here."

"Don't you think it's about time you bought a new vehicle?"

"I can't afford a new vehicle."

He stuck out his hand. Josie searched the pocket of her purple fleece jacket and tossed her keys to him.

"I'll catch a ride with Kate," she said.

As they left, Jake wondered if Kate had really slept with Sam Smythe.

He was tired. They'd been up all night and Angeline's head kept bobbing in the Land Rover like she was on the verge of dropping off, or maybe that was just a way of avoiding any conversation with him.

"I didn't mean to explode at Josie like that," he said.

Angeline raised her head. "Just what is your relationship with her?"

Jake didn't answer.

"And Katherine Leonard, what is your relationship with *her*?"

"It's nothing."

"You lived with her, and you say it's nothing? Is there anyone you haven't slept with?"

"Angeline, we're just friends. At one time she might've meant something more, but not now."

The road narrowed and turned gravelly. Jake eased the brake, turned down Seagirt Lane, and ground to a halt. He sat in the truck and stared out the window at the rows of tents.

"I didn't spend my life in a monastery, I didn't have anyone to care what I did as a kid. Some people have to take love where they can get it. Not everyone is as fortunate as you."

Her eyes were like fire or ice. Maybe it was time he gave up. He got out of the truck and when she didn't, he went around and opened the door for her.

"What do you know about how fortunate I am?" Angeline exploded "You think I'm so fortunate? My father has cut me off as long as I want to do archaeology. I have no money for graduate school next year, I can't work for Clifford Radisson now, and my parents are getting a divorce. Is that fortunate?"

Jake stared at her, on the verge of a hysterical laugh. "Let's set the record straight, once and for all. I am not sleeping with Josie. I am not sleeping with Kate. All of that is past history. I haven't slept with anyone in the last three months except you. You're the only one I want, but since you won't have me, I guess I'll have to get used to sleeping alone."

The sun was well into the sky and it was broad morning. The sparrows were doing their chattery thing and his head felt like the hole Radisson had blasted in the beach.

"I was not taking a shower with Josie. She was rubbing some

ointment on my shoulder. I happened to injure it quite badly when I
tried to pull you out of that hole."

***

Jake jiggled the flap to Angeline's tent in answer to her moan. "Do
you need a few minutes? I'll get you some water."

He left and Angeline removed her sweater which was damp from
being slept in. The shirt underneath it was wilted. She removed that
too, and rubbed the limp cotton over her face.

How long had she been asleep? Was it even the same day?

"Can I come in?"

She was naked from the waist up and rummaged around in her pile
of clothing for something to wear. She pulled a red T-shirt over her
head, then pushed the flap aside to let Jake in. He shoved an enamelled
basin of water toward her. He watched her, and when she didn't give
him the signal to stay, he went outside to wait.

She knelt in front of the basin, grabbed her hair and twisted it into
a short pony tail, and fastened it with an elastic band. Cold water went
flying, then she mopped her face with a towel, dipped her toothbrush
into the basin and brushed her teeth. She changed into shorts and
tucked in her shirt before heading outside.

"I phoned Tom," Jake said. "The assessment is in."

"But I haven't written up the faunal material yet."

"And I never wrote up the artifacts. Josie did. He was here, and she
gave him preliminary reports while I was in Seattle and you were in
Toronto."

Angeline kicked the basin she had brought outside forward with her
foot. His eyes went from the Native print on her shirt to her face.

"I'm sorry," he said. "Lookout Island has been sold."

His gaze swept past her over the dome of her tent to the abandoned
shell midden. It flitted back, then landed on Josie's navy blue tent. The
door suddenly flew open and ejected the co-director in a purposeful
trajectory toward the house.

"Her contract at the university is up. She's sort of hanging in limbo.

She just found out they don't have the funds to re-hire her this fall."

A few paces from her tent, Angeline stooped to pour the used water onto the grass. Josie could do something so underhanded, so deceitful, and Jake had the capacity to forgive her.

"Josie turned thirty this year. It's hard not knowing what direction you should take when you've invested so much in one thing. I think it's time we gave up the fight over the theme park. Everyone needs a job, I can see that now."

Angeline couldn't believe what she was hearing.

"What time is it? Did you get your brakes checked out?" she asked.

"It's three. And I was on my way to pick up my truck now. I was hoping you'd come with me."

"I will, but we have to go back to the cave."

"It's too late. I got it straight from the horse's mouth or should I say the Office of the Regional Archaeologist of the Heritage Advisory Board of the Archaeological Assistance Division for Culture Communications and Tourism that the theme park is a go."

"What about the cobbles? The Raven. He's here, I can feel him."

Jake laughed. "You're worse than me. Forget what I said last night. All that postulating was just the raving of a drunken fool."

Angeline started toward the parked cars at the side of the gravel road. "If you don't want to come with me, then give me Josie's keys and I'll go myself."

"Why does all of this matter so much to you?"

She stopped, turned around, and glanced down at the design on her chest. This was her favourite T-shirt. Red, with a black eagle and raven fighting for the salmon. He was looking at it too.

"Do me a favour," Jake said, approaching her. "Don't wear that today."

CHAPTER TWENTY-EIGHT

A Steller's jay dropped from a hemlock branch high above the roof of the trailer to a lower one where it whistled to its mate. Clifford Radisson placed his binoculars onto the portable table in front of him.

"What exactly did Katherine Leonard say?" he asked.

The contractor lit up a cigarette. "She went to the site to say good-bye to the crew before going back to Seattle. Lalonde wasn't there."

Radisson's men were taking a coffee break. Several of them were smoking at the edge of the wide excavated depression and a couple of the older workers were drinking coffee out of metallic thermoses.

He turned from the trailer's large window. "What time was this?"

"Early this morning. Around eight I think."

"Where did he go?"

The contractor shrugged, then grinned. "No one knows. Too bad Kate doesn't talk in her sleep. I could find out something more next time she's back."

Radisson had thought Katherine Leonard would be more discriminating than to sleep with Sam Smythe. But her behaviour was consistent with her personality. Her tastes, from what little he had seen, in fashion, jewelry especially, were vulgar.

She had agreed to come to work for him when the negotiations were formalized. She was a good informant, especially now that she was involved with Sam Smythe. Still, he was having second thoughts. He wasn't sure he wanted someone of Katherine's less than discriminating judgement working for him.

"Don't worry Mr. Radisson," the contractor said, jerking a thumb seaward. "I don't think they can miss the new pictures, if that's where they've gone."

"I should have sent someone else," Radisson said. "You're a miserable excuse for an artist."

Sam Smythe tapped ash to the floor, undiminished. Radisson went to his desk. "Use an ash tray."

"You've got one?"

"Over by the sink."

Smythe returned with a metal ash tray and sat down. He tapped his cigarette. "I don't know why those damned archaeologists keep going back there. Lines and squiggles are lines and squiggles to me."

The tip of the contractor's cigarette blazed orange. Neither did Radisson. Unless Lalonde and Angeline had found it.

"You could send the Coast Guard after them. They'll be illegally trespassing."

Radisson shook his head. That wasn't what he wanted. And he wasn't going to put guards up around the cave either. He wanted all of the archaeologists working for him.

He stared to his left, east of Otter Cove, at the sea, and rose to fetch the binoculars. A small boat glided across the water between the marina and Lookout Island. Two people sat inside it.

Rage. He suddenly felt rage.

The man did everything wrong.

He disparaged opportunities to earn revenue for something as archaic as principles. He was kind to little old ladies. He was friends, *friends* of all things, with women - fat women, slutty women, *all* women.

He would rather lose his job than see a theme park on Cedar Island. He did not understand the concept of capitalism, free enterprise. Entrepreneurship. He was an academic. A head-in-the-clouds academic. But there was something else. In one particular way Jake Lalonde was exactly like Clifford Radisson.

From the moment that they'd met, he had felt the affinity *and* the antagonism. He had felt how this one man could impede his ambition.

It was absurd. He, Clifford Radisson, had the financial means, the political clout, the charm, the wit, the power. But something was drawing Lalonde to the cave, just as Radisson had been drawn.

He returned to his desk, rocked back on the chair, while Sam Smythe puffed smoke rings into the air. Problems. Problems unanticipated, problems unresolved.

Connie Amos had not relented. She would not sell her property to him. That was fine. If she wanted to continue to live here he would build her a castle to live in. If only she wasn't so friendly with Jake Lalonde.

"Mr. Radisson?" Sam Smythe was smoking in his face.

"Go back to work," he said. "I have some thinking to do. Come back in thirty minutes. I'll have an errand for you then."

The contractor got up, snuffed out his cigarette and went outside. Radisson sat forward on his seat leaning his elbows on the desk.

Angeline was with Jake. He had frightened her by killing the raven, by losing his temper. Instead of running to him after he had saved her from Sam Smythe, she had run to Jake.

He rose and went to the rear of the trailer where the Eagle mask lay on a small table. As he touched it he felt a surge of familiarity.

The mask was a symbol of power. This power was inherited, passed down from generation to generation. It had belonged to a chief of the Haida Nation. Now it belonged to him.

Connie Amos did not believe him. He had proof. He had recognized the heraldic figure on that totem pole picture she kept hidden.

Just as he knew the Eagle was his, he knew the Raven belonged to Jake. He understood the motivation, the underlying drive propelling them both in the same direction. He understood Jake's affinity with the Raven mask and the rattle. He remembered that day on the beach when he had landed his helicopter, the bout of temper concerning his purchase of the masks.

He understood.

He knew.

Which was why he had taken them away.

The power in these masks was as real as the artisans who had made them. Their power was older, wiser, more reliable, than the back-biting rat race he lived in today. He wanted to bring this power to the fore. He wanted to show this power in a way that everyone else in this wretched world could relate to.

RAVENSWORLD. Ironic. He had chosen to name the theme park for Lalonde. Now there was only one thing left that Jake Lalonde had, that he wanted.

A large yellow crane moved outside, lowered to clear away trees and debris. A man in an orange hard hat gestured to the crane's operator to back up. This was the site of a mega gift shop that would soon be swarming with shoppers. In another few days the ground would dry up and they would pour the foundation.

Radisson walked back to his desk. If archaeology was a process of gathering evidence and interpreting the clues, then he would give those two archaeologists the puzzle of their lives.

He picked up the phone, dialled, and listened to it ring.

"Government of Washington. Heritage Advisory Board," the receptionist at the other end answered.

"Good afternoon," Radisson said.

A rap sounded at the door. It eased open and a head popped in. "Sorry, am I disturbing you?"

Radisson hung up the phone before the woman at the other end could ask him to hold. He smiled. "I was just trying to call you. Please, come in."

"The UNESCO office contacted me," Tom Jelna informed him. "Cedar and Lookout Islands have been jointly nominated for World Heritage status. They're sending a committee to evaluate the sites next week."

CHAPTER TWENTY-NINE

Jake looked down the hill to the sparkling sea. Across the water the marina lay quiet. The air was sharp. Summer was waning and the odour of decaying leaves mixed with cedar and fir. He crouched down and picked up a large nail. It was blunt on both ends. He dropped it into his pocket and lifted the unlit Coleman lantern from the ground. Angeline passed him his silver flashlight. He turned it on, and entered the cave.

They moved slowly, cautious of the protruding stones and the deathly silence. Jake listened for the dripping. It was there, echoing, loud because of the stillness, and he had a sudden urge to flee.

He thought briefly of handing Angeline the flashlight and letting her explore the cave herself. He listened to the eerie sounds of their breathing.

It was damp in here, like it always was. It smelled strongly of the sea, but this time the odour seemed fresh. He set the Coleman lantern down and turned it on.

The carvings were still there, still the same. The ovoid eyes stared down. At the far end, dancing on the wall, the tales of the Raven mocked him. Jake didn't dare go any deeper into the cave. He stood rooted where he was, close to the entrance, far enough away so that the Raven couldn't touch him.

Every time he came in here he felt like he had entered something forbidden. Every time he looked at these etchings in stone, his heart froze.

They belonged to another time, another world. A time when the will of nature took precedence over that of men. Fresh air gusted once, then again from somewhere deep inside the earth. He told himself desperately that this was nothing more than a cave.

All the signs of humanity were in here beneath the etched symbols. The firewood, the fake petroglyphs. The stones.

The light flickered, moving in a shadowy dance. Jake circled the walls, the ceiling, the floor. Why had she wanted to come back? Her eyes glinted, caught in the beam of his flashlight, but showed no sign of what she was looking for. She moved toward the far wall, to the Raven abducting the Salmon Princess.

His light flashed, poured onto the floor. Still there. The cobbles, those damn cobbles were still there. Five of them. Dark spaces, glittering round stones, the skeleton of a bird. Why did these images belong together? Jake crouched down and touched one of the granite cobbles that was rolled up against the side of the wall. Light spilled downward catching sparks of fool's gold.

"Another picture's been added to the wall," Angeline whispered.

Jake let the cobble roll gently to the ground. He rose, and went to study the etching where Angeline stood.

"Not being very discreet about this, is he?" she asked. The image was familiar. It was grotesque, eeric, vicious. The claws of a large hook-beaked bird digging into the breast of a smaller one, wings arced behind.

"He must have added that one before Parks Services sold him the island," she said. "That isn't a myth is it?"

Jake shook his head. It reminded him of Angeline's red T-shirt. The one he had told her not to wear today. It had made him uncomfortable seeing that T-shirt again. It had reminded him of the way Radisson had looked at her when they'd first met on the beach. Jake studied the carving carefully. The Eagle battling it out with the Raven. The prize, the Salmon Princess.

He dropped the flashlight as a rattle and boom shook the ground. Something knocked him off balance. Angeline jumped, cried out.

"What was that?"

"Listen!"

Jake jerked his head up as a crash outside jarred the cave and a rumbling came down the hill. His heart leaped into his throat. Things rolled and slid and shook the hollow cavern. The walls threatened to topple down on top of them. A surge of adrenaline coursed from his gut, and he threw his arms around Angeline, and dropped her to the ground.

The sky was falling. He huddled over her. Thunder boomed and rocks rolled and dirt thudded down the hill. The roar went on interminably, then silence. Jake looked up.

"Are you all right?" he asked Angeline, and when she nodded, he slowly rose to his feet.

He groped in the dark but the flashlight had rolled between two lumps of stone. Without bothering to fetch it, he stumbled blindly to the front of the cave. He struck his fist into blackness. There was a solid wall of rock and rubble where the entrance should have been.

At the far end of the cave, light pooled over the floor and slowly tilted upward making shadows loom from the humps of stone as Angeline righted the lantern. Now came movement and the sound of grating rock.

She located the flashlight and made her way over the hummocks of sandstone. Her hand reached out to test the wall of rock and earth.

Jake kicked at it and a tumble of soil slid down. He clawed, using both hands, until his nails filled with dirt. The wall barely changed its configuration. He had barely made a dent in it. He thrust his hands in, scooping until his knuckles were scraped and his palms bled.

No use.

Angeline stayed where she was, watching him. She touched his shoulder. "Stop it. We can't get out that way."

Blood smeared on his jeans as he wiped his hands, and his fingernails stung. In all his nightmares he had never thought he would be confronted with suffocating to death, buried in stone.

Jake looked into Angeline's eyes which were strangely serene. She took his hand with the one that wasn't holding the flashlight and turned it over to look at his wounds. They weren't bad. Just scrapes and minor cuts that hurt like hell. She clamped her fingers over his and held them tight. Suddenly all the pain eased into the back of his mind.

"I don't have anything to bandage you up with," she said.

He pulled her into his arms and wrapped them around her. She buried herself in his shirt, then lifted her head and looked at him steadily.

"Come back here with me."

Angeline led him back through the cave where the stone ceiling domed over their heads. It seemed smaller now that he knew they couldn't get out. The rock above felt lower, the walls closer. Without daylight from the opening, the cave was suffocating. Yellow light washed the walls in an orange warmth, the colour of the sandstone. The etchings seemed sharper, the fake ones standing out. The pillar of stone rose sharply from the ground. Jake trembled. He wanted to run, to flee. There was no way out. If there was any way out of here–

"Can you smell it?" she asked. "Over here. There was always fresh air coming from over here."

Angeline got down on her hands and knees and crawled behind the towering column of stone. Jake hesitated. Stared. The light flickered making the images on the wall beside him flutter. He blinked. He suddenly felt compelled to search the void beyond that pillar. Slowly, he put the Coleman lantern down.

"Jake," she whispered urgently. "Come down here." Then he was on the floor behind her.

She lay on her stomach and snaked through a tunnel in the pitch blackness. Jake thrust the flashlight after her and felt her reach back to take it. This was where the fresh air was coming from. He could feel the coolness like a sea breeze.

She was out on the other side, standing upright in the dark with the flashlight waving in front of her.

Images flashed in his brain. He stood very still, feeling a sudden wave of vertigo.

He must have risen too quickly. Blood must have left his brain, pooling in his legs. He squeezed his eyes shut, then slowly opened them and took the flashlight from her.

The space they were in was a large domed cave, larger than the one they had just left. Light poured over and across the ground, moving this way and that. In the centre, a black cavernous void gaped.

A tingling assailed his fingertips and travelled up his arms. He inhaled, clenched his free fist and looked down. A whistling sound came from somewhere beyond. The smooth sandstone basin ran about seventeen feet over the length of the floor and eight feet wide. When he moved, the narrow beam hit a gleam of water. He estimated the depth to be about six feet.

"Jake, are you all right?"

He didn't answer.

"Jake!"

"I'm fine."

He waited until the sensations ebbed, then followed the circumference of the pool with the flashlight.

About two feet down from the rim a circular frieze of petroglyph faces blinked in a frozen dance. He got down on his belly, resting awkwardly, shoving large scattered stones out of his way. He paused, shut his eyes. When he opened them, he saw several dark bands in the walls, left by retreating water.

At the top of the stone bowl, high above the top rim of the frieze, was a darkened band. It was probably formed when spring runoff filled the pool and completely submerged the etchings. Later in the year when rainfall lessened, the water was as it was now, only about a foot deep with the petroglyphs high and dry. The winter band of striations was directly at the lower rim of the petroglyph carvings.

Whoever had carved these pictures here had done it in the dead of winter, partly submerged in cold water.

Angeline whispered, "A shaman's pool?"

Jake nodded. In his search for the Raven myths, he had come across many a mention of the use of pools for ritual cleansing. The exact location of these pools was secret. The shaman's experience was a very private ordeal, not shared with the common man.

"Jake?"

"Yeah," he said, feeling the dizziness return.

"What's the matter? Aren't you feeling well?"

He needed a drink, but he didn't dare drink from the pool. Besides it was too deep. If he fell in there . . . He shuddered. Something was pushing, pulling him toward the pool.

He took another deep breath, waited, listened to the silence.

"Go ahead," he encouraged her, "What were you going to tell me?"

Angeline looked at him, concerned. "I was just going to say that Radisson thought if he could distract us, disgust us with those fakes, we'd forget about the cave and he could buy it. Are you sure you're all right?"

She knelt down beside him. "Can I see that?"

She stuck her hand out for the flashlight and tilted it. On the floor all around the rim, hard globular objects, rocks that had stuck in his abdomen as he had leaned over to examine the water marks, lined the pool.

The *cobbles*. They twinkled now in the dim light all around the edge of the pool.

"Where's the other flashlight?" Angeline asked. "We're losing power. I don't know how much longer these batteries will last."

Jake steadied himself, rose to his knees. "I left the Coleman lantern in the outer cave. Try turning the flashlight off for awhile. See if that recharges it."

He touched a glittering cobble, lifted it and cradled it in his hand.

"Wait," he said.

These were the same stones as were in the outer cave. The same as the one they had dug out of the pit at the wet site. Jake touched the black smudge in the centre of one of the cobbles. Someone had built little fires in these and had fed them with oil.

Angeline passed the flashlight to him, and he put the cobble on the ground. He circled the walls inside the pool.

There were five figures etched into the stone. He recognized all of them. According to the Tlingit, the world began in black chaos, but *Yehlh*, a spirit who chose to present himself as a raven, created men and stole light, fresh water, and fire from the other spirits to give to humanity. Jake knew the myth and every version of it.

The creation of the world.

"That spiral. That's where sunlight comes from. And that – It's the Raven."

Angeline had identified the mythical being as clearly as he had. The petroglyph undeniably showed *Yehlh* in his bird form.

"That stick thing is fire, the burning branch he stole from the sun," he said. Linked with the Raven was a symbol made of three concentric circles which represented the earth.

"And there," Jake moved the light unsteadily around the pool, "is *Hoon*, the North Wind. The figure beside him, the wolf, is *Kun-nook*, the guardian of freshwater. The Raven stole freshwater from him."

A shaman's pool depicting *Yehlh* creating the world. A northern myth from Alaska.

"He travelled, Jake, from one end of the coast to the other. It fits your theory. That was his house in our wet site, where we found the granite cobble and where Joe dug up Connie's Raven rattle."

He passed the flashlight back to Angeline. She stood at the edge of the pool pointing to a carving of the Raven stealing the light.

Petroglyphs were the closest thing that prehistoric Native people had to anything like writing. A series of pictures telling a story. The Raven had a star-shaped object in his open beak, and was shooting, wings taut, straight up toward the sky. Right behind him was the curved beak and hooked talons of the Eagle.

"That should be east," he said, breathless, "if I'm not completely disoriented." The direction the sun rose and where the Eagle made the Raven drop the sun. "Shut the light off."

She didn't have to. The weak batteries caused the bulb to flit and flicker one last time. Blackness descended, then suddenly the whole cavern sparkled like a million diamonds.

"Phosphorescing microbes," Angeline whispered.

The domed ceiling over their heads looked like the night sky. Like the Milky Way in a universe of endless velvet. Jake could swear there were constellations up there. Up, way up, almost directly above the pool a crack of light, shaped like a fingernail, illuminated the blackness. That must be where the runoff trickled down to fill the pool. He could see exactly why this cavern had been chosen by the shaman.

Jake pointed to the crescent of light that looked a lot like the moon.

It was an opening to the outside. Daylight. The cave must extend to the edge of the cliff which was why no one had ever found it before and why the walls were still intact. Angeline touched his arm. From the east wall just as the Raven had indicated from the sunken stone frieze, a sliver of light shot into the dark chamber.

"There's a block of stone there," she said.

She was right. The light beamed into the chamber around an obstruction that diffused the light from outside. It was, he hoped, a way out.

There was a low narrow tunnel exactly where the Raven had indicated it would be. The opening was circular and in the surrounding darkness radiated light like the sun. But it was too small for Jake to get his shoulders through.

Angeline got down on her knees and disappeared through the opening.

CHAPTER THIRTY

The buttress where she stood was mostly rock. She squinted into the distance. The sea between the two islands was a turbulent blue capped with white. Her arms ached, knowing she would have to row that distance to find help.

She edged back against the mountain and made her way to the mouth of the first cave. Several small trees had been uprooted and the corpses of shrubs lay everywhere.

"Jake!" she yelled at the dirt and rubble.

How deep was it? How much manpower was she going to need to dig him out?

Not a sound came from within. She paused. Listened. A Steller's jay called hoarsely, then the drone of bees. She looked back, once, then started down the hill.

The windless air carried voices up from the shore.

"Don't worry, this will work." It was Sam Smythe speaking.

"I just want to scare them away. That's all. Are you sure they weren't in the cave? I really don't want them hurt." The man who answered wore a navy blue baseball cap that covered his face.

Angeline waited, tense, praying they hadn't heard her. She could make out the contractor clearly. He was struggling with the mooring, arguing with the other man. She moved slowly, stumbled on a rock. Smythe looked up, then resumed unfastening the mooring from a branch. The two figures were silent now and the contractor shoved the boat off the beach before climbing aboard. The dinghy bobbed in the water just offshore. Smythe yanked on the cord of the small outboard motor and cursed.

"We should have rented one from the kiosk," the man in the baseball cap said. "Instead of borrowing this leaky old thing from those kids."

Smythe tried again, then a third time. On the fourth go, the engine roared to life.

They were in clear view now as the boat slid away from the shore.

The contractor guided the dinghy through the shallows. The man in the baseball cap sat in the bow facing her, but Angeline couldn't make out his face. She couldn't take to her own boat until they were safely out of sight. They crossed almost to the opposite shore, then angled sharply to the left.

***

Jake stared at the glittering blackness, the dead flashlight cold in his hand. He switched it on and a weak orange light flickered, blinked out. He lowered the handle onto the stone floor. He had to get back to the outer cave. If he fell into that hole–

Light glowed rosily beyond the tunnel. Jake crawled back through the tight opening and sagged to the floor by the Coleman lantern. The eyes in the stone were watching him. The walls closing in. He had a sense of unreality. A feeling of absolute loneliness. This was what it was like to be alone with your own brain.

He slumped against the stone pillar. If this had been the Raven's final stop, if that had been his house they had found on the wet site, where would he have gone to die?

He had to go back in there. Had to muster the energy, the courage to search that cave. He picked up the lamp, sucked in a huge breath, and snaked on his hands and knees through the rocky passage. The inner chamber flared up in warm orange light. On his feet now, he moved over to the pool, and gazed down. He jerked involuntarily, stumbling backward, groping behind with his fingers, searching for the reassuring feel of rough stone. The Raven had already told him where the sun was located, maybe he would also tell him where his final resting place lay.

Jake walked around to the other side of the pool, and focussed. He focussed with all his mind. Death was part of the cycle of life, so if the wall facing him, when he and Angeline had discovered the pool, depicted the creation of life, then the base of the ellipse should depict death. The Raven was an integral, essential element, a motivator in the creation of life. If he was mortal, it made sense for him to memorialize his own death. And how could that best be done except to etch it in stone?

He saw it. The figures circularly arranged. The fisherman with the line in his hand, and his wife, neck and back arched. In the centre was the halibut, hook dangling over its mouth. Below, forming the bottom of the ring, was the Raven. Only here, he did not rest with his head and beak curved to the woman's spine. He was crushed, curled into a ball, surrounded by fish.

The Raven had been punished for copulating with the fisherman's wife. He had been beaten to a pulp, torn limb from limb, then cast into a latrine. When that didn't work, he was trussed with cedar bark fishing line, weighted down with stones, and hurled into the sea.

Jake didn't have to shut his eyes to remember this vision. He knew. The Raven was coiled into a ball at the bottom of a fish-filled sea. Had his last request been to have his remains dropped into the deep?

Somehow, Jake didn't think so. A man with an ego as grandiose as the Raven's would want his remains to be visible and accessible because undoubtably he'd believe that people would come to pay their respects.

But the picture of the Raven drowning at the bottom of the sea nagged at him. Maybe not at the bottom of the sea. Maybe at the bottom of something, anything that held water. Like the pool. Could *Yehlh* (for that was the name he had decided to give the human Raven) have been buried in the stone pool?

Yehlh's bones may have been lying around waiting for someone to find them for thousands of years. He had to find out. He had to get down there, find *Yehlh*'s bones and then get himself out of here.

The water was only about a foot or so deep. He should be able to see the bottom. The first time they had shone the flashlight down, neither he nor Angeline had seen anything at the bottom of the pool. At the time, they had not been looking for anything. This pool was seventeen feet long. They had only glanced casually at the bottom of one part of it – the centre area, opposite the creation myth.

Jake moved around until he stood above the death scene. He

dropped to his belly and lowered the lantern into the pool as far as he could reach without falling into it.

Directly below the tale of the Raven's humiliating death Jake's lantern lit the water. At first it was difficult to see anything because the light radiated upward and out, not down. But as he tilted it to get a better view, the water rippled, shivered.

***

Her pulse began to quicken. They were not docking at the marina. They were puttering around in the middle of the goddamn channel.

Angeline drew her hair out of her face and tried to think. She hadn't heard the clank of tools as they got into the boat, so maybe they hadn't taken any away with them. Maybe they had left something here she could use.

She crawled her way back up the hill. At the top, she gazed seaward. The two men had not gone very far. They were pretending to be fishing or something. She could see long poles extending from each of their hands. Again, she wondered who the man in the baseball cap was. She had heard his voice before. Maybe even spoken to him. He was sophisticated even when he cursed. His speech, like Jake's, had the intonation of someone who was educated.

Angeline stared hard over the channel. Taking the boat was totally out of the question. It was already five-thirty or six o'clock. If Smythe and his friend stayed there all evening, they would see her.

Around the other side of what used to be the cave mouth Angeline found what she was looking for. She kicked away loose branches and dirt and uncovered a shovel – no, two shovels, a crowbar and a pick. There was also a grubby old Cordura backpack.

She rummaged through it. There was a canteen, some granola bars and a half dozen dried pepperoni sticks. Her lips were parched, and here was water. She hesitated. These things belonged to Sam Smythe.

***

He almost shrieked. Because even after all that deducing, Jake wasn't really expecting to see anything. The skull of a man, eye sockets hollow, was staring, grinning at him, with most of his teeth intact. The bone was pocked and discoloured, but human. The rest of the skeleton was there too. This was *Yehlh*, the shaman. The dark image of Jake's dreams.

Jake moved the lantern in an ellipse around the circumference of the pool and peered into every corner. Mostly the water was still and empty except for a few fallen stones.

A couple of feet above the skull a dark pointed shape loomed out of the shadows. Jake's lips parted and he steadied his breath. If that was what he thought it was . . . He looked closer. It was.

He crept back in the dark through to the tunnel and dragged himself into the first cave. It was silent in here and even more dead than the grave of *Yehlh*. Now that he had experienced the real thing – the shaman's pool, everything else seemed artificial. He glanced at the wall where Radisson's man had faked the petroglyphs. He pulled out the nail he had kept in his pocket and measured it up against the etching of the Raven abducting the Salmon Princess.

Most of the carvings decorating these walls were fakes.

But not this one.

Jake turned, stared across the cavern to the towering pillar of stone.

***

Angeline elbowed her way through the black hole. Everything was dark at first, then sparkled as her eyes adjusted. The crescent moon was there, high above the cave floor, though dimmer now that daylight was falling. She tried to remember where the rim of the pool was. It was bordered by those granite cobbles so if she stayed on her hands and knees and crawled to her left, eventually she should hit the wall and not fall in.

Angeline's pupils dilated fully to the reduced light, and she could see the weak flicker of a flashlight at the edge of the pool. She groped her way over, lifted it, stood, and just as suddenly dropped it as she glimpsed a horrible face beneath the water.

Jake came to her out of the darkness, lowered his lantern to the floor and wrapped his arms around her. She sagged against his chest and felt the tears squeeze out of her eyes.

"I thought you were dead," she said. "I thought I saw someone in the pool."

"It wasn't me." His smile died even before it had surfaced. "Is something wrong? You got back pretty quick."

She nodded, trembling.

"What happened?" he asked.

She told him what she had seen.

Angeline went back to where she had left the shovel while Jake followed with the light. "I couldn't leave, Jake, they're sitting in the middle of the channel. Fishing."

Her shoulders slumped. It had suddenly occurred to her who the man in the baseball cap was. "I think Tom Jelna's with him."

She sat on the floor and removed the canteen from around her neck, and Jake squatted.

"Are you sure?" he asked.

"Yes."

They stared at each other for a long second, then she dragged herself to her knees and crawled through the tunnel back outside. When she returned, she brought the backpack, a shovel and the crowbar with her. She began to remove the food and handed over a granola bar. Then she leaned against the wall wearily and listened to Jake eat.

"Why would the Regional Archaeologist want us dead?" she asked.

A paper wrapper crunched as Jake crumpled it into a ball and stuffed it into the pack. He wasn't sure that he did. He rose, dusting his hands off on his jeans and led her back to the pool.

Angeline looked to where Jake pointed with the lamp to the scene of the fisherman and his wife.

She had seen this image before.

They lay uncomfortably on their stomachs side by side just above the Raven's death tale while the lantern flitted across the surface of the pool. In the water below there was nothing but wavering shadows. She suddenly jerked back. She had seen it again. A reflection, not hers. And not Jake's either. Unless he had become the devil himself. She lowered her head, peered once more into the brown glassy depths.

"It's him," she whispered. "The shaman. You were right all along."

Light struck a dark oblong object in the shadows just above the body. The object was familiar, ending in a long straight beak. The water mysteriously rippled, yellow bleeding into black. An eye appeared, and Angeline looked up sharply.

"The mask from the Cedar Island Museum!"

"And look there."

Connie's rattle lay on its side near the skeleton's hand, the head of the Raven prominent, the man and frog, tongues linked. And the Eagle staring out of its belly.

Jake met her eyes and Angeline recognized the grim set of his jaw. He got to his feet and walked back to the east entrance to fetch the tools. She watched him go back to the inner chamber with the crowbar, the lantern, and the shovel. The backpack remained on the floor, and she left it there and crawled out to the setting sun.

One more hour of daylight. She hoisted the pick and loosened some earth. A tapping came from inside the cave. She slammed down with the pick almost wrenching her shoulder as the impact reverberated through her arm. She heard a muffled sound in answer and a tapping, closer this time. She kicked at the loam, found a loose rock and clanged the back of her shovel on it. The tapping ceased and Jake began digging.

It was almost dark, only a pale purplish glow shone through the trees. Angeline had managed to make something of a dent in the earth and from the nearness of the sounds inside the cave, so had Jake. Behind her some kind of frog was croaking and insects, crickets maybe, chirped. The hairy branches of firs spiralled black against the sky. Below, in the channel, it was dark.

The pack was still on the floor when she returned to the cave. She groped about for the canteen. A dribble ran down her chin as she drank, then she made her way along the invisible stone wall to the opening of the other chamber.

Warm light shone from within and Angeline followed it to where Jake stood hunched over the handle of his shovel. She removed the canteen from around her neck and handed it to him.

"I think they're gone," she said.

"Back to the marina?"

"Possibly."

"You look dead on your feet," he said. "Come here and sit down."

She sat on the lumpy ground and drew her knees up to her chin. "What time is it? Do you know?"

He glanced at his watch. "Nine fifteen. We'll be out of here in another hour." He mopped his head with the edge of his T-shirt and studied her. "Do you want to call it a night? If those two have come back to check on their handiwork, it might be best for us to stay low until morning."

Angeline took the canteen from him, and drank. "Won't someone come looking for us? Won't Josie wonder what happened to us when we don't come back?"

Jake shook his head with a grim smile. "What's more likely is that she'll assume I took you to a hotel for a night of sordid debauchery."

If there hadn't been another opening to the cave, they really would have died in here and nobody would have known.

He took her hand and drew her up until they were standing face to face. Angeline knew Jake was exhausted too. His face was haggard and streaked with grime. His hands were scraped and bleeding again from the effort of digging. He let her go and bent down to retrieve the shovel. She suddenly remembered he had not been feeling well.

"Jake?" He glanced over at her, then positioned the shovel. It was clear he was not going to tell her a thing. There was no point in even asking.

The night was black and still. Angeline felt a chill creep along her arms. She glanced nervously around, then drove her shovel in.

The sound of metal chipping on stone was coming from inside. Jake must be really close to breaking through. She started to scratch away at the loose earth on the left side of a boulder until their shovels clanged together. Then a tumble of soil slid down from above covering the place where they had met. She scraped at the rubble, clawed at it till tears streamed down her cheeks. This just wasn't going to work; every time they broke through more dirt came sliding down the hill.

She forced herself to keep shovelling. Silty earth sucked in, like a mole burrowing down. Jake broke through again, and this time the hole stayed opened for him to crawl out.

CHAPTER THIRTY-ONE

They were almost back at Cedar Island, gliding along the obsidian water, still and black as road ice.

Had the brakes to his Bronco been tampered with? Had the Regional Archaeologist deliberately collided with him that night he was returning from the library? The eroding cliff at the First Salmon Ceremony on Gooseberry Island had dropped a rock big enough to kill. And then there was the accident at the sinkhole – And the cut rope.

Jake looked around, but no boat followed. It was typical for Radisson to let someone else do his dirty work for him. One thing was certain. That rockslide was deliberate. He stroked again. The going was slow. After two hours of digging his body was screaming for rest.

Tom, Kate, and Josie had gone to school with him. Tom had always been a rival, both for the women in his life and for the limited scholarships. Later, they had competed for jobs. While Jake had become a professor, Jelna had chosen an alternate route and become a bureaucrat. They were no longer competing for the same things, and Jake refused to believe his long-time colleague wanted him dead.

He stopped rowing, rested his shoulders, and gazed across to the bow of the small rowboat.

"You're exhausted," Angeline said. "Let's trade places. I'll row for awhile."

Jake started to rise, but tipped the boat so perilously that they both changed their minds at the same time.

"It's not much further," he said, and sat back. He did not want to risk knocking them both into the drink.

The oars splashed, sounding loud in the dead of night. The lights of the marina winked. Jake steered the dinghy to the lee of the dock. As they ground on the rocky shore below the marina, he watched for movement.

He fastened the mooring to a projecting stone and gestured to Angeline to get out.

"Not there," he whispered as she headed toward the dock. It was better to wait until morning before returning to camp. They needed to rest.

He led Angeline down the rocky beach to a sheltered area consisting of smooth flat stones and a couple of dried logs.

"It's not exactly the Hilton," he said. "Do you think you can sleep here?"

He kicked away some dry sea wrack and lay down on his back on the sandstone. Angeline settled in close beside him. He stared up at the sky and studied the moon. It was coming into half phase now, cool and luminous, the colour of dirty snow.

"When did you lose your mother?" Angeline asked.

Jake rolled over onto his stomach and propped himself up on an arm to look at her. "I guess I was around one or so. Why?"

"Do you remember anything about where you used to live? Or about her?"

He didn't remember anything much except someone singing. It was like a lullaby but not something mothers normally sang. It was . . . he didn't know, about fishing? "I have a vague image of a white house with, I think, a big porch."

"That sounds like Connie's house."

Connie had told him she wasn't his mother. The authorities in Seattle had given him a name – Susan Tom. Why couldn't he find any information on this woman who was supposed to have brought him into the world? Who was she? What had happened to her? If she was dead, as they claimed she was, why couldn't he find her grave? The only thing he knew for sure was that he had inherited the crest of the Raven. He rolled down onto his back.

"Do you think Connie might have known your mother?" she asked.

"No," he said. "Why would she keep that a secret?"

"I don't know." Angeline looked over, hesitating, and lowered her lashes. "Maybe you and Radisson are– "

Suddenly Jake sat up, turned, grating his jeans on stone and stared at her.

"Think about it. That captain had a Haida wife."

He wanted to laugh outright, but something stopped him. To imagine that he and Radisson were both descended from some nineteenth century white sea captain, immortalized on a Haida pole, was absurd.

"The captain married in 1837," Angeline said. "There'd be all sorts of records to verify it. You told me he worked for the Hudson's Bay Company. You could easily find out. I wouldn't bother to ask Connie though. There's something about your family history that she doesn't want you to know. She's protecting you."

"No," Jake argued. "That means I'd be related to Martin Moon. Marina would be my cousin. Wouldn't somebody know that?"

"Not necessarily. It was a hundred and sixty years ago." Angeline raised herself on her elbow. "It makes sense. Why else would she have that totem pole picture with the crest figure of the captain? Why does she want to give it to you?"

Jake had never seen the picture and the only reason he knew of it was because of her.

He slumped down. He was tired. His limbs felt like jelly. Fear and physical labour turned muscles into jelly. Angeline lowered herself beside him. He leaned over and brushed his lips against her forehead, making her open her eyes. He smiled briefly, turned until they were lying back to back. He tried to take deep regular breaths but his body resisted. He was tired of speculating, tired of the whole thing.

He stared at the stony beach and the charcoal sky edging the sea. He felt Angeline's arm slide around his waist.

Carefully, he rolled over and looked into her face. His hand went to her cheek. Shadows hid any dirt there, though it wouldn't have mattered. Nothing could mar her beauty. Even if she was hit by a car or struck by a disfiguring disease.

"Are you okay?" she asked softly.

"Yeah, why? Don't I seem okay?"

"You weren't feeling all that well inside the cave."

"I thought we were going to die." He laughed.

"But after that," she insisted. "When we found the pool."

He couldn't tell her there was nothing wrong except that he was afraid of his own dreams.

"You found the Raven," she said.

She tucked her head under his chin. The intimacy made him feel slightly uncomfortable. He fidgeted, and looked away. She moved closer. He raised his arm and she settled into it.

The rock dipped slightly under his back, worn smooth by the whirling action of the tide. At the pub the other night she had said he could be descended from the Raven himself.

Was it possible?

Jake shivered.

CHAPTER THIRTY-TWO

Angeline finally told him what had happened in Toronto.

In the early morning light she described how Radisson had lured her to his hotel room and used the contractor to terrorize her. But she had no proof, except a gut feeling that he had orchestrated the whole thing.

"What proof do you need?" Jake demanded. "Smythe stalked you at the zoo. He tried to scare you into signing the contract. Why else would he do that?"

They were speeding along Beach Road, the horizon a wet pale red beneath a dark sky. Jake was not letting the developer get away with anything more. Radisson would not have the pool. He would not have the theme park. Not if Jake could help it.

"He killed the bird," Angeline said.

"What?" Jake almost ran them off the road, but quickly regained control of the wheel.

"He caught that injured bird, the one with the broken wing that we saw on the beach. He kept it in a cage. He snapped its neck in half right in front of me."

Jake's voice came frighteningly low. "That bird was a *raven*."

Jake accelerated and recklessly took the next curve in the road. He slowed and shifted gears. Twelve years, thirteen, he had searched for clues to the Raven. It was not going to be easy. But he hated Clifford Radisson, hated him for hurting Angeline. He couldn't kill the man so he would kill his dream. Even if it meant the destruction of his own.

"I'm going to take you back to camp. No – I'm going to drop you off at Connie's. Stay there till I come back."

The road wound into mist, emerging on the other side to a cold wind. Jake breathed in the damp air. It was Sunday. Not that many people were around. Today he wouldn't be missed at the site. He jetted down a straight stretch of road. At the end of it, to their left, a white house came into view.

Angeline looked for movement inside the kitchen. Jake stopped the truck, reached over to open the door for her. She paused before getting out, looked back at him.

"I know what I'm doing," he said.

***

Connie watched Jake's tail lights disappear in the distance. It wasn't even six o'clock yet. As she rounded the corner of the house from the beach a figure approached.

"Angeline, what are you doing here so early in the morning? Is everything all right?"

Connie led Angeline into the house and started to get breakfast and tea. Connie frowned as she listened to Angeline's story. It was worse than she had thought. He was worse than she had dared given him credit for. She could not believe he was capable of these acts of pure greed.

"In the bright light of day, it all seems absurd," Angeline said. "Maybe it *was* an accident."

Connie was past believing that the rockslide was an accident. She had stayed out of his life. When she had first seen his name in the newspapers, she knew she had lost him forever. It was her own fault. She had given him up. Was this her punishment for abandoning her child?

"Have you seen what they've done to Otter Cove?" Angeline asked. "It's horrible. Like a bomb exploded at the top of the beach."

Connie shook her head. She had known that eventually it would come to this. But she had hoped the archaeologists could find a way to stop it.

"I'm scared," Angeline said. "I think he's– "

"He?"

"Radisson. No, Jake. I think . . . Can you stop him?"

Connie stared at her. Someone had to have the power to stop him. If not Radisson, then Jake. From what Angeline had told her, Jake had been caught up in a violent emotional storm, leaving nothing to reason. No. She shook her head. She had to trust him.

"Don't let your imagination get carried away, Angeline," she said, trying to reassure them both. "He's a sensible, capable, intelligent– "

"No, he's not. He's as crazy as Radisson. I have to stop him. I have to stop them both."

Connie reached out and touched Angeline's hand. If Connie didn't do something . . . the poor girl was watching her, eyes pleading.

Connie couldn't tell her anything, give her any reassurance. Everything Clifford Radisson had done was legitimate. She had tried to deny it. For years she had denied her bond to him. But when he finally confronted her himself, when he recognized the totem figure, she knew for certain. He had as fair a claim to the descent of the Eagle as Jake had to the Raven.

"Clifford Radisson hasn't done anything wrong," Connie said. They had no proof.

"But that's what I'm worried about, Jake *might* do something wrong."

Connie hoped Angeline would not realize the truth. Would not question why she did not want to act. Jake must hear it from her.

She moaned. It was true. He was about the right age. Ten or twelve years older than Jake. There was nothing remotely Native about his physiology, and though her own dark skin and eyes denied it, she was only three quarters Native. His father was White. It explained his obsession with things Native. It explained his desire to build on her island. It explained his recognition of the photograph. Oh Paul. How could they have conceived such a child?

"Go and find Jake," Connie said, and left and went into the bathroom.

Angeline followed.

Above the tank the picture hung as it had for thirty years.

"Give him this." Connie removed the photograph and put it into Angeline's hands. "The captain's wife was Haida. The union produced several descent lines. One was Shaman Moon's family. Another, was mine."

***

"Angeline, where've you been?" Josie asked. "And where's Jake?"

"He had some errands to run. He'll probably be awhile. Can I ask you something?"

Josie looked at her curiously and gestured her into her tent. "What? I'm going into town to do my laundry, I didn't have time yesterday, do you want to come?"

"No thanks. Do you know if Clifford Radisson's on the island?"

"I believe he is." Josie stuffed some grubby T-shirts and jeans into a dark green backpack, then cast a worried look across the tent. "I have something to tell Jake. When is he coming back?"

Angeline wondered at Josie's concern. Jake, it seemed, was wrong. Josie *had* worried about them last night. "Have you seen Tom Jelna around?" she asked.

Josie glanced down at a pair of whitish socks. "He's in Seattle. What made you think he was here?"

"Oh, I thought I saw him the other day. Is Clifford Radisson still staying at the Surf Lodge?"

Josie nodded and tossed the socks onto her clean pile. "What's the matter, Angeline? What happened to you and Jake last night?" Her eyes softened uncharacteristically. "I was worried when you didn't come back. I thought you might have had another accident with the Bronco. I've been telling Jake for the past year to get a new truck."

Angeline smiled, reassured her that nothing was wrong and went outside. A creepy feeling sidled up her spine.

Josie came out of her tent loaded down with her pack, and Angeline asked for a lift.

"What's that?" Josie indicated the photograph Angeline still clutched in her hand.

"Oh something Connie wanted to show Jake."

"Can I see it?"

Angeline passed Josie the plastic laminated picture. Josie studied it and handed it back. She dug her keys from out of her pocket and opened the car door.

"Is there something wrong?" she asked.

Angeline wished to God she could tell her. But she couldn't.

***

Otter Cove was as silent as a graveyard. The wind whistling through the trees and the sparrows chirping above the cliff didn't make the devastation look any less horrific than it had yesterday. There was only one thing to do. Only one place he must have gone. She would have to go there too.

The splash of the oars sounded eerie in Angeline's ears. There were no voices and no people anywhere. The man at the kiosk was not at work yet, so she had borrowed a boat, one which, against the company's regulations, somehow had had the oars left in it. The gulls were quiet like they knew this was no ordinary Sunday. No fishermen were out on the water either.

Angeline glided toward Lookout Island. Somewhere above her head a familiar droning stirred the air. A helicopter. She didn't look up. She was rowing backwards and couldn't see what lay beyond. Ahead of her the silent marina gently dissolved in the circling mist. The choppy sea snapped at her oars. She peered over her shoulder to judge the remaining distance to shore. A raven landed on top of a shaggy cedar.

Angeline continued rowing. She sloshed some seawater onto her lap. A few drops landed on the photograph lying on the seat beside her.

***

The hole they had dug last night was still there. The mound of dirt and rubble, bits of tree and shrubbery sat tall as a reminder of their efforts. The tools lay scattered exactly where they had left them. Jake picked them up and thrust them just inside the cave entrance. A hoarse woody croaking raked the air from below. The raven was trying to tell him something. It flew high in the sky, did a tumbling dive and barrel-rolled over the top of the mountain.

Jake crawled through the gaping aperture and blinked at the dark. He had to do this quickly before he lost his nerve. He could not shake the wariness off. Every time he came in here he felt the shaman beckoning.

The Coleman lantern sat on the floor where Jake had left it last night and he lifted it now, switching it on.

The lamp dangled precariously over the stone rim. A soft mist rose from the pool where Jake knelt. The time was near. But the shaman was never a real sorcerer. He was not a wizard, a god, or a spirit. He was mortal.

Jake rose and looked around the rocky cavern. *Yehlh* couldn't save himself thousands of years ago, anymore than Jake could save him now.

If only he had found the grave of *Yehlh* last year. Before Radisson had come here. He could have found out the truth. Tests to date his age, his year of death, his health. Anything to tell him more about the shaman who, over the millennia, had become myth.

***

The black bird crowed like a rooster sounding the dawn of day. "Quiet!" Angeline wanted to yell at it. The whirring sound faded. There was nothing in the sky. She needed silence if she was to find Jake without scaring the bejeezus out of him. She didn't know why she was overcome by this need for secrecy. There were no boats on the channel, and nothing except one other dinghy was docked here.

She rowed a short distance around the island just in case. The air stirred just as it had every time she had gone inside the cave. The boat banged into the shore and she reached out to grip the stone it hit. It was level enough to land and not too rocky, and there was also a cedar sapling to fasten the line to. She stepped gingerly out of the boat, ankle deep in salt water, her running shoes tied and looped around her neck. She heaved at the hull.

"Hello sweetheart," a voice said.

Ice flowed to Angeline's fingertips. Slowly, she turned her head.

Twin eagles tattooed in black and red twitched on the arm reaching for her. "Not who you were expecting?"

She stood rigid, unable to move or to make a sound. Her bare feet began to freeze in the cold water.

"Let me help you," the contractor said.

Clifford Radisson stood behind Sam Smythe, smiling.

***

From where Jake hid in a thicket of fir trees, he saw Angeline shaking. Seconds passed and she didn't take the proffered hand. Sam Smythe gave her an ugly smile, hauled her onto the shore, and lugged the dinghy the rest of the way onto the rocks.

They let her put on her shoes. She suddenly vaulted up from where she crouched over her laces and stepped backwards. She was trying to put some distance between herself and the men. Radisson caught her arm and dragged her over to where Sam Smythe had gone and was twisting a piece of rope between his hands. A small branch cracked under Jake's foot and a raucous cry came from above.

The raven.

Sam Smythe hooked Angeline by the waist, felled her to the ground. "I like it when you squirm," he said, locking her with one arm while he fondled her with the other.

"Stay put," Radisson ordered. He removed a knife from his belt, and the high polish on the blade flashed in the sun.

So this was how Radisson would get his revenge. He knew he was being watched. That meant Jake had to do something quick before the developer decided to goad him more.

Jake frantically scanned the swaying branches in front of his face and the dead fall on the ground. Sticks and stones. Little stones. Pebbles. He didn't have a gun, he didn't have anything remotely resembling a weapon. He moved, sending rubble coursing down the hill.

"What was that?" Smythe asked.

Radisson raked the top of the mountain and flashed a look of emotion so uncharacteristic of him that Jake shuddered.

"Where is he?" Radisson asked Angeline in a smooth flat voice.

Her face was pale.

"Where!" he shouted.

She cowered on the ground with the contractor's arms tight around her. His voice changed, turned quiet. "You should have stayed with me. You shouldn't have tried to fight me. I could have given it all to you. Now I'm just going to have to take what I want."

He picked up a long dry branch and snapped it into three pieces on his knee. He motioned Sam Smythe to haul Angeline to her feet, and to hold her with her arms wrenched up behind her back. Sitting in full view on a boulder, and with the sharp knife, he began to whittle away at one of the broken pieces of wood. He scraped until it formed a point. He blew the parings away and examined his handiwork. Then he dropped it to the ground and proceeded to do the same to the second.

Radisson picked up the last piece of the branch and whittled at it, stripping ribbons of bark away, then dry, white wood. When he was done he placed it alongside the others. He sat and contemplated his work. His eyes stared blankly at the stakes before shifting to the knife in his hand. He tested the edge of the blade on a fingernail and winced when it cut.

The man was insane.

Radisson's head shot up almost like he could hear Jake's thoughts. He picked the first stake off the ground and studied Angeline. Her face went white. He turned the stake over in his hand and tested the point.

"Over here," he said, kicking away some dead fall and tapping the ground with his foot.

The contractor dragged Angeline to where Radisson squatted and they both stood watching him. The developer held a large rock in one hand and with the other, positioned the stake on the ground. He glanced up to relish the terror on Angeline's face. He hammered it in, then rose and stood in front of her.

Smythe was holding her, arms still twisted behind her back. His eyes ran over her body, and Jake's heart boomed in his chest.

She was wearing the shirt. The two solid birds in black, the one with a violent streak of turquoise across its belly against the background of red.

"I've always liked that T-shirt," Radisson said, softly. "Take it off."

Angeline stared in horror. Jake's foot slipped, sending a crackling twig down the hill.

Radisson smiled.

"Smythe," he said, quietly. "Let her go."

The contractor released his hold on her. Radisson jerked his chin uphill. Smythe understood and began to climb. Jake moved with each step Smythe took, heading downhill at the same time that the contractor made his way toward him.

Leaves crunched, twigs snapped. Branches were thrust aside and projections of bare rock scaled. Dead fall rolled down the mountainside, moss and ferns were crushed. The wind blew, rustling the leaves, then Sam Smythe stopped. He listened and so did Jake.

Radisson was holding the knife in one hand, his eyes fixed on Angeline's.

"I've waited a long time," he told her.

Jake could almost hear her heart hammering in time to his own.

"I don't want to hurt you. I never did." He held the knife, tilting the blade so that it pointed just under her chin.

"I just want to make love to you."

In all this time Angeline hadn't uttered a word.

"I want you to *want* me to make love to you."

Jake grabbed a deep breath, the raven screamed, but before he could move, Smythe's body crashed into him.

White stars showered all around.

CHAPTER THIRTY-THREE

Everything blurred. Jake spit leaves out of his mouth and looked up. The contractor weighed as much as he did, and every time Jake moved, his head throbbed and the knife cinched deeper.

"Get up," Smythe said.

He rose, knife still at his throat, and stumbled down the hill. Radisson threw Smythe a rope, then hooked Angeline with a strong right grip.

He fought having his hands tied, and Radisson said quite calmly, "You fight, Lalonde, and I hurt her. And believe me, I don't want to hurt her."

He flexed his muscles, swelling them as much as he could while Sam Smythe bound his hands behind his back, shoved him to the ground and tied his feet.

Radisson turned back to Angeline. "The T-shirt, darling."

"Leave her alone," Jake growled.

The knife came up and under his chin. He was still on the ground with Smythe's forearm crushing his sternum.

"Unless you're some kind of a *magician*," the developer taunted. "I'd say you're in no position to barter."

Radisson released Angeline and turned her around to face him.

"Honey, I don't want Smythe to cut him in front of you." His brows rose sympathetically in a false entreating gesture. "Take off the shirt."

She looked desperately at Sam Smythe. "Please, not in front of him."

Radisson signalled to the contractor to heed her request.

"And Jake," she begged as Smythe turned away. "Please don't make me do it in front of him."

The developer pierced her with his cold colourless gaze. His brows lowered, the clear irises darkened.

"Are you in love with him?" he asked.

Smythe turned his head back to watch her answer. Jake caught her eyes and Angeline looked down at the ground. She was breathing rapidly.

Radisson's face flushed purple. He grabbed her by the shoulders and shook her. A tear streaked down her cheek.

His hands dropped to his sides, the knife clutched in his right. Rage contorted his features and he looked at the contractor.

"You want her? She's yours."

"NO!" Jake yelled.

The contractor went hurtling to block Angeline from escaping. Radisson ignored them. He measured off four feet on either side of the stake he had pounded into the earth earlier and marked the spots; then he retrieved the two other stakes and hammered them in. The three stakes formed a triad.

He went over to Smythe who straddled Angeline's waist and had flipped her flat on her back. He grabbed her arms and held them securely over her head, then he nodded at Smythe who slid down her body until he was sitting on her legs. The contractor reached over, pulled up her shirt, and put his hand on her zipper, a vulgar smile on his lips.

The zipper came down. She wore white lace panties cut low at the hips, concealing practically nothing. As Jake watched, her denim shorts were peeled over her thighs.

Smythe got to his feet, holding Angeline's shorts in both hands. He forced her legs into the air. Using the momentum of her struggling and leaving her underwear intact, he stripped the shorts to her ankles.

"Bring her here," Radisson said.

The triad of wooden stakes projected from the earth. Smythe picked her up with ease and roughly placed her down. They turned her over, thrashing, until she was on her hands and knees. Then Smythe held her while Radisson tied her wrists together to the first stake. Before they could secure her feet, she kicked out, yanked up the stake – And ran.

***

Angeline sprinted up the hill past the trees. The contractor followed.

He was running fast. Below she could hear yelling.

"Get up," Radisson bellowed at Jake, "I've freed your feet, now get up. And, don't even think about trying to escape. I'm right behind you."

Radisson still had the knife. If she could make it to the cave, she could hide. There were stones to shield her, and if she found her way to the inner cavern, she could escape through the other opening.

Closer came the crack of breaking twigs and rolling pebbles. Jake and Radisson toiled up the scree behind her. Angeline turned to watch for Sam Smythe. He jumped from the bushes and seized her.

***

Lights flickered, flame leaped up from the stone bowls that Sam Smythe was lighting inside the cave. Jake wrestled with the ropes binding his hands behind his back. From where he lay, he saw Angeline bound to the stone pillar clad only in her T-shirt and panties. Her hair hung over her cheeks, and she knelt on her hands and knees. Beyond her yawned the tunnel to the shaman's pool.

Radisson returned from the inner cavern and flaunted the Raven rattle. He crouched beside Angeline. He put the rattle by her head, the hooked visage of the raptor leering up at her, while something dripped from far away.

"How many times did you do it with Jake?" he asked, softly.

He motioned to Sam Smythe to join him, and both men crouched by her head. Radisson glanced down, and the contractor lowered a hand and touched the drawing of the raven covering her breast.

The fires surged, tossing shadows up to the ceiling. A cold draft rose from the floor.

"Little fishies swimming around inside the dark pool–" Radisson's voice cut the silence. "Nine months, Lalonde. Then we'll see which one of us has won."

Shadows moved on Radisson's face, sharpening his features. His lids lowered to Jake's groin, then to his own. "I think she has the same effect on both of us." He turned back, dipped his head, and cupped Angeline's chin. His tongue flickered out, wet and pink, and he kissed her on the lips. "This wasn't how I wanted it," he told her.

She recoiled, and his expression went dark.

"How many times did Jake fuck you!"

He cupped her jaw in both hands and forced her to look at the contractor. "If you don't answer me, I'll give you to him!"

The contractor grinned, then his mouth drooped as he realized his boss had no intention of giving him Angeline.

Radisson went behind her and pushed up her shirt. He reached forward, under, and filled his palms with her breasts; then both of his hands slid down her back to her bottom. He stroked the white silk and she shrank back, trying to twist out of his reach. He moved up closer until his nose almost touched her. A finger circled the small of her back, dug under the elastic around her hips, made a half circuit from side to side. It found the lace around her leg, traced the curve to her inner thigh.

His eyes locked with Jake's.

He got up and walked to where Jake lay staring from the ground. "What do you say, *Magician*? Do you want her?"

He called over his shoulder to Angeline, "Who do you want darling? Me, Smythe or Dr. Lalonde here? Make your choice, or I'll make it for you."

Jake struggled with the ropes that tethered him. Radisson went back to Angeline. She shut her eyes, repulsed by his face. He hooked her head in his arm and drew out his knife.

She whimpered.

He hesitated.

If he didn't do it, Radisson would let the contractor rape her. Radisson held the blade to her throat, and his hand trembled. "Say you'll do it!"

He drew her hair away, exposing the whiteness of her neck. He pressed the blade against her skin until a drop of blood appeared.

"It doesn't end here, Lalonde. Another generation."

CHAPTER THIRTY-FOUR

Jake jerked wide awake. A tremendous pain coursed through his neck to his brain. His head throbbed, his arms ached, his legs felt like no blood had passed through them for hours.

He moaned and tried to move. Rubble stuck to the side of his jaw. He was lying on his side, hands bound behind his back, panic flooding his entire body. His breath caught and he thrashed at the cruel bindings. He hit something soft.

"Jake! Keep still!"

Angeline knelt behind him, wrestling with the rope around his wrists. He torqued and stared anxiously up at her face.

"It's all right. They're gone."

Her neck below the soft bob of hair had a small cut and a smear of dried blood. The T-shirt fell to the top of her thighs, and with her hair slipping to shield her neck as she bent down to reach his wrists, there was nothing to show for Radisson's brutality.

"Where did they go?" he asked.

Her eyes moved toward the pillar of stone.

"To the pool?"

She nodded. "Fifteen minutes ago, I think."

Jake's feet were bound but he managed to sit up with her help. His head boomed. He must have taken quite a blow but he couldn't remember being hit. He looked up at Angeline as she hovered over him and tried to read her face.

"Are you okay, Angel?"

She nodded, and sat on her haunches, and reached out to touch his brow. "I was a bit worried about you, though," she said quietly. "You really took a bump on the head."

He turned until he fully faced her. He couldn't remember a thing. He didn't want to remember. The only thing he wanted to know was that she was all right, that they hadn't harmed her, hadn't touched her, hadn't–

"They didn't– " He couldn't even say it. His mind reeled with the vile images of Radisson's smile and Sam Smythe's leer.

Angeline shook her head rapidly, looked to the rear of the cave at the black tunnel, then back at him.

"Don't you remember? After he did this– " She touched her neck. "You told him you planted the dynamite. Then that creep kicked you in the head when you wouldn't tell him where you put it. I guess they think they can stop it."

It was the only thing he could think of to get them away from her. Jake jerked at the bindings and shifted his gaze from the Native design on her T-shirt.

"How did you get free? No. Tell me later. We have to get off this island." Jake struggled ferociously with the knots. "We *have* to get out of here. Now!"

Angeline found a sharp piece of rock and slammed it down on another to break off a sharper edge. She sawed back and forth on the rope behind his back till it twanged free. He sawed the ropes from his legs himself, then grasped her hand.

He was about to spring to his feet, but stopped. She was so calm. She clutched at his heart. He held her hand in both of his like it was the most precious thing in his life.

"We'd better go, Jake. They'll be back any minute."

"Wait." He searched her face to see how much she knew. "I wouldn't have done it," he said.

Her eyes were the clearest brightest eyes he had ever seen. "He had a knife to my throat, Jake."

She touched her lips with her tongue. Her face was so close, he was so scared. In the next moment the whole world could come crashing down on him and he wouldn't care. As long as nothing could ever hurt her again.

"I love you," she whispered.

Sam Smythe's head emerged from behind the pillar. His sudden reappearance shocked Jake and Angeline apart. Radisson came close behind the contractor.

"Where did you hide it?" the developer shrieked, lunging toward them.

The urgency of what Jake had done suddenly struck too. He grabbed Angeline by the hand and yelled, "Run!"

They stumbled out of the cave and barrelled down the mountainside. At the bottom they wove through the forest till they hit the beach. Angeline dove into her boat and grappled the oars. Jake untied the mooring and shoved the dinghy into the water.

If Radisson had come by helicopter it was nowhere in sight. The boat that Jake had come in was still there bobbing against the shore. Radisson and Smythe were plummeting toward it, hollering at the top of their lungs. Jake got there first, slipped the nylon noose from the shrub, and shoved it into the sea. A tremendous wave rolled up and sucked it almost immediately beyond reach. Jake sloshed through the chilly water, fell on his face, and stroked to the boat where Angeline waited.

"Row!" he yelled, spitting up salt and clinging to the side of the dinghy. "Don't wait for me. Row! Now!"

She rowed and he clamoured aboard, but they weren't moving fast enough. The tide had turned, sending the current against them.

"Switch with me!" he bellowed, dripping water as he rose.

Angeline stood up, dangerously wobbling the dinghy. As he made his way aft, another boat approached. It was Connie and Josie.

"Turn back!" he yelled at them. "Get out of here!"

Fear filled Connie's eyes. "Jake, what have you done?"

He waved frantically for them to go back, locked the oars, and furiously started to stroke. They floated closer.

On the shore, desperate curses flew as the dinghy Jake had released slipped around the curve of the island and vanished.

Connie's boat banged against his.

"Clifford Radisson has done terrible things, Jake," she said. "But please don't let him die because of *my* mistake."

The boats rocked apart. Connie's mistake? How?

"Show him the picture, Angeline. Show it to him. Please!"

Angeline pointed to the bottom of the boat where a plasticized photograph floated in three inches of water at Jake's feet.

"Where did you get this?" he demanded.

Connie's dinghy sank perilously low. She wasn't a good enough sailor to manoeuvre the craft fast enough to rescue Radisson. Even if she was, with Josie on board, one more person would capsize them.

"Jake, please. Don't let him die."

He stared at her. At the picture. Connie nodded, eyes beseeching.

He brought the boat about. The developer climbed aboard, dripping. Then a tremendous explosion shook the air, and Angeline hunched over, shielding her head as Jake rowed with all his strength.

The summit of Lookout Island tumbled down the cliff and into the channel. Rubble and earth, trees and shrubs collided with the sea. Near the shore seabirds squawked and screamed. A salmon leaped into the air. A bump from the right lurched Jake's dinghy forward into Connie's boat.

A pair of blue eyes reached out for him. It was Josie. Twelve years she had been his friend. He missed her.

"You didn't have to do that," she said, her voice cracking with emotion. "I was coming to tell you. I put in a nomination weeks ago to declare Lookout Island a World Heritage Site. I was waiting to hear from them before I told you. I knew if it was so important to you there had to be a reason."

He reached over across the two boats, crashing their hulls together. He gave Josie a tremendous hug. Something he had not given to her in years.

"I'm sorry." She sobbed on his shoulder. "I was going to tell you last night, but you didn't come back."

Above, in the sky, an eagle circled the jumping fish. On the shore, the rock slide stopped. The eagle rose, wings magnificently outspread. It swooped down, lunged at its prey, and missed.

"Thanks," he whispered into her ear.

It was too late. Jake stared at the destruction. He could hardly believe what he had done.

CHAPTER THIRTY-FIVE

"Where's Smythe?" Radisson growled.

Jake looked around. The contractor was nowhere in sight.

They rowed back to the island, but Smythe wasn't among the ruin either. They scaled what was left of the slope. Only Angeline fit into the small opening at the summit, and when she crawled through it, she found the entire cavern and the pool intact.

The cave with the etching of the Raven abducting the Salmon Chief's daughter was buried in a pile of rubble, but *Yehlh* still grinned in his watery grave; the mask floated by his side; and the stone frieze of petroglyphs circled the pool unmarred.

Josie said to Radisson, "I had a long talk with the people at UNESCO. If this island is granted World Heritage status its ownership reverts to the State."

Jake welcomed Josie's change of heart. What had brought it about? She had not suspected the treachery in Radisson, or known of the attempts on his life, or seen the brutalization of Angeline. He thought about the wooden stakes the man had sharpened so methodically. He thought about the tall pillar; the triad of stones.

"What did you think I was going to do to her?" Radisson feigned outrage. Then he smiled. "We are the same, Dr. Lalonde. Obsessed with our projects."

Fairgrounds, zoos, theme parks. And torture. Jake had no words to describe what he felt for this man. He had staked Angeline to the ground.

Angeline stepped into Radisson's face. She opened her fist and revealed what she had retrieved from the cave.

Radisson's hand shot out and she dodged him, drawing the rattle back. He went for her wrist, but before Jake could react, she swung. The rattle struck the developer in the face, landing him flat on his ass. In its waterlogged state it crumbled to the earth.

Jake retraced his steps down the hill which was strewn with rubble and uprooted trees. When the developer reached the base of the mountain, he stared out to sea. The Coast Guard was on its way and Tom Jelna stood at the prow of the cutter.

Jake went to stand beside Connie, and she met his eyes sadly, then she gazed at Radisson's back. "Please don't do anything more until I've had a chance to talk to him."

She walked over to the edge of the water and touched Radisson's shoulder. He looked at her as she spoke to him and something changed in his stature. He shrank. They left together and walked along the rim of the beach.

Angeline came over and Jake took her hand. He looked down at the photograph he held in the other, and felt again a spark of familiarity. Clifford Radisson had recognized the totem figure too, and Jake no longer wondered why.

***

Connie opened the windows wide in her sunroom to let in the screech of the gulls and the roar of the sea. The tide was out, and rocks covered in barnacles rose in humps and mounds, forming living pools.

Jake looked down at the table in front of him. The photograph with the carved human figure on the totem pole aroused a curiosity he hadn't felt since that first inkling, years ago, when he wondered if the Raven might have once been a man.

At the base of the pole was the black bird himself and perched on his head was a supernatural ancestor, the Wolf. On top of *his* head was the Beaver, and then came the captain in his sailor's britches and cap. Jacques Lascelles was the captain's name, and was possibly Jake's great great grandfather. Crowning the pole was the Thunderbird.

"Almost three decades ago, a white woman brought a half Native boy to me," she said. "He had whooping cough, and was close to death's door. The woman told me that when she took him into her home the photograph had come with him. She asked me to keep it for fear of it getting lost. One day, she said, the boy would come to claim it. So I kept it for years, but the boy never came, then a few years ago

I had it laminated to protect it. Before your mother died, Jake, she left this with you. You were the boy I nursed back to health thirty years ago."

Jake had never searched terribly hard for his mother's grave. But when Angeline had shown him this photograph, he knew it belonged to him.

"That song you used to sing to me when I stayed with you," he said. "Is it Haida?"

"No." Her head shook slightly. "It's a Tsimshian lullaby. Your foster mother, the one who brought you to me, said you used to like it as a baby. She worked with the Tsimshian, she and her husband. They were anthropologists."

"I've had so many foster parents. I can't remember or even know if I knew what they did for a living. Anthropology, huh? Maybe that's where I got my interest in archaeology from."

"Do you have an Indian name?" she asked.

"*Nankilslas*. He-Whose-Voice-Is-Obeyed," he mocked. "I guess I was destined to become a professor lecturing a bunch of bored students, though I can't say they do what I say, particularly."

"One of the Raven's names," Connie said.

Jake laughed bitterly. "I'm sure my mother gave me that name more likely because I screamed all the time so she had to pay attention to me and then got sick of it."

Connie shook her head. "I don't think it was like that at all."

***

Before dawn broke, Jake slipped from his tent and looked down at the newly arrived journal he held in his hand. He gave it a comforting squeeze, walked over the grassy hummock to sand, and stopped at the foot of the tide. Angeline appeared on the dewy rise where the first rays of the sun cast long shadows.

"You're up early," she said.

"So are you. Did you sleep okay? I tried not to wake you when I got up."

She smiled, and walked down the slope to join him. "What will happen with the theme park?" she asked.

When UNESCO saw the pool, he told her, they would halt construction on the project. It might take a year or so to do the evaluation, meanwhile everything would remain as it was. Smythe had disappeared, whether killed or escaped, nobody knew, but Radisson no longer had his henchman.

"I never realized how desperate he was," she said. Just because I wouldn't - *didn't*, want him, he had to terrorize me. But he couldn't even do it himself. He had to use Sam Smythe because he didn't want to lower himself to that level. He thought if he used other people it absolved him of responsibility."

Jake didn't say a thing. If she wanted to think it was that, then he wasn't going to contradict her. If she didn't know what Radisson had really intended for her, then he was never going to tell her.

"I don't know what Radisson would have done if you hadn't told him you'd rigged the cave with explosives, but when they left to look for the dynamite– " She stopped and her voice hushed. "I thought they'd killed you when that monster kicked you in the head. I just knew I had to free myself, so I sawed the rope against the rock and it broke."

Jake wrapped his arms around her and buried his face in her hair. Emotion shook his entire body and he knew she could feel it.

"I know the blood tie is distant," Angeline said. "But do you realize you now have family?"

Yes. Connie, the Moon family, and another cousin too. But the last he could not bear to acknowledge. He suddenly remembered he had something to show her.

"Look." He handed over the journal.

"What's this?"

"Page 82."

She flipped to the page and gazed down in the growing light.

"It came in the mail yesterday."

"The Marten Lake raven bones, you got your article published! With this kind of validation from your colleagues, the government will have to fund your kind of research."

He shrugged. "I've decided to take a leave next year so that I can go to the Queen Charlotte Islands and find out something more about my mother."

Carly came running over the hummock of grass. "Kate's on the phone from Seattle. Guess what? Jelna resigned. He's in the psychiatric ward at Seattle General. Something about stress, personal problems. She's now Regional Archaeologist!"

Jake's jaw dropped half an inch, then recognizing the irony, he laughed. "I'll be there in a second. Ask her to wait."

He had never asked this before, but now, he wanted to know. "Why archaeology, Angeline?"

"Because the past links the present with the future. Because despite our obvious ineptitude, humankind has survived for a very long time. I want to know where we come from and where we're going to."

Jake smiled. "I guess you realize when you show that Siberians came to the New World because of the salmon, you'll be fair game for the critics?"

"I've always been fair game," she said.

***

The reporters thronged forward around the entrance to Seattle's downtown courthouse. A three-man police escort attempted a protective ring. Well-known billionaire caught up in explosion on sacred burial site! What was Clifford Radisson doing there? Who was involved? How could Radisson even think of building on such precious heritage land?

"No comment," the lawyer barked, backhanding a microphone from his client's face.

The San Juan Islands were not Clifford Radisson's only concern. Other places had tourist potential. RAVENSWORLD may not materialize tomorrow, next month, or next year – but soon.

A mere setback. Things to smooth over with the police. Until the assessment was done, and the commotion died down, it was still his land. He had paid for it. He would surmount the obstacles as he had done in the past, show Connie Amos he was not what she thought he was. He would show everyone - *especially* Jake Lalonde - just what it meant to be the president of Radisson Enterprises.

He shoved a particularly annoying journalist out of his path, and got into the limousine.

EPILOGUE

The woman with the eyes of the forest sat in the rocky crevice of her shelter, and sought wisdom from the grey lake that rippled from the harsh north wind. A slick-furred marten peered over a ridge of barren earth, and scampered into the dusk. The stone bluffs banking the water reminded her of the night when she left the magician to his fate beneath the twinkling stars of his cavern.

Yehlh had brought light to the world, and then had returned to the dark. Eight moons she had journeyed by land and by sea to seek his homeland. Soon she would reach her destination. Another moon, across the wide strip of sea, and she would be there.

On these northern isles the child would be born, for she was alone now. Her companion had left her early this morning to join his master in the realm of the spirits. She put a stick of hemlock to the fire flickering before her, and brought it into the cave. There on the ground lay the raven, his smooth black feathers brushed back by her own loving hand. Beside him a stone glittered, the shadows etching a shallow depression on its worn surface. She touched the stick to the stone, and watched the oil catch and lick into flame. She had spent the day preparing his grave, and with her own hands had scraped away the hard earth.

She laid him now in his bed of rock and placed the lamp beside him. It flickered and surged and consumed the oil, and died. With each handful of soil she scattered, she prayed for his safe passage; she prayed he would return to the land from where he was born. She had faith, and remembered her own words, the conviction that had given her the courage to go forth and seek her own destiny. The magician still had a future. His enemy had taken her body but not her heart. If the forces of his spirit world were stronger than that of this earth, then the life she carried within her would surely be his.

She rose and felt the child kick. Tomorrow they would journey to the land of the Raven. Tomorrow they would seek out the islands where she would raise the magician's son. She would tell the stories of the Raven to the boy as she had done for these past eight moons. She would speak his name so that he would never leave the homeland of his father.

He would possess the power of creation to render images from wood or stone. He would know the healing art of laughter as his sire had done. As for her, she would teach him kindness and courage. Above all things she would teach him forgiveness. She would teach him to cherish the name of his father. All of these stories she would give to him on the islands of *Haida Gwaii*.

ACKNOWLEDGEMENTS

The Northwest Coast, a land of temperate sea, towering forest, and ranging mountain is home to a trickster, a common black bird. Long ago this bird inspired a cycle of stories the influence of which we see today in the art, mythology, and dance of Native Peoples. From Alaska to British Columbia, Washington State to Oregon the image of the Raven persists. The idea for this novel was inspired by the culture and myths of the First Nations, and by the diverse archaeologists with whom I spent so many memorable years working on the B.C. coast. My story is fiction, but the practice of raven ritualism could have had a prehistoric origin. In 1991 two raven burials were discovered by Dr. Jon Driver of Simon Fraser University in a Palaeoindian site in northeastern British Columbia that date to circa 10,000 years.

To create my fictional world, I drew on the works of Franz Boas, John R. Swanton, Wilson Duff, Phillip Drucker, Beth Hill, Bill Holm, Pat Krammer, Ruth Kirk, Hilary Stewart, and Wayne Suttles.

I am grateful to Antanas Sileika who nurtured this story at its earliest stages; and to Joanne Kellock, my literary agent, who sadly passed away before she could see my novel in print. She dedicated much time and insight into the shaping of the manuscript.

To Aubrey Cannon, whose archaeological knowledge, critical eye, and appreciative smile made this book my greatest adventure, thank-you.

About the Author

Deborah Cannon was born and raised in Vancouver, British Columbia. Her love of the Pacific landscape and of the Northwest Coast Native myths inspires much of her fiction. She is published by Simon Fraser University's Archaeology Press, the Canadian Journal of Archaeology, and the Canadian Writer's Guide. Her fiction appears in Farsector SFFH in conjunction with Fictionwise.com. **The Raven's Pool** is her first novel. The sequel **White Raven** is soon to be released. She lives with her archaeologist husband and her two shih-poos Ming and Tang.

Available Soon:

White Raven
by Deborah Cannon

It's a bad time for archaeologist, Jake Lalonde, to visit Skidegate to search for his mother. All she left him was a picture of a totem pole that upsets everyone who sees it. The Queen Charlotte Haida are embroiled in a logging dispute; dead animals are turning up everywhere, rekindling belief in the legend of the Seawolf; and an Elder decides they must kill a seal to put an end to the talk.

Available Now:

The Raven's Pool
by Deborah Cannon

Obsessed by Northwest Coast Raven mythology, a ruthless developer threatens to destroy Jake's and Angeline's lives. Clifford Radisson's motives are darker and more sinister than anything the two archaeologists can imagine.

Ask for this title at your local bookseller, or order online at www.trafford.com/robots/04-1332.html

ISBN 141203504-X